THE
ROAD

Also by Henry Beetle Hough

THE
ROAD

Henry Beetle Hough

HARCOURT, BRACE & WORLD, INC.

NEW YORK

For Betty

THE
ROAD

THERE used to be a sign at the bend in the lane—NOT A THROUGH WAY—DEAD END. Barry Johnson put it up after he moved to Dinton Center from Boston and built a house for himself and Gretchen about a dozen years ago. Before that, nobody cared whether anyone tried to drive through the lane or not; few ever did, that I remember, and these few were either curious or lost. They weren't going anywhere. It was interesting to see people get lost in a lane like ours, and we regarded the event as a diversion rather than as an intrusion.

That time, a dozen years ago, must have been an age of innocence in Dinton Center, though we didn't think so—or wouldn't have thought so, if the point had been raised. Katie says that innocence can never exist at any given moment, on account of people's suspicions, and you have to wait for the moment to have gone by.

As to the lane, the truth is that it did lead to a number of places, and you could have navigated its whole length if you happened to have an ox cart or stout shoes. It never was passable by automobile. It led to the salt marshes and wild cranberry bogs, and beyond these, if you persisted, you could get to the Point where the summer hotel had stood and had burned like Rome or Chicago or like Baltimore in the autumn of 1904. I mean we had a fire as proud as any of theirs, and people still refer to that night's blizzard as the Great Hotel Storm.

The Point, however, could be reached more easily by a longer and better-mannered road than our lane; this way, though not hard-surfaced, had been so trodden by antiquity that frosts no longer disturbed it much. It made an arc through West Dinton and then twisted back to the Point as an afterthought. Going to the Point, though, was not a consideration that weighed on anyone's mind in our time of innocence. There wasn't five cents' worth of difference whether you went or you didn't.

On our lane the bouncing Bet bloomed in July—Gretchen Johnson always referred to it as "the phlox"—blue chicory in

August with the full lilt of summer and, always, goldenrod and elegiac purple asters in fall. We had sweet fern, Mayflowers, sassafras, and near the bend an overhanging cluster of swamp maples. I don't remember hearing any of the old people say that the lane was beautiful, though I knew they all thought so; in the Dinton tradition it was presumptuous to plaster adjectives upon the landscape except in school or church talk. You never extolled anything that was native; you took it for granted.

A country lane was a country lane, and that's what ours was until one Saturday afternoon when Barry Johnson put up that sign. Then, although we had no inkling at the time, it became suburban. My God, how suburban it became!

I remember Barry coming toward me, hands in the pockets of his shrubby tan slacks, the turtle neck of a snappy blue sweater giving importance to his long jaw and in some measure to the rest of his face. It was Katie's view that Barry was implausible, but I thought just the opposite; plausible was exactly what he was.

"There really aren't such people," Katie said. "He doesn't convince me. He's wasting his time."

"I guess he doesn't much care what impression he makes on you, Katie, dear."

"Naturally I speak only from my own point of view, one I consider appropriate to the country. If he has one, let him go to a suitable place and tend to it."

"You mean he's implausible because he's young and handsome and successful. Because he wears good clothes and is intelligent and has good manners . . ."

"Those are all excellent reasons," Katie said, looking at me distractedly from where she stood at the front of the stove—an old-fashioned, cast-iron range it was, representing a phase of Katie's cast-iron convictions. She was engaged in inventing a new cracker.

"I imagine the world is full of his kind," I said. "He puzzles you because he's the first of his type in Dinton Center. He's a suburbanite."

"It would take more than him to puzzle me. You mean he really is a suburbanite?"

"Of course he is."

"I don't like it. I don't see why it has to happen to us."

I thought of no reply at the time and, as a matter of fact, have thought of none since. I didn't feel prepared to elucidate the philosophy of a situation that would necessarily involve so much of the industrial revolution and the latest bankruptcy of the New Haven Railroad.

"Hi, fellow!" Barry said to me in greeting, using a form of address to which Katie objected strongly. I wasn't keen about it myself.

He had walked down the lane from his house to ours, a distance of perhaps fifty yards and a descent of several feet. Anciently, and our house was of that order, builders had chosen low, sheltered sites; the moderns, like Barry and Gretchen, looked for elevated places with views.

"They can see farther," Katie said, "but they burn more furnace oil on account of more exposure to wind." She didn't say anything at the moment, though. The response was mine.

"Why, hello, Barry," I said.

"Gretchen wants to know if it's early for crocuses to be in bloom."

"The middle of March? In Dinton? No, Washington's Birthday is the legal date for the first crocuses hereabouts."

But I don't think Barry had listened to my reply. "Say, Gid," he went on, "have you noticed any special traffic on the lane lately?"

"Traffic? Good grief, no."

"I don't mean automobiles or trucks or anything like that. As a matter of fact, I mean a tall guy with red hair and sort of loose joints. That is, he has a free way of walking—throws his legs out as if he didn't care whether he got them back. I've seen him half a dozen times, and I can't help wondering where the hell he thinks he's going. You haven't seen him?"

"No. Have you, Katie?"

"Um," said Katie.

"Funny thing is, I've never seen this man anywhere on the lane beyond our house. By the time I cross over to look out the west window, he's disappeared. Do you suppose he cuts off through the hedge?"

When Barry spoke of a hedge he didn't mean privet or any of that conventional ilk; he meant the natural hedgerow of sweet and pungent Dinton things such as sweet pepper bush, sumac, wild cherry, black alder, arrowwood and so on. I don't believe the thickets produced an item that Katie couldn't make wine or jelly out of, or pick a bouquet of at some time in our interesting year.

"Why would he go through the hedge?" I asked.

"Oh, maybe to get to Spinney's place."

"Not likely."

"No, I suppose not."

Henry Spinney, whose house stood third and last on the lane, derived from that old and easily recognizable school of the contrary-minded. I'm not sure whether he had other principles, but he had this one: to object. It was surprising how much territory a principle like that could cover, and in Henry's case it was backed by the experience and perverse will of a retired pilot of the old Fall River Line.

A retired steamboat pilot or mate is very likely a type, but on the Fall River Line a pilot was also a gentleman. The chances were he could baffle you with the fruit of his extensive associations, even with some foundations of a broad culture. In addition, I think there was a polarity, as between New York and Boston, in Henry Spinney. You might say it was significant that Dinton stood about halfway between.

Katie and I had never been in his house, or he in ours, though we had lived nearby for many years. We were the perfect neighbors.

So it was unlikely that anyone would be seeking Henry Spinney either on the lane or cross lots through the hedge. Anyway, I remarked to Barry Johnson that if I saw his mysterious stranger I would let him know.

"I'd like that, Gid," he said. "Gretchen says she's never seen him, and pretty soon I'll think I'm haunted by a private apparition. Meantime, I guess I'll put up my little sign again."

"What do you hear from Ruth Ellen?" Kate inquired, switching the subject in polite Dinton fashion. Ruth Ellen was the Johnsons' seventeen-year-old daughter who, having marched for peace and civil rights, starred in hockey at the Dinton High School, and worked as a nurse's aide at the Cottage Hospital, was now at Rose Manor Junior College.

"She doesn't write often. I guess she's all right," said Barry.

He walked away, and the worst happened. He did put up his sign, but this time the lettering was somewhat different: NO THRU WAY—DEAD END. Katie said the altered form showed the rapid descent of world culture.

"A little more and we're t-h-r-u," she said.

But that same morning, after Barry had left, our conversation was about the mysterious redheaded stranger.

"Funny about that," I said. "Barry says the man always disappears. He never sees him any farther along the lane."

"I should think not," said Katie.

"What do you mean by that?"

"Some things are clear as daylight. This man can never be seen farther along the lane than the Johnson house because that's where he stops."

"Without Barry knowing?"

"Naturally. He doesn't want to see Barry—he wants to see Gretchen. He hides in the garage until Barry is out of the way."

"How long have you known this? Why didn't you tell me?"

"Lift that stove lid. Put in that hunk of oak wood."

She never did say why she had kept mum, but I felt sure that the real reason lay in the pride of superiority of her sex. She knew I would find out eventually, and then she would preen herself with having known all along.

"I'm amazed at Gretchen," I said. "I can't believe it. Maybe this stranger is just selling magazine subscriptions or vanilla extract."

"And hides in the garage until Barry leaves?"

Katie shrugged while she gave her mixture in the kettle on the top of the stove a few more vigorous stirs.

"I think I may have something this time," she said. "But if I really, really have, I refuse to market any of my crackers through the chain stores."

"You think Barry's a fool."

"Of course he's a fool."

"Because he has no doubts about the fidelity of his wife?"

"Don't be dull, Gideon, my love."

"Suppose our positions were reversed, ours and the Johnsons', I mean. . . ."

"They couldn't be, as you well know. For one thing, no red-headed stranger or any other stranger would be running after me, and . . ."

"You're more attractive than you think," I said. "If you'd only stop leaning over a hot stove all day . . ."

"Shut up. I feel more creative here at my stove in my own kitchen that I would in bed with old Adam himself."

"Katie!"

"Besides, I prefer things as they used to be around here. We had plenty of original sin in the old days, as I recall, and it was one of the primal conditions. But you don't have to exercise any fine perceptions to see how unoriginal sin is crowding out the other kind. I say it's cheap. The trouble is, fundamentally, that the Almighty intended Dinton to be at least four hours from Boston. The Old Colony Line made it in three hours, the New Haven lengthened it out again because the New Haven never believed in haste, and now Route 3 makes it an hour and twenty minutes if you want to drive like whoop-it-for-hell as most people do. What can you expect? The inevitable result is a stranger dodging around in our lane, waiting to fornicate with Gretchen Johnson."

If I felt unequal to expounding the philosophy of things to Katie, she had no such backwardness with me. I did not know whether I agreed entirely, but there was a weight of logic and emerging history on her side.

Our conversation then stopped short. She sent me to the attic to look for extra baking tins.

Upon reflection I found myself obliged to admit that my own arrangements had in some way established the pattern for what was now taking place in our lane, and in Dinton, and perhaps more broadly in the world outside. For a good many years now, I had been in the employ of an old established wholesale grocery house in Boston, an altogether famous firm of which I had come to be an established and not far from old executive. The house at Dinton had come to me from my forebears, and Katie and I found it convenient to live there while I went to Boston, at first six days a week, then five days a week, and finally three days a week.

Therefore my goings and comings followed the same lines of geography as Barry Johnson's. It might be said that we were both commuters. But I was a countryman going to work in the city, and Barry was a city man coming to sleep in the country. I don't know how significant the difference may seem to others, but to me it formed a Great Divide. Civilization splits upon such distinctions as this.

When I mentioned the matter to Katie, she seemed to give me credit for discernment; she doesn't often do this.

"Come to think of it," she said, "I used to hear of Dinton people going to the city for Fourth of July to see the fireworks and watch the parading. Now it's all the other way. Every holiday that comes along, Dinton gets a spillover from Greater Boston, whatever that is, and our own people stay put. You might say there's a reversal of gravitational pull affecting the tides of our subculture."

"What's our subculture, for heaven's sake?"

"It's the only culture we've got. It's all sub."

I did not think that our manner of life, Katie's and mine, much resembled Barry's and Gretchen's. Gretchen lived in suburbia and was closely concerned with crocuses, tuberous-rooted begonias, and chionodoxa. She belonged to a contract-bridge club, the P.T.A., and had been named to a committee to get up a Dinton League of Women Voters. Katie lived in the country, and her flowers, such as daffodils, lilacs and hardy perpetual roses, were mostly descendents of those naturalized by Dinton ancestors long ago. They were all easygoing. She belonged to the Dinton Historical Society and the Women's Club, and hadn't been to a meeting for years.

Both women were college graduates, Gretchen of Wellesley, and Katie, a good while earlier, of Wheaton. It might be said, though here I offer an extremely subjective and probably prejudiced opinion, that Gretchen went on escalating, which was the modern thing, and Katie had come down to earth. But maybe it was just that time was on our side.

Katie's experiments in the kitchen, though they seemed likely to continue indefinitely, had already been productive enough to satisfy most ambitions. Through my Boston firm I had been helpful in placing two of her concoctions with manufacturers who distributed them under their own trade names: Aunt Drusilla's Tea Cake Mix, and Non-Caloric Versatile Thins, though the Versatile Thins had died aborning. Customers seemed to get fat on them, or such was the report. Anyway, Aunt Drusilla's Tea Cake Mix had achieved national distribution. Katie's morose passions were aroused, however, because the baking concern had begun adding peanut oil to the formula. Mention peanuts to Katie and she would usually scream.

I pointed out to her more than once how much she was indebted to the new civilization of which Barry and Gretchen Johnson were representatives. She must look upon them not as monsters of the evolutionary process but as customers.

"Rats!" she said. "Everybody has to eat." All sorts of people still said "Nuts!" but no one else of my acquaintance ever said "Rats!" It was an heirloom expletive. It was also an affectation.

Katie and Gretchen each considered the other disoriented. If both were right, they possibly had something in common, but the very nature of their bond would prevent their discovering it. As for Barry and myself, we got along all right. Whether we had much or anything in common didn't matter; we always pretended that we had. Barry would always say, "Hi, fellow!" and I would always behave as if he had spoken a language common to us both. Maybe he had. Katie said once that men are the least common denominator.

❧

All this more or less introduces a scene that unfolded, as if by dramatic necessity, a few days later. I had plunged out into some unseasonably warm weather, inviting the relaxation of communion with nature in March, not always allowed by our Dinton climate. Not far beyond my door I met Henry Spinney carrying an axe in one hand and in the other Barry Johnson's sign, which he had chopped off midway of its supporting post.

"Nice morning, Henry," I said.

"Oh, hell, yes," he said. "I suppose you've seen this damn thing."

I shall dilute Henry's profanity. It wasn't especially ornate, and the words are familiar, though not always used as enthusiastically or as publicly as he used them. I doubt if his steamboating experience had enriched the vocabulary, drawn from seafaring tradition, to which he had been born. But he used them with the added emphasis of individual proprietorship. He had made them his own.

"Yes, I've seen it," I said.

"Stupid bastard," said Henry, referring to Barry Johnson.

I felt I owed a certain duty to Barry, so I ventured the lame remark that he wanted privacy.

"He don't know how to get it," Henry Spinney declared. "I want privacy, you want privacy. So far as I know, we've had a pretty reasonable article of privacy and a fair prospect of hanging on to it until this goddamn fool with his fancy neckties and toothbrush mustache thinks he has to put up a standing invitation to the contrary."

"He meant the sign as a sort of warning."

"Dinton people don't want to be warned. They're extremely goddamned averse to being warned."

"I know, Henry, but aren't you exaggerating the importance of a small matter?"

"Exaggerating, hell. What's small on Boston Common or Central Park is big as all hell in Dinton. A small matter like this can bust the town hall and courthouse wide open, and after that they'll go to work on the Statehouse. My God, before this is over, Washington is likely to hear about it, and we'll have a goddamned committee of congressmen eating rare steaks at the Central House at the expense of the taxpayers. We're going to have people here, all on account of this sign, and you might as well make up your mind to it. It's going to be as if the earth were tilted and the whole population sliding down toward us."

In principle, of course, Henry Spinney was right, but it seemed unlikely to me that the sign had been much noticed or even that it would have been much noticed if it had stayed in place a while longer. I said something to this effect, but my words bounced back from the broad beam of Henry Spinney's personality.

As I remember it, all officers and dignitaries—the terms in this case are almost indistinguishable—of the Fall River Line were impressive figures, and they all gained their impressiveness from horizontal rather than vertical measurement. I can recall none that was above medium height, but there was hardly a limit to the width or breadth of any of them. This was entirely different from corpulence; you couldn't have found a fat man among them, but they had spread out like pianos until you wondered how they could negotiate ordinary doorways. Henry Spinney belonged in that company. His legs were at the corners of a powerful dead end of anatomy.

"If regulation isn't the root of all evil, it's damn close," said Henry. "We don't want to regulate ourselves into any damn mess of trouble around here."

"What are you going to do with the sign?" I asked.

"This," said he, regarding the offensive object balefully, "is going into my fireplace, and I'm going to watch it burn."

"Are you planning to say an incantation over the ashes?"

He grinned, and I might say he grinned both happily and furiously.

"I can think of a goddamned good one," he said.

When I reported all this to Katie, she merely looked at me with emphatic inattention.

"We'll cross that bridge when we come to it. Don't go into the living room without wiping your feet."

As soon as he noticed the rape of his sign, Barry Johnson came over, as of course he would.

"I can only suppose it was an act of malicious mischief," he said, "though Gretchen says the village boys have always been polite to her. Neither of us can think of any grievance anyone in Dinton can have against us. I tell you, though, Gid, I can't afford to keep paying for signs if they're just going to disappear."

"I don't think it can be expected of you," I said.

"In my own mind I'm wondering about that redheaded chap. He could have done it."

"Have you seen him lately?"

"Not exactly. But I think I've seen footprints that are most likely his. Gretchen is as puzzled as I am."

"She is?" said Katie.

"Yes," said Barry. "Did you think she wouldn't be?"

"Intuition, maybe," said Katie. "That's what they always say about a woman, but you can't expect it to work every time."

"Are you going to put up another sign?" I asked.

"I'm going to see what I can do up in Boston. Maybe a metal one."

He went away, and Katie said, "Why didn't you tell him the truth?"

"Just cautious, I guess. Why didn't you?"

"Too much bother. If he had the sense of a countryman instead of a suburbanite, such as that is, he wouldn't need to be told."

❧

Barry did find an attractive metal sign in a hardware store in Boston. White embossed letters against a green background said, in the same objectionable idiom Barry had employed, NO THRU WAY. But before he posted this prefabricated warning, which, after all, was not confined to our lane but part of a far wider conflict, the course of events had lurched forward. That's what Dinton events do; they lurch. They don't flow.

The active agent appeared in the person of Ellie Kempton, highway surveyor of the township of Dinton, a skinny, conniving and agreeable character who was comfortable to have around only when the town had voted an unnecessarily large road budget both for maintenance and new construction.

The highway surveyor didn't do any surveying. He superintended the streets and roads, approved his own bills, and spent an appropriation second in size only to that for health, education and welfare. Welfare used to cost more than streets, but that was when people cared nothing about any streets but the ones they lived on and would haggle over every penny. In the automobile age it didn't take long for streets to outstrip welfare and even compete with schools.

When I answered Ellie's knock at the back door, he said, "Come out here a minute, Gid. I want to show you something."

"Who is it?" said Katie from somewhere in the front of the house.

"It's Ellie Kempton," I said.

"What does he want?"

"I don't know. I'll be back in a minute."

"Women are curious. Always were, are and will be. Funny about women," Ellie remarked, though he intended his observation not as sagacity but merely as conversation. Conversation had to be carried on as a possibly useful distraction from the main issue, whatever the main issue happened to be. Usually it was money. Ellie was a pretty fair sample of your up-to-date dollar-and-cents man, evolved from a Dinton rootstock.

I put on my hat and coat and stepped out with Ellie until we both stood in the middle of the lane.

"You know, Gid," he said, "if we work it right we can get a good widening and a hard surface on this street."

"What street?"

"I call it a street. It's all laid out on the town plan."

"The town plan has only a remote relation to facts," I said.

"Just the same, I believe the town will accept a new layout of this street and improve it."

"Why on earth should anyone want to improve it?"

"Real-estate values. Bring more taxable property onto the books of the assessors. You've been kind of neglected out this way. It's about time the town spent something for your benefit. Goodness knows, you've been paying enough taxes for other people."

"Ellie, you know damn well that Katie and I don't want a lick of work done on this lane. Henry Spinney doesn't, and Barry Johnson doesn't. We like it the way it is."

"You probably haven't figured on the possibilities. There's the potentiality of growth."

"Growth be damned. Why do you have to come around mixing in a neighborhood like this?"

"There's been talk. It's an old right of way. You can find it on the town plan. People don't like the notion of it being closed off."

"Nobody's planning to close it off."

"That sign," said Ellie.

"All it said was that the lane doesn't lead anywhere."

"It leads plenty of places for those who are allowed to feel free to use what is an old right of way, so shown on the town plan."

"We'll fight you, Ellie. We're all dead against you."

"I'm not so sure about Henry Spinney."

"I am."

"Have you talked to him lately?"

"I sure have."

"Well, you talk to him again."

"I will."

"There's something big that's started rolling, and I don't know as anything can stop it."

"What are you talking about?"

"Building roads. People living in the world today use roads. You use roads. I use roads. Roads have got to be built."

"Not here, for God's sake."

"Here, same as everywhere."

"Ellie, there's something you're not telling, and I'm not going to ask you because I can see you have no intention of telling. But I'll find out, and I expect it isn't going to take me very long. I know every smell in Dinton, night or day, summer or winter."

"It's only roads. That's what it is. Roads is what modern civilization is all about."

"Aren't you forgetting politics?"

"Well, the politics in this case was taken up by Mr. Johnson posting that sign."

"All the same, giving you the benefit of the doubt you're not entitled to, this is going to be war. Somebody will get hurt."

"I'm sorry to hear you talk that way, Gid. I suspected you'd swing in with us, same as Henry Spinney. He sees the need. He knows you can't hold back progress in Dinton any more than other progressive communities."

Ellie departed, and I was eager to see Henry Spinney. But before I could find him—he was away on a Boston trip that day—it turned out that Katie and I had to work off a sort of conference with Barry and Gretchen Johnson. They hadn't seen Ellie, but they had heard the news in town; that's how fast the conspiracy against our lane had gained headway. We sat in our living room, as consciously formal, important and threatened as an equal number of delegates considering the latest crisis in international relations.

"I think what puzzles me most," said Barry who had begun speaking as the natural leader of the group, "is that people in Dinton don't seem to resent the prospect of having to pay for an entirely unnecessary road. As I remember it, when Gretchen and I first came here, the voters were tax-conscious. You could sense that good old thriftiness as part of the way of life. Now Gretchen tells me the talk she heard in the post office and stores was all in favor of putting a hard-surfaced road through here."

"People are the same everywhere," said Katie. "They like roads. They don't care where the hell the roads are or where they lead."

"Katie's right," I said. "The last thing a man will economize on in his own home is liquor and automobiles, and the last thing he'll economize on publicly is roads."

"I don't think we have to surrender to cynicism," said Gretchen with her attitude of chill collegiate good sense. "We can always appeal to reason, and reason does prevail when it has a chance. . . ."

"Like hell it does," said Katie.

"Katie!" I said. "Please!"

"We've got to explain, to communicate," Gretchen went on. "I know you feel strongly about this, Katie. We all do. I realize that when people are talking as I heard them today, the odds seem pretty hopeless. But we have the best case, and we can make them see it."

"Perhaps you're right," said Katie hypocritically.

I wasn't following Gretchen's words so much as her configuration, and I may as well put that plainly. I'd had hardly a glimpse of her since Katie's disclosure about the redheaded stranger, and when you learn something like that about a pretty woman, you take a renewed interest in her—and a different sort of interest. If you're a man, you do, and it matters not about age or moral philosophy. Gretchen was far prettier than most women, with a lot of youth and health thrown in. She kept her darkish hair brushed back from her forehead, but not entirely; it fluffed in places. Her greenish eyes looked at you confidently and, maybe, frankly. I wondered about that. I thought the romantic reservation was present.

She wore a creamy tweed jacket over a blue blouse, and a mixed blue-and-brown tweed skirt. This costume seemed to do more for her figure by making you remember it than another could have done by disclosing it more candidly. You remembered it from the early days of the Garden of Eden, or at least from your first discovery of Eden's legend.

"I don't know whether Gretchen's plan would push too fast," said Barry. "She's all for forming a committee. But I wonder if the menace is really as serious as we assume. We don't want to head off a stampede if . . ."

"It's serious, all right," I said.

"I can't think why," said Barry. "I can't conceive of a thing like this gaining such headway in Dinton overnight—I mean, without any reason at all."

"Just one little item," said Katie. "No t-h-r-u way."

"My committee idea is really to make use of the movement already started toward a Dinton League of Women Voters," said Gretchen evenly. That is, her words walked a sort of tightrope, and you looked at them up there and out there. Yet they weren't altogether real to me and did not keep away my forbidden thoughts about Gretchen's flesh. "After all, this is a civic cause. It's logical to join the two together. The League can get a better start with an issue."

"What do you think, Gid?" asked Barry.

"With Gretchen carrying the ball I'm all for it," I said.

"And you, Katie?"

"If the women don't do something, nobody will," said Katie. "I will say that to me committees are poison, but so is DDT, and I hear it's still being widely used."

"All right, that's settled," said Barry. "Gretchen will go ahead, and meantime I'm going to make it a point to talk to the selectmen, the people at the bank, and some others. How about you, Gid?"

"Oh, I'll make myself heard. I've already talked with Ellie Kempton, the road surveyor."

"I think the thing that should worry us more than anything else is Mr. Spinney's attitude," said Gretchen.

"Yes, I can't understand Spinney," said Barry.

"What about him?" I asked.

"I haven't been able to contact him myself yet," said Barry, "but I hear him quoted as saying the hard-surfaced road may turn out to be a good thing."

"I'm seeing Henry as soon as possible," I said.

"Well, that's good," said Gretchen. "You're much the best one to see him."

This was how our conference went, but of course we didn't stop there; we went over the same ground three or four times more, and Katie brought in coffee and some unidentifiable concoction of her own, and I watched Gretchen settle back comfortably on our sofa—yes, it's a sofa, though the name is old-fashioned—and cross her lovely legs, and double them up, and change from one fluid pose to another. I was bored with the conversation, but since I had Gretchen to watch I wouldn't complain.

Then Katie brought the session to a close by asking, "What do you hear from Ruth Ellen?"

Barry looked at Gretchen, and Gretchen carefully didn't look at him. "Ruth Ellen is planning to come home for a few days," she said.

"It isn't midterm, is it?" Katie asked.

"No. She's just coming," said Gretchen.

"Her mother told her she could," said Barry.

"Certainly I did," said Gretchen. "If our daughter's judgment is that she should come home for a few days, well, I think we just have to respect it."

"Oh, yes," said Barry. "That's the way to run a college. No attention to rules, no respect for authority."

"But Barry," said Gretchen, "we don't absolutely know that the dean told her not to come."

They were now on the way to the door, and we heard them taking the discussion out with them and across the grass to the lane and even a distance after that.

Katie picked up the soiled coffee cups and took them to the kitchen. I followed with an ash tray completely filled with Gretchen's lipstick-stained butts.

"It's too bad you don't get to serve on a committee with Gretchen," said Katie.

"Why?"

"Mini-skirts, mostly."

"Katie, you have a wicked tongue."

"I wouldn't swap you for your predatory eye," she said.

I saw Henry Spinney the next day. It surprised me to find that his house was thoroughly Victorian. The room in which we sat had gilt wallpaper with curlicues, tacked-down carpeting that was now believed to hold the germs of generations, an overstuffed sofa in flowered covering with ostentatious buttons holding its bulges, antimacassars on the chairs, and gilt-framed paintings of waterfalls, sheep in the highlands, Arabs charging in the desert, and all that sort of thing. Even the large crystal ash tray on the heavy-legged mahogany table beside which Henry sat with his cigar belonged to the setting, as I could remember from childhood.

All this, I thought, had been contrived, and at first it puzzled me to fit Henry into such surroundings. Then I realized that nothing had really been contrived for him; he had been born to it, and had lived and, one might say, flowered in it. And there was a spiritual kinship between this room and a major theme of Henry's life, with which I now realized there was a close association—the Fall River Line.

In detail, of course, Henry's living room did not resemble any of the lush, rococo public rooms of the wonderful old side-wheeler *Priscilla,* but the over-all identity was close. The effulgence of a day gone by, not in the too remote past but in the middle distance, lived on here—more than lived on. It continued a flourishing survival, and Henry, with his odd, thick, squat figure, his cigar, his sometimes austere, always well-dramatized authority, formed the most vital part of it. For there was real vitality in the New England version of Victorianism despite all evidence against such a belief. I knew. I had felt it. I saw it now.

Henry sat in his shirt sleeves, and the shirt was an old-fashioned stiff white one with starched cuffs, temporarily open around his wrists, with heavy gold links dangling. The links might have been presented to him upon his retirement; they were that ceremonial or monumental. He had discarded his necktie for comfort, and the collar was likewise open. I remembered some of the old lore about "dress shirts" and how my mother had disliked ironing them. That shirt of Henry's represented the old-fashioned subordination of the female; she was born to wash and iron for just such men as he, although I realized that few remained extant.

"I thought you and I ought to have a talk, Henry," I said.

"I expect we should, Gid. Can I offer you a cigar?"

"I was born too late for your taste in cigars," I said, "and besides that, you have to remember that in me the blood of old Dinton has pretty well run out."

"You don't fool me, Gid, but never mind. What are these goddamned asinine Johnson people going to do now about all the trouble they've started?"

"Well, the first thing is going to be a committee."

"Good. That's as good as anything."

"Will you support it, Henry?"

"You know damn well I won't have any part of these goddamn time-wasting committees."

"You think it won't amount to anything?"

"Gid, you don't need to ask that. You know as goddamn well

as I do that only one thing is nearer to zero than a committee, and that's a petition. But you have to get 'em up, no two ways about it. Are they going to circulate a petition?"

"They could."

"Tell them to go ahead with a petition—on stiff paper—long sheets like they use at the courthouse. Tell them to have Judge Holley draw it up."

"I'm willing to pass the word along. But Henry, I want you to tell me what you said to Ellie Kempton. Did you give him the impression that you were backing him up in this scheme?"

"I'm not responsible for the impressions of a man like Ellie Kempton. He sees what he wants to see and hears what he wants to hear. As soon as he came through that door I told him he and his goddamned kind were a drag on humanity. I told him he was more goddamned foolish and vicious and mercenary than any other man born in Dinton in this century. I told him my ideas about this lane, and they're the same as yours and the same as they always have been. You know that, Gid."

"Well, go on," I said. "There's more to it."

"More of the same, and it all ran off Ellie's back like rain off the roof of my kitchen ell. You don't get anywhere blowing off your mouth to Ellie or his kind—he knows he's got his hand in the pocket of the taxpayer, and all he cares about is keeping it there."

"If he can stand up to you, Henry, he's better than most."

"He just looked out the window with no more expression than a dried herring. That's Ellie's style. I know the breed."

"Well, what happened next?"

"I asked him who he was thinking of getting for an appraiser, and he stopped looking out the window in a hurry. 'An appraiser?' he said, surprised. 'You're damn right,' I told him. 'An appraiser. You don't think any property along this lane is going to change hands to make a street without its being appraised, do you?' He looked at me and I could see the light bursting in that back-room brain of his. 'What property?' he asked me, though already he had seen some of the possibilities. 'The town will never vote to put hard surface on this lane the way it is,' I said. 'The money would be thrown away unless there's a widening to at least twenty-five feet. That's why I'm so strong against the hard surface. I don't want any goddamned boulevard.' "

"You baited him, Henry. You deliberately baited him. You wouldn't have mentioned appraising, which means money, if you hadn't wanted him to rise to it."

"How he took it is his lookout."

"Henry," I said, "you did just what you intended to do. You started him thinking about appraisals, land damages and so on. You practically invited him to consider how much of a promotion he can make out of this peaceful lane of ours. Naturally he would suppose you were only going to hold out for what you can get."

"Just so, Gid. Ellie would have come to the real money part of it sooner or later. Might as well have the subject raised right at the beginning."

"You're not expressing the whole of your thought, Henry."

"I don't need to," he said, putting his head back and exhaling a thick plume of cigar smoke. Then, looking at me with as much or as little candor as I might elect to perceive, he went on, "If we don't jail one or two of them before this is over, I don't have the mentality that a man of my age and experience is supposed to be possessed of. Ellie has a line into the Statehouse. He knows that when land damages and highways were hitched together in Massachusetts, it was better than gold in California or nuggets in the Klondike put together, and no real inconvenience attached. He don't even have to buy a shovel. At most he'll open a new bank account in his wife's name."

"I don't know," I said. "Ellie has that kind of shrewdness, all right, but it seems to me you're counting on things not likely to happen."

"I'm not counting on anything, Gid. I'm just making moves the way I see the odds."

"It would surprise me if Ellie or any of them around here did anything you could jail them for. . . ."

"You mean you'd be surprised if they got caught at it."

"Yes, I suppose that's what I mean."

"Look, Gid, there's one more circumstance. I can see what's in your mind. You still think I'm setting a needless course into squally weather. All right. But look, did you ever know any great run of Dinton people to be on the same side of any issue as Henry Spinney?"

"That's because you choose to be contrary-minded."

"Maybe I do and maybe I don't. In this case, no matter what, I choose to do some navigating and let Ellie and all the rest of them do the guessing and worrying. If I want to, I can come about quick in heavy weather. I like heavy weather, Gid. I was raised to it."

The next time I saw Henry was at the first meeting of Gretchen Johnson's committee, which was held in the grand-jury room at the courthouse on a Saturday night in early April. I did not want to attend the meeting, but Katie insisted that I could not shirk so clear a responsibility. After she had me safely involved, she announced that she would go along also. She expected me to try to back out at this juncture, since there was no need for both of us to undergo the experience, but I lacked the spunk.

We sat on the last of the golden-oak benches on the side of the room nearest the door, though not with any expectation on my part that early escape would be possible. The other benches filled up well before eight o'clock, the time set in the notices, and those present were an odd mixture of the people you would expect to show up and those you wouldn't. You would expect the Garden Club members, the articulate civic faddists, and a few who loved meetings—any meetings—but you would not expect the root-and-branch conservatives, Jared Bartlett and his wife, Charlotte, and Mrs. Almira Hunter, for instance.

For that matter, I would not have expected Henry Spinney, but in he came, dressed in a blue serge suit that looked vaguely nautical. I didn't notice him at first because Mrs. Bronson Alder, one of Dinton's more aggressive clubwomen, had leaned over us as if to impart a confidential message.

"Gretchen has done an awfully good job putting this meeting together," she whispered. "She's done a perfectly wonderful job."

As soon as Mrs. Alder and her importance had moved on, Katie remarked to me, "It appears that everyone nowadays is doing a good job. You hear that word everywhere. The minister does a good job, so does the driver of the mail truck, the junior-high-school principal, and the man who repairs old sofas—I forget his name. When I was growing up, the language wasn't so limited. A job was a job and not just a flowery manner of speaking, except I remember how my father used to say that our dog Plutarch had gone into the front hall again and done his job on the red carpet. I . . . ."

"Katie," I said, "will you be quiet?"

"Look," she said, nudging me, and that was when I saw Henry Spinney. Almost at the same moment Gretchen Johnson rapped for order.

She, of course, had been faced with the problem of what to wear, not only because of her own image, as they say nowadays, but because her attire would set the tone of the meeting. She could have made it fussily clubbish or sensibly civic or any of several variations. It might be subject to satire around town in any case, but by appearing as unaffected as possible she avoided trite adjectives and the more familiar degrees of antagonism. She hadn't dressed down, and she hadn't dressed up. Her rather plain but by no means inexpensive blue wool dress had a severe neckline. I thought it was probably just right.

"You all know why we are here," she said. "I hope that this evening we shall be able to arrange a formal organization, but before we proceed with that I think some informal discussion will be helpful. The question of unnecessarily widening and surfacing a beautiful little country lane is just an instance of what we as citizens and taxpayers have to face in dealing with our government today."

This sounded like the beginning of a familiar propaganda talk, but Gretchen quickly balanced the "unnecessary-expenditure" theme with really warm expansiveness on the other side. She wasn't against improvement, or even against bond issues and new functions of government. She was, and you believed her, for a better world, beginning with Dinton.

"Now," she said, "since the matter of the lane is what has started us off on what I hope will be a real program, I think we should have some exchange of views right away before going any further."

Mrs. Alder rose up promptly, breasted the air waves, or whatever air waves the grand-jury room accommodated, in the manner of a battleship, and proceeded to define the issues. She defined the issues aloft and right down to the ground, and no matter if you looked at them from up or down or right or left, they were the same issues. Yet she didn't say exactly what they were, though they involved our institutions, conservation, economy in government, natural resources, future generations, traditions, the good sense of the people of Dinton, and more streetlights in the business center of the town.

Her reference to the people's good sense was dangerous. You can drag your oratory along as much as you like, but when you mention good sense, you arouse suspicion. Whose good sense is open to doubt? Who questions it, and how much sense has the questioner got? It's true that Dinton has its share of flightiness and eccentricity, but what town hasn't? If you want to attack something, the thing to do is to stick to morals, a field in which weakness is prevalent the world over; you mustn't suggest that Dinton people are weak in their heads. I could feel the defensiveness of the audience. I don't know whether Gretchen felt it, or whether her instinct prompted her to gloss things over.

She called on Mrs. Herbert Clifford, who was skinny, tart and respected. Mrs. Clifford rose and said, "Anyone would lay out so much as fifty cents on that lane ought to be put away for good. We taxpayers have got enough to contend with." Then she sat down.

This was real progress for our side, and there seemed to be an excellent chance that others would follow Mrs. Clifford's tone and style, as people are prone to do at meetings when they recognize something easy and popular has been said. If this should happen, we could all listen a while, the meeting would elect Gretchen permanent chairman with authority to name her committee, and we could all go home and turn on the TV.

Gretchen sensed the right ones to call on, and for a little while we made excellent westing. But then Charlotte Bartlett got up without being so much as recognized.

"I'm against spending town money as much as anybody in this room," she said, with a slight quaver in her voice because she was shy about speaking in public. That quaver was worth a lot; it broke the momentum that had been heading all in one direction. "My husband and I suffer from taxes. But what I want to know is how would they manage if two oil trucks should meet head on in that little narrow lane, the way it is now?"

She sat down. I remembered what I should have had in mind all along, that Jared Bartlett always counted on having his trucks hired for any new road work in town.

Jared himself stood up and said, "I don't know as improving that lane—that road—would cost so much town money. We could get it under Chapter 90 so's the county would pay a quarter and the state would pay half."

Mrs. Alder scented the familiar challenge, her nostrils vibrating, and she stood up to answer it in the familiar way. "It won't do to imagine that what the state spends has nothing to do with our pocketbooks here in Dinton," she declared. "The state gets its money from us and people just like us."

Somehow this truth—for truth it must be, though it falls upon most ears as the most abstract of logical exercises—has never yet retarded any local desire for state funds. I was prepared to hear someone say that the state was bound to spend the money anyway, and if Dinton didn't take it, some other town would. But Gretchen proved her skill at chairmanship. She left the state money dangling and invited the attention of the meeting in a different direction.

"The question has been raised about oil trucks meeting in the lane," she said. "I think we would all like to hear more about this, and I will ask Mr. Spinney to comment."

Henry hoisted himself to full view. His broad face had no coarseness, and indeed there seemed a refinement of molding about his nose and eyes, the mark of a man born to observe and consider. His skin had never lost a basic suntan glow, and his chin would have been the envy of many a general.

"Now as to oil trucks," Henry said. "It's very true, as any of you can see, if two oil trucks meet in that lane no power under heaven can get one past the other. No two ways about it, one truck has got to back up, union rules or no union rules. This puts me in mind of the situation in Bulawayo, South Africa. In a wild region like that they needed oxen to haul their wagons, and they used to have sixteen or eighteen hitched in a span, as they called it. Now, turning one of these outfits was no easy affair, as we can all realize, and when Bulawayo was laid out, the streets were made wide —so wide that an eighteen-oxen hitch could be turned around as desired any place at all, so as to head in the other direction.

"In a matter of a dozen years or so, they stopped using oxen and wagons, because lorries—that's their name for trucks—had come to practical application there as everywhere else. So you might say the wide streets served no real purpose any more, except that—and I ask you to note this—at least six oil trucks could pass, side by side, at one time. It's an advantage Bulawayo has, laying it over any other settled place on the face of the globe."

Henry sat down and, as may be imagined, there was silence. We had all heard what he had said, yet it was altogether unclear what he had really said, or how seriously it should be taken. I suppose many of those present decided that they were—to use an old expression—being had. This was my own view. Henry was in his usual form; but although the business about the oil trucks would come up again eventually, no one in Dinton would want to touch it again right away.

The first to rally was Mrs. Clifford.

"I hear talk about state money," she said, "but since when would the state lay out money on a blind-alley road? That lane don't go anywhere, and the state has need enough of all its money for roads that do go places."

"That's true if you don't look far enough," Jared Bartlett replied, hitching himself halfway up from his bench. "Naturally, the state would want to make it a real through way, and that's how it should be, maybe, except for the selfishness of a few people. Under Chapter 90 we can get that road opened all the way to the Point. I'd like to know what better progress there could be for the town."

"How would you get past the Crying Swamp?" Mrs. Clifford demanded.

"You'd go to the west of it," said Jared Bartlett.

"You would not," said Henry Spinney, without taking the trouble to rise. "You'd go to the east."

"How do you figure that?" demanded Jared. "If you tried to go to the east you'd be bogged down for two, three years. No state engineer would be fool enough to put his O.K. on that route."

"Some people admire state engineers, but as for me, I've no use for them. I say the voters of this town of Dinton can settle what routes they want. What's the state got to do with it? They expect you to lick their boots up there in the Statehouse, but you don't have to do it."

Gretchen rapped mildly for order. Her composure had been shot from under her, but she held on to appearances fairly well.

"I don't think," she began, "I don't think . . ."

Mrs. Clifford interrupted. "West or east," she said, "I hold that it's all downright foolishness."

Mrs. Abbot Parker, who had sided with our forces at the beginning, was now tempted to show her superior knowledge. "There's a line of hummocks that leads right through the middle of the Crying Swamp—well, not the middle exactly, but off a little to the southwest—and you could build a ridge of high ground by following those hummocks. That's where the dirt road ran when I was a girl."

"Never was a dirt road!" declared Mrs. Clifford.

"There was so," said Mrs. Parker.

"You call that old cow path a road? I've been out that way as much as anyone in this room. I guess I know," said Mrs. Clifford.

"Ella, of course you know," said Mrs. Parker. "I'm not trying to dispute you. If it was a cow path, it was a cow path. All I'm saying is that's the best approach to solid ground."

"Maybe it is and maybe it isn't," said Ella.

"We aren't getting anywhere, Madam Chairman," said Jared Bartlett.

"Sounds to me as if Brother Bartlett was trying to cut off free discussion," said Henry Spinney. "I don't know where else there is to make headway if we can't talk it out right here. Seems to me you could go either east or west of the Crying Swamp so long as you went far enough either way. It might be you'd end up with a loop both ways if the Chapter 90 money held out."

"Listen, Henry Spinney," said Ella Clifford, "this is supposed to be a short way to the Point."

"It isn't supposed to be anything yet," replied Henry. "We're just talking about it. As to this matter of routes, you have to re-member that Oliver Holcomb will ask for damages if you cut through his cranberry bog."

"Cranberry bog nothing," said Jared Bartlett. "Oliver Holcomb hasn't picked a cranberry there for years. The whole place has gone back to wild swamp."

"That may be fact, but it's a hell of a long way from being good sense," said Henry, ornamenting his language a bit more than this. "It hasn't been worthwhile picking cranberries in that Godforsaken place because there's no way of getting the barrels shipped out. With a new boulevard such as this gathering is now contemplating, the economic future of the region will be what you might call assured and rejuvenated. A man will be able to ship cranberries, bog iron, cows or peat-flavored whiskey, all with equal ease, and have the stuff unloaded at the door of any Boston store, bar, speakeasy, or the Statehouse itself. He will be able to pass as many oil trucks on the way as he has a mind to."

I suppose Jared saw that if he argued with Henry he would be arguing against himself, so he kept still, even though it must have gone against the grain to allow so extravagantly implausible a statement to stand uncontradicted.

The meeting went on for a while, and I could go on with this account of it, but not without an accumulating burden of repetition and confusion. There's no more popular subject in Dinton than town landmarks as they used to be and the memories that men and women have of them in the old days. I don't believe a landmark or any approximation of a landmark between our lane and the Point remained undiscussed at that meeting. But at last Gretchen's gavel fell for the final adjournment.

She had her committee all right, with herself as chairman and authority to choose whatever members she wanted to serve with her, but she also had a fouled-up prospect and an opposition party that would certainly include everyone who stood to make a dollar out of any road-building work in or near the town of Dinton. There was also the challenge that had been raised as to the best route for a highway leading through our lane to the Point, and at this season of the year, when life in Dinton was uneventful, there would be people who would take sides on the issue entirely apart from any question of the merits of a proposed road or the common sense of spending anyone's money on it.

～

When we got home Katie and I were both hungry. A meeting in Dinton is a great worker-up of the appetite. So we went into the kitchen, and Katie got out the bread, some of her beach-plum jam, cheese and various other things, and put the kettle on to make tea. She was having an affair with tea along about this time.

"I remember when I read *David Copperfield* the last time," Katie said, "how Dickens remarked that when there was an argument and somebody began to lug in a bushel of wheat as somebody always did, he dropped out and admitted himself licked. He never could cope with those bushels of wheat or think of anything on the other side to top them. Well, that's the way I felt when Charlotte Bartlett lugged in the two oil trucks. I predict it will be many a long day before we get rid of those oil trucks."

"I'm afraid you're right," I said, "in spite of Henry Spinney."

"Or because of him, you might as well say. Like as not people will begin arguing for a road wide enough for seven abreast. Why should Africa be ahead of Dinton?"

"It won't be that bad."

"I don't see why it won't. Bushels of wheat have gone out. It's oil trucks that suit the public ideology. Suppose you tell me straight off anything more influential than oil trucks?"

"The water's boiling," I said. "I'd like some tea so long as I can't have coffee."

"We ran out of coffee, and I didn't think to buy any more." She didn't think. I let this familiar misstatement pass. She was having an affair with tea but she would never admit it.

Just about then there was a sound at the kitchen door. The door opened and Gretchen's head appeared. "May we come in?" she asked.

"Come right along," said Katie.

Gretchen had Barry with her, he having arrived at a late hour from Boston.

"He won't believe what happened at the meeting," she said.

"Oh, that!" said Katie. "That was just the beginning."

"What do you mean, just the beginning?" Barry asked.

"Let's eat first and then fill in the pauses with talk," Katie suggested.

"Yes, I would like something," said Gretchen. "I feel weak and famished."

She took off her jacket and hitched herself up on the counter —in Dinton we are more apt to call it the dresser—beside the sink, swinging her nimble legs. Barry tilted back in one of the kitchen chairs, Katie swished about for a bit longer, I settled on the woodbox, and we were ready for a post-meeting analysis.

"I felt the thing was getting out of hand," Gretchen said, "but I didn't know what I could do about it."

"If the fire alarm had sounded just then, it would have been handy," said Katie.

"Nothing short of that could have helped much," I said.

"I don't get it," said Barry, his young forehead wrinkled with concern—unnecessary wrinkles they were, but that was the way of the times. Katie said we lived in a wrinkling generation, a remark as superficial as any she ever made; probably she was really thinking about tensions. "I thought Dinton was simple and honest and different. From what Gretchen tells me, half the town is ready for a transaction in unadulterated boodle."

"Dinton is a microcosm," said Katie.

"I see the situation more as a matter of personalities," said Gretchen.

"You can say that again," said Katie.

"I hope that's it," said Barry, "because you can always appeal to a man's good sense and basic decency. After all, there's a traditional soundness in Dinton. Isn't that so?"

"If any two can agree on what soundness is," said Katie. "Hair-splitting is more traditional than almost anything around here."

"I see what you mean, but even so you're much too cynical," said Gretchen. "Now let's take the arguments about which route would be best for a road from here to the Point. What's the reason for the talk running off at a tangent like that, away from the main issue, which is whether there will be any road at all?"

There wasn't any ready answer, because most things don't go by reason. Barry hadn't half listened to her. He continued to worry about the idea of a meeting in Dinton being so irresponsible—that was the word he wound up with. Katie, after having agreed with him at the beginning, veered around and began getting more and more argumentative.

"You shouldn't have come so far from Boston if you don't like the kind of meetings down here," she said. "Now in Brookline or Dedham you could have had something measured right out to your taste, nice and conformist."

"I doubt it very much," said Barry. "You've got me all wrong if you think I'm after conformity and sophistication."

"Well, I'm not able to name off those Boston suburbs in the right order," said Katie. "Never could. But I expect if you could have come out just the right distance from Park Street or Tremont or whatever, you could have found exactly the sort of talk you have in mind. Boston thins out as you get away from it, and you can find the right mixture if you travel just far enough. I imagine it's the same around a good many of our big cities."

"I think you have a certain element of truth there, Katie, but there's a lot more to be said."

"Always is if you don't know when to stop," said Katie. "I suppose there has to be a Boston. As for me, I've lived all my life on the rim, and the outer ripple has just begun to show itself in Dinton."

"I'd like to see for myself what the countryside is like between here and the Point," said Gretchen. "I can't seem to visualize the Crying Swamp or the hummocks, if they do exist, or anything else about it. I'd like to know who's right. If the subject is going to be debated, I ought to know firsthand a lot more than I do now."

"Yes, you sure ought," said Barry.

"Could one get from the end of the lane to the Point on a bicycle? I used to ride a bicycle a lot."

"Not a chance," I said.

"Then walking is the only way, I suppose. What would you say the distance is?"

"Between four and five miles."

"Well, I could make that easily. Will you go with me, Gid?

You can show me exactly the places that people are talking about."

"When?" I asked.

"Why not tomorrow? It looks as if the weather will be good. Or is tomorrow one of your days in the city?"

"No, it's one of my days in Dinton. I guess I can go. As a matter of fact, I'd like to. I haven't walked to the Point in a good while, and I'd like to see how things look nowadays."

That was how, without premeditation, the joint expedition of Gretchen and me to the Point was decided upon. Katie was looking at me, and I could look right back. The idea wasn't mine; I was completely innocent.

As the Johnsons prepared to go, Katie said, "How soon is Ruth Ellen coming home?"

"She isn't coming. She's staying right at school," Barry said.

"She isn't coming right away," said Gretchen, "but if our daughter feels there's some reason for her to come home, she's certainly coming. That's definite."

"There isn't any reason," said Barry.

"You mean you don't think there's any reason."

"I know damn well and so do you," said Barry.

After they had gone, Katie said, "They don't even quarrel like Dinton people. They quarrel like husbands and wives you see on television."

"When do you watch television?"

"When I have my hair done," said Katie.

"Well," I said, "they're suburban. That's just about the whole of it."

~

Now as to Gretchen Johnson, up to this bright spring day she had been no problem of mine, and she wasn't to become so until midafternoon. Until then, I may say that I indulged in anticipation and not foreboding. I had seen her under various circumstances but, to put it plainly, never quite apart from a masculine fantasy old in me as in mankind.

One could say that my impression of Gretchen had been literary rather than realistic. Knowing about the redheaded stranger, I had placed her in a dubious but delightful frame of reference; seeing her preside at a meeting, I had taken note of her crisp competence—and of the divergence that so fascinatingly occurs to separate the flesh and the intellect; and watching her as she swung her legs in the kitchen, I had felt her conforming to my view of a modern young wife, a sum total of many items but not the sort of whole that one ought to contemplate too aggressively.

Her first words when she arrived to keep our appointment were "We should be back by suppertime, don't you think?"

"Why, yes. As a matter of fact, we don't need to walk all the way to the Point unless you really want to."

"I think we'd better."

She was dressed in dark-blue slacks, a neatly fitting blue sweater with a modified turtle-neck collar, a bright-red scarf around her throat, and what I guess were sensible walking shoes. She swung a small jacket across one arm. I thought at first she was hatless, but later I discovered she did have a red felt saucer on the back of her crown.

"Be sure to keep out of the bushes," said Katie.

Gretchen eyed her as if wondering if she really meant what it was perfectly clear she did mean.

"I don't think we need to worry much about poison ivy at this time of year," I said.

"Well, it pays to take care," said Katie.

"I expect it does," said Gretchen.

"Shall we be off?" I said. "Time's awasting."

It wasn't so much time that prompted me as it was a desire to get Gretchen separated from Katie. We let the kitchen door slam behind us and walked out into the lane. Traditionally, a walk to the Point was nothing much, but this one promised to be an adventure heightened by the beguiling spring atmosphere.

Henry Spinney watched us from a post in his yard where he had been raking leaves. His unbuttoned coat hung loose, exposing the upper part of a suit of heavy underwear. As we came abreast of his place he waved but said nothing, and I was aware that his speechlessness was itself a comment.

The lane didn't really end. It ran into gentle wildness and then into the open countryside, but even then one could find the mark of an old trodden path, which Gretchen and I followed, she in the lead. The order of our going satisfied me, for I preferred to see her rather than not to see her.

I have described the atmosphere of the afternoon as beguiling, and so it was. But spring is an uncertain season around Dinton, and by the time Gretchen and I had covered a mile or so, with briers nagging at our legs and the sense of an old wilderness surrounding us with whisperings and solitude, clouds had covered most of the western sky. We traversed boggy places where the hard ground seemed about to end, though hummocks and ridges still carried it on intermittently. Dead trees rising from black pools reminded Gretchen of a blasted heath, and she spoke with distaste.

I don't know how it is to enter a new wilderness; I suspect there may be both awe and adventure, and probably much else. But one can hardly help feeling a witching reminder that others have gone before and that their legacy survives in a ghostly, hypnotic fashion.

I had been accustomed to this feeling from childhood. In Dinton we were brought up in awe of the Crying Swamp. But Gretchen's experience was new. She seemed to listen anxiously, and although there was plenty to hear—the pounding of surf on the Point in the distance, the edginess of the rising southwest wind, the crinkle of thickets and copses and glacial kettle holes pretending they were occupied, whether or no (and except for song sparrows, rabbits and ghosts, how could they be occupied?) —the general effect was one of expectant silence. Something was always about to be uttered, and the loneliness of that conquered, puritanized and deserted landscape accumulated the farther one ventured into it.

"We should have come in the morning," said Gretchen.

"I don't know. The shadows would have been pointing in the other direction, that's all."

"Oh, but look at the sky. It makes things so bare and gloomy."

"The whole promontory of Dinton is in mourning. You can't expect to outwit as ancient a fact as that."

"In mourning for what?"

"Well, I guess all mourning goes back to the same things—lost causes, lost lives and lost souls."

"What a cheerful companion you are, Gid! What lost lives are you talking about?"

"You see that depression over there? It looks like some of the glacial potholes, but the fact is it's a cellar hole. There's an uncut slab of stone that served as a doorstep, and close by there's a lilac bush that will be blooming in a few more weeks, as I suppose it must have bloomed a couple of centuries ago for the people who lived in the house that was above the cellar hole. The story is that the woman smoked in bed—a pipe, of course—and the bedclothes caught fire. The house burned down with the family in it."

"Don't you know any history that's cheerful?"

"Some, but tragedies make the best stories, and this region is the very darling of tragedy and mystery."

Gretchen was still walking ahead, and for the moment neither she nor I had noticed that there was no longer a discernible path; rather, we could have had a choice of ways, all uncertain and none well trod. Unused to the country—any country, but least of all to ours—she had no sense of the sun in the sky or the feeling of wind direction or even the guiding rhythm of distant surf. Having no awareness of any of these, she allowed herself to turn and follow what was perhaps a deer track or the remnant of a cow path, and led us down a sudden, unexpected slope into a pothole that was like a basin. We were quickly at the bottom of that depression, a fringe of bare sumacs looming on the farther side.

Within a range of moderate heights, depths and distances this

Dinton landscape presented relatively marked, impressive con-
trasts; and although we had descended perhaps no more than
twelve or fifteen feet, it was easy to imagine ourselves, if not at
the center of the earth in some treacherous crater, at least trapped
at the bottom of a pit hardly less compelling of awe. Gretchen
uttered a sharp cry and grabbed my arm. We stood together looking up at the fretwork of posturing sumacs.

"I guess we'd better go back the way we came," I said. "We
shouldn't have turned when we did."

Gretchen let go her hold on my sleeve as if reluctantly, though
I didn't yet realize the degree of her fear; I took it for no more
than timidity. I led the way up, up to the sky and the view and the
not altogether natural world of the Point heath.

"Aren't we almost there?" Gretchen asked.

"To the Point? Well, no. We've still to come to the main part
of the Crying Swamp."

"What was that bog we passed back there?"

"Just some swampy land—it connects up, over beyond."

The apprehension in her face seemed ludicrous, for the ghosts
of Dinton are ghosts of no violence.

"Don't worry," I told her. "The swamp isn't likely to be crying
or even sobbing this afternoon. It only moans and whimpers on
dark nights or when a gale of wind is blowing."

"What makes it moan?"

"Nobody knows. Probably in the beginning there was some
tree scraping against another tree, or the screech owls were hoot-
ing, or swamp gas bubbled. Or maybe there really was a mur-
dered Indian squaw or a mad adventurer who came here to die of
his wounds. Why, Gretchen, what's the matter?"

"Gid!" she said.

"Don't mind our demonology, Gretchen. It's a folk art. One
Dinton theory is that between here and the Point there are no
hollows. Every low place is a holler. One deep, black kettle hole
is called Soskin's Holler because an Indian of that name was
killed there by his son-in-law who drove in a skewer from one of

the old man's ears to the other. It's said that if you go there on a dark night at the proper time of the year and rap loudly on the ground three times, a voice will answer, 'Judgment, stranger,' followed by a frightful scream."

Gretchen couldn't say anything now, for her teeth were clicking together like a child's on a bitter morning. At last I began to understand. Her fear was really within herself. For a minute at least I forced myself to realize this truth and to regret my harping on Dinton superstition.

We had come to that bench mark of civilization at which the struggle against the external, whatever the external—if anything —may be, meets and joins the internal struggle in which there are also kettle holes and Crying Swamps. The aspect of a straggled, lonely scene around us, reinforced by my heedless tales, had matched some corresponding landscape in Gretchen's hidden and natural self. The fences of her sophistication did not run that far back into the primitive, and no doubt there were byways and forks that represented choices never made or fates never yet confronted.

However it was, I had a badly frightened Gretchen on my hands, and all at once we were beyond the point of no return, for she could less bear to turn back than to keep on our course toward the Point. Distance mattered less to her than her inner alarms.

So I became as reassuring and protective toward Gretchen as I could, though I felt little response on her part, and we traversed the region of the Crying Swamp, which stretched out, after all, only for the distance of a quarter of a mile. The only cries we heard were of herring gulls overhead. If you want something dismal at any season of the year, I can recommend the swamp with its blasted trees, hummocks and black pools. Gloomily, I wondered how we should get back, since the farther we proceeded the more impossible it seemed to Gretchen to turn again.

We were beyond the swamp when the sun came out again, bright and clear. We sat down to rest on the almost flat side of a boulder that rose from the ground like a monument. At least, I thought, I had the sense not to tell Gretchen that her disturbance was all nonsense. Such things never are, and I don't know that any of us would be much helped if they were.

"You can see from here," I said, "how the argument started about the best route for an extension of our lane to the Point. The Crying Swamp does present a puzzle, except maybe to an engineer."

"Yes," said Gretchen without any interest whatever.

I thought how extraordinarily pretty she was as the sunlight fell upon her in all its gilding. But of the kinds of romance the world offers, I could imagine this interlude in which I found myself with Gretchen as the very least. The whole affair was stupid, and I must pretend that it wasn't; moreover, the fact that Gretchen was drawn toward me for protection did not make us closer. The opposite was true, as I saw clearly.

We had started out again with landmarks of the Point in sight, though still tantalizingly far, and I had taken Gretchen's arm to direct her past a boggy place, part of an old slough, as Dinton people like to say. Her foot slipped and she stepped into the mud.

"You fat fool, look what you've done!" she exclaimed.

But as soon as the words were uttered she turned contrite. She touched my cheek with the palm of one cold hand and said, "Oh, Gid, I'm sorry!"

So then we were close, the barrier between us removed; and I laughed and put my arm around her middle, and we walked along side by side until briers and rocks made it necessary to change to single file. But even this was no real romance, though it provided an indulgence I had not expected. The epithet Gretchen had used didn't seem to me offensive; it was nothing compared with Katie's realistic language. No man should deny that he is a fool, but I always did deny that I was fat.

Though the distance now shortened, all was not plain sailing. I don't know whether Gretchen's emotional difficulties welled up again in anticlimax or whether she was suffering a reaction, but it seemed to me that she was about to become physically ill. In this my judgment proved correct; she did become physically ill, and I held her while she held me until her retching was over.

We were both quite calm thereafter, and in a few minutes we emerged on the Point and stood on the site of the old hotel, looking seaward across the breaking surf. The view and the zestful salt air must have been a restorative, for after a few minutes Gretchen seemed completely herself, whatever that might have been. We sat on a rock, green-lichened, among the bayberry bushes. I don't know what Gretchen's thoughts were, but mine were of the time of day. If we didn't move rapidly toward home, we were bound to be out long after darkness had fallen.

It wasn't the time, though, but the way of our return that worried Gretchen. She said, "I suppose you know I can't possibly go back through all that again."

I did know. "Of course, there's the long road to town, but it's well named. It's a hell of a long road."

"I feel like staying right here."

"That's all right for the time being, but shouldn't we have some plan?"

"Barry won't worry. He's so sensible." By the way she pronounced the adjective, with its sudden tone of bitterness, I noted that it was not a compliment. "How about Katie? Is she sensible?"

"Well, she's got sense."

"That's different," said Gretchen. "You're lucky to have a wife with sense. I wish Barry had sense."

"If we stay here," I said, "we will probably be discovered sooner or later by a couple of handsome young men in a helicopter, and Barry and Katie can turn on their radios and hear how Mrs. Barry Johnson, thirty-eight, pretty suburbanite, and Gideon Lester, fifty-two, Boston food executive, were sighted by an air-rescue team on remote and desolate Dinton Point after having subsisted forty-eight hours on roots and nuts. . . ."

"Who said I was thirty-eight?"

"I don't know. Aren't you?"

"Maybe somewhere around that, but I don't care to make a public display of it. I'm thirsty. Is there any drinking water around here?"

"There's a clear spring over by the bluff."

We walked across the crisp moss and stony soil where the winds prevented any less hardy texture, and at first Gretchen tried to drink by lifting water from the spring in her palm. This didn't work so well, and finally she lay on the ground and put her lips to the water, as I remembered doing many times in my boyhood. I admired her accomplishment of a genuinely country procedure.

"What are we going to do? Really, I mean," she asked.

"The practical thing would be to walk back the way we came."

"I can't. I know how idiotic I must appear to you, Gid, but I can't."

"I know you can't. I'm not an amateur Freud, but I can recognize an aversion when I see it—or a compulsion. I suppose you're neurotic."

"No, I'm not neurotic. I have very, very few phobias or fixations of any kind, and I'm practically always able to rationalize them. I simply don't know what's come over me, but whatever it is, you can't expect me to straighten it out in a minute."

"So I suppose the alternative is to start along the recognized route to town. We might be picked up, though I can't imagine how or why. If we aren't picked up we can bivouac at some agreeable spot until morning."

She made a face, but I took it that her silence meant acquiescence.

"It's settled, then. Do you feel like starting now?"

"Better now than later, I suppose."

My foreboding proved unfounded. We were not exactly picked up, but within a surprisingly short distance we came to an automobile parked by the side of the road, without lights, in the deepening gloom. The occupants, whom we aroused rather awkwardly, were a teen-age couple from Dinton, a boy and girl fortuitously unrecognized by me. They hastily put their clothing to rights, making this business more obvious in their anxiety than it need have been, and appeared eager to drive us to Dinton. A sense of guilt can beget the greatest courtesy. But of course there was a tacit bargain—they would assist us, and we would never be parties to a disclosure of the gratifying sin in which they had engaged.

I thought there was only one explanation I could offer to Katie about my belated return home, the truth, and I wondered how she would accept it. I needn't have felt any concern. She laughed when she saw me come in, and she kept laughing until my dignity would not permit me to offer any explanation whatever. Eventually, I knew, her curiosity would require a complete accounting, but at the moment I was by no means complimented by her offhand estimate of the circumstances. They had been ridiculous, but she had no right to assume so.

The next afternoon we had a more or less accidental, informal meeting of the residents of the lane, and Barry Johnson thanked me for looking after Gretchen. He thanked me with a significant, man-to-man expression that brought me closer to the feeling of a great lover than anything in my career up to that moment. He said Gretchen's ankle had been subject to weakness ever since a skiing accident a few years previous, and you could never tell when it was going to give out.

He offered the explanation, which for her own reasons was the explanation Gretchen had made to him, as if he considered it no less fishy than he thought I considered it, and as it really was. I replied guiltily that I was glad to have been of help and that Gretchen had behaved extremely well under the circumstances. Why she had drawn upon this trite invention instead of telling the truth I could not at first imagine; then I realized that the affair fell within a context of the suburban world that required certain conventions. Guilt of a sort was to be assumed, in any case, and the social requirement was simply to put on a good face.

I noted, too, that the truth wouldn't have allowed Barry this exercise of broad-mindedness. I still thought the situation stupid, but Gretchen knew Barry better than I.

Katie listened to the concluding exchanges of the conversation, glancing at me with a knowing look that I declined to acknowledge. We all should have been on secure ground then, but Barry turned suddenly to Henry Spinney.

"I intended to ask you this before, Mr. Spinney," he said. "Have you happened to notice a stranger walking through the lane now and then—a redheaded man who just seems to disappear?"

"Disappear?" asked Henry.

"Well, yes. I can't discover that he's bound for any destination. I don't know where he does go."

"No mystery about that," said Henry Spinney, and both Katie and Gretchen looked at him with startled eyes. "No mystery. It's Beelzebub, that's who it is. I've always understood he had red hair and a sort of thin face, and I don't know where he could better spend his time than right here in our lane."

⤳

Now that I had become aware of Gretchen as an individual instead of a type, though perhaps stereotype would be the better word, I of course knew her less well. Understanding is likely to be in inverse ratio to familiarity. I supposed now that she must be a complex instance of the modern woman hidden under the convention imposed by suburban living, in whom shadow and substance, drift and purpose, fact and affectation, could be confused and transposed. But I realized that the primitive would not have been much tamed or disciplined, in spite of appearances, and a certain insight might be gained if one looked carefully for the primitive.

But if by chance or perception I had been able to decide anything about Gretchen's personal composition, it would have been addled hopelessly on the morning later that week when I drove to Boston with Barry. He undertook to explain her to me. His attitude seemed almost fatherly, and I realized uncomfortably that he was proceeding on the mistaken assumption that my afternoon and evening experience with Gretchen had been romantic and that we had lain together bodily in some imagined spot of invitation on the way to the Point. If his ideas fell short of so explicit and impossible a fulfillment, he was nevertheless determined to be as tolerant and mature as any extreme situation could have demanded. I took it that the difference between his attitude and Katie's was exactly that between being sensible and having sense.

I should like to have said, "Barry, for God's sake, where between the lane and the Point on a fairly raw spring afternoon could any man and woman have managed a posture of lovemaking without unimaginable inconvenience and hardship?" Oddly enough, what deterred me as much as anything from saying just this was a feeling that I should be letting Gretchen down. I was not going to be the one to tell him her charms were less allconquering than he thought they were. It is also true that he made me feel I had missed an opportunity that I have encountered more often in books than in my own life. So I listened with embarrassment and increasing annoyance.

Gretchen, he said, had been brought up strictly, too strictly, and in school and college had become overintellectualized. She had also rebelled against the puritanism of her parents, as a result of which some unconscious volition led her not only to refuse certain restraints but to violate them. All this didn't really mean anything, though. Or, at least, it meant merely a wavering of the border line between reality and fantasy.

The rest of his analysis seemed to me just as garbled and pat, just as naïve and uninformed as this. Yet if he had challenged me to do better in explaining Katie, my own wife, very likely I should have bungled as badly as he. So I mustered the good sense to leave the whole matter alone. My life with Katie had involved mostly the handling of situations, not of a person, for I had realized from the beginning that on most levels she was and would remain too much for me.

When Barry and I reached Dinton again that afternoon, Katie, Gretchen and a strange blond girl were standing in the lane. I say the blond girl was strange, even though I recognized her as Ruth Ellen Johnson, who obviously had arrived home at an unexpected time in spite of her father's objections. I never got over this impression of strangeness, even though I came to know her so much better than would ever have seemed likely. In appearance she wasn't much like either of her parents, and I judged that not only her corn-silk hair and blue-gray eyes but also her quick, lively expressions and the interchangeable grace and awkwardness of her body, particularly of her arms and her long legs, must have derived from genes that had skipped a generation on both sides of the family. But she was young, and youth in itself had become strange to me.

She brushed her father's cheek with her lips in what was by definition a kiss, but nothing more and probably something less, and turned her attention to me. The late sun gave her hair and skin a reflection of gold, and I realized for the first time that although she was not pretty—I don't suppose she was at all pretty—she was sometimes lovely. I repeat that she was young, a fact her appearance and attitudes kept repeating and emphasizing, but all the same she had matured a good deal since I last had seen her.

"When did you get home?" Barry asked.

"About an hour ago."

"Did you drive?"

"Oh, yes, I drove."

"How'd you come?"

"Most of the way on Route 138. Oh, of course I started on 15, and then I cut off on 24."

"You would have made better time on 32," said Barry. "You would have missed all that traffic going into Boston."

"There wasn't much traffic."

"There usually is. It's generally better to take 32."

"I don't care much for 32."

"You should try it when you go back. There's a loop now that takes you around Athol. All you have to do is keep watching for the overpass."

From the expression on Ruth Ellen's face, I didn't think she was going to try 32, but the conversation was interrupted pretty crisply by Gretchen.

"We've been looking at the lane," she said.

"A state D.P.W. truck was here this afternoon," said Katie.

"You see them everywhere," said Ruth Ellen in her newly mature voice—newly mature to me, I mean. It sounded rather soft and distant. "I don't know anywhere in Massachusetts that you don't see D.P.W. trucks."

"Not here," said Katie. "Not up to now."

"Let's all go into the house and have a drink," I said. "Let's drink to Ruth Ellen's homecoming."

I knew right away I shouldn't have said that, for it brought up a controversial subject; yet as soon as the antagonistic expressions on the faces of all three had passed me by, I began to notice that Barry, who had so strongly objected to Ruth Ellen's breaking away from school at an odd time, was much more quickly reconciled to her arrival than Gretchen was. I thought at first this was because Barry reacted more easily to the Martini on the rocks that he accepted in our living room than Gretchen did to a conservative Scotch and soda. This may have been so, but the division of feeling continued throughout the two days of Ruth Ellen's visit.

꙳

I rose earlier than Katie the next morning, and as soon as I had gone into the kitchen for my orange juice, I noticed Ruth Ellen sitting on our back steps. Her dress was of blue the color of the sky, and I express this romantically because that was the way I felt.

I opened the door. Ruth Ellen glanced over her shoulder, smiled, and patted the step beside her.

"Sit," she said, and I did.

"Daddy thinks you're having some sort of affair with Mummy," she said, and to have something like this said to me first thing in the morning was mildly traumatic. "Obviously that's not true. In fact, I'm not even sure he really thinks so."

"Obviously untrue?" I heard myself asking.

"You know what I mean."

"I don't know, and I don't think I want to know."

"Anyway," she said, "I can see that Daddy is trying to put me off the track. I have a good idea what's really happening, and that's why I simply had to come home."

"You mean . . . it's your father who's having an affair?"

"You can see he's the type."

"What type?"

"Well, it all depends. Temperamentally or financially or psychologically—all three, maybe. I guess his alienation began before he was born. Novels are written about men like him. You know what I call them? I call them the seducing generation."

"More so than earlier generations?"

"Natch. Because of urbanization. Because their civilization is all set up for it. I don't suppose you can help me, but I had to confide in someone, and it had to be a man, a man older than myself."

"If it's advice . . ."

"No, for God's sake, it isn't advice. Advice comes under the head of communication, and there's too damn lousy much of it."

"Then what?"

"Well, if you did have an affair with Mummy . . ."

"That sounds to me like one of the oldest and stalest of theatrical devices," I said.

"Old but ever new. Besides, what makes it entirely different is the fact that he's standardized and you're not."

"Both standardized and alienated?"

"Right. He needs to be jolted. Shock treatment. Do you think you might at least show an interest in Mummy?"

"I already have," I said. "In fact, Katie has commented on it."

"Good. I don't know why I should feel so responsible, but I do."

"I think you're an unusual young woman."

"Girl," she said, correcting me. "Yes, I am. A lot of us are. Don't for God's sake, say anything about revolt—there's no revolt about it. There's just a new maturity, and high time. Can you understand that?"

"Yes, I can."

"Daddy's against you in this business about widening and surfacing the lane. You know that, don't you?"

"I certainly don't. He's our most powerful defender of the *status quo*."

"Yes, yes, I know. He thinks he is, too. But look at him. A man with his attributes, who dresses as he dresses, who lives the conventional life he lives, and—maybe most of all—who works in Boston, is in favor of roads. That's his civilization. He's part of it. He's a creature of it."

"Are you suggesting that your father is capable of treachery?"

"I'm only suggesting that he's capable of being exactly what he is. He's on Route 128, and you'll never get him off it."

I didn't know whether my qualms of giddiness were due to this conversation or to the fact that my system needs breakfast as soon as I get up, and I hadn't had any. Just the same, I would gladly have continued this conversation, and felt disappointed when Katie opened the door and looked out.

"Well!" she said. "Well! Come on in here, the two of you, and have some coffee."

So we did, and Ruth Ellen, sitting at our kitchen table and chatting, was as innocent and carefree as she had been as a little girl. But, I wondered, had she ever been? How soon do those keen, quick purposes, with or without complete accuracy of the perceptions that are always combined with them, become plainly evident in the congenitally endowed female? I couldn't guess. I watched the bright innocence of Ruth Ellen's smile as it was turned toward Katie, and I was aware that her feet were resting on a rung of her chair and her body was gracefully and comfortably contorted. She was all youth and fun. She hadn't a care in the world.

After she had gone, Katie said to me, "What were you two talking about?"

"I'm damned if I know," I said.

"Oh, that!" said Katie.

⤫

The next time Barry and I drove to Boston our conversation didn't consist of much. Ruth Ellen had gone back to school, and he supposed that her trip home had just been some sort of compulsion, and anyway it was all over and didn't matter any more. I mentioned my opinion that she was an unusual girl, and Barry said he guessed she was, but it didn't show in the reports sent to him from the school. He said she was a reserved type, and you could never tell what she was thinking.

Barry and I separated at a parking lot in Boston, and I walked along Kneeland Street to Tremont and the Common and began my business hours by peeling an apple. The fact that the apple was paid for by my company is not an important point. This was, irrespective of all else, the sort of executive I had come to be, and I suppose I could be it in Boston more easily than would have been possible in any city of a different tradition.

Late that afternoon a business card was brought to me indicating that a man named Lorenzo E. Sparrow awaited my convenience for an interview. I had only to glance through the transparently glazed office partition to see Mr. Sparrow himself. Except for his plumage, or hair, which was of an indeterminate mixed-brown hue and therefore sparrowy, it occurred to me that he was not well named. His jowls were not at all birdlike, his cheeks were ruddy with the overblown contours of good living, and when he approached my desk I became aware of an abdomen that he seemed to carry as he would an inconvenient burden. His drooping jacket did not want to remain closed over it.

I'm afraid I said, "What can I do for you, Mr. Sparrow?" But this worn formality is almost indispensable in business.

He did not reply directly. He said, "How's everybody down in Dinton?"

"All right, I believe."

"I used to know Dinton—used to go down there for a weekend or two every summer. My brother-in-law worked in a laundry on South Main Street. What was the name of it, now?"

"Probably the Eagle," I said.

"That was it. Eagle Laundry. My wife and I used to go down and visit with him. Nice, lovely town, Dinton—all kinds of possibilities. I could see it even back then. Only one thing lacking—access. That's all Dinton needs is access."

I realized that Mr. Sparrow's acquaintance with Dinton was of the least possible degree. I doubted that he had been there more than once.

"It seems to me Dinton is accessible enough for anyone," I said. "I never saw anyone have any trouble getting in or out. The Civil Defense people say it can be evacuated in twenty minutes by land or sea, and in eighteen minutes when school is in session."

"Oh, you can get there all right. But then where are you? What can you do except drive up Main Street?"

"You can park your car and take it easy," I said.

"Yeah, I know. But people nowadays like to go places and see things."

"Mr. Sparrow," I said, "what are you trying to sell?"

He ignored my question, but in a way he was responsive.

"Beaches, ocean, open country. You know. Some guy drives a quarter of a mile in Dinton, sees a view he likes, and first thing you know up goes a forty-thousand-dollar house. Fifty thousand —maybe more. All the way up. That's a nice piece of taxable property for you Dinton folks. You can run your whole town on a few propositions like that, let alone what they mean to contractors, artisans and so on."

There was a familiarity about Mr. Sparrow's style, and although I did not identify it until later, I may say here what it turned out to be. He was fashioning himself into a Massachusetts statesman, the modern, practical, and two-sided type, a far cry from the tradition of the Adamses and Hancocks, which ended a long time ago. His language did not come up to form. Though he used words such as "artisan" and "access," which you can follow through a conversation in the manner of radioactive isotopes through the circulatory system, his blatant crudity, once you were aware of its peculiar consistency, became as unmistakable as Bulfinch's gold dome with floodlights glaring upon it.

"Are you in the building business, Mr. Sparrow?" I asked.

"No, no. I'm a man who likes to see things move ahead—I don't care where it is, anywhere in Massachusetts. If you don't forge ahead, you slide back. Now I happen to be pretty close to the D.P.W. There's Chapter 90 money that can be had for improving roads in Dinton, or we might even get a new bond issue. Don't say it can't be done, because it can be done."

"I'm afraid you're right," I said. "If the recent history of our state proves anything, it proves an infinite capacity for financing stupid things."

"I don't get you," said Mr. Sparrow, and though I felt he would be shrewd enough in most things, I was not surprised.

"The point I want to make," I said, "is that I hope to God you and the D.P.W. will keep the hell out of Dinton."

He recoiled as if in bewilderment. "You got to have good roads," he said, opening a prospect of roads without end, ever widening and lengthening, following a course of improvement and devastation that would run through all civilization. If anyone had asked me, I would have had to say that the man had vision, and in this I felt outclassed. As cheap as the commodity had become, vision was something I didn't hanker after. He regarded my heresy with a certain puzzlement, and then I could see him turn crafty.

"Take the matter of values," he said. "You want to look into values. You'll find your eyes opened."

"Values? I don't believe you and I can agree. . . ."

"The hell we can't, Mr. Lester. You're a businessman. Well, my line is real estate and appraising. I'm an expert at it, and if there's a highway system in Dinton, I'm the one can see that you folks don't come out on the short end of land damages."

This was open enough, certainly.

"On your trips to Dinton did you happen to meet our highway surveyor, Ellie Kempton?" I asked.

"No, I never met Ellie, but he's been in touch with me lately. I was recommended to him if he wanted somebody who knew values and also knew his way around the Statehouse."

So the fuse laid by Henry Spinney with that talk about appraisers had burned this far and was glowing brightly. I considered what possible means there might be of stepping on it and extinguishing the glow.

"He works hard for you people, Ellie Kempton does. I can say to you straight out that he's a good man."

"Do they think well of him at the D.P.W.?"

"They will before this is over. Listen, Mr. Lester, what I'm giving you is straight talk. You rate as a topflight, hard-nosed citizen down in Dinton. You've got influence. I don't mind saying that Ellie Kempton asked me to talk to you—he wants me to introduce you around at the Statehouse. He wants you to get the whole picture. . . ."

I don't think I was listening. Mr. Sparrow launched into much re-used language, the kind that makes one's eyes glaze and one's attention retract or stray elsewhere. I was aware of such phrases as "updating your primary roads," "personal injury totals," "shorten distance by saving time," "transportation as one of our most vital raw materials." Mr. Sparrow was soaring, but finally I felt him touch ground again and heard him say, "Don't tell me you'd rather have schools than roads, because you can have both."

"I wasn't going to tell you that. Why the hell should I?"

He looked at me with astonishment, apparently because the

relative merits of schools and roads had been, in his experience, a topic of unvarying importance and interest.

Now that I had gained the initiative I decided to keep it. Without waiting for Mr. Sparrow to rearrange his propaganda material, I said, "Let's have one thing clear, now and forever more. I have not the least intention of being introduced at the Statehouse by you or anyone else. I regard the Statehouse with as much abhorrence as any other house of prostitution."

Maybe this was going too far, but I had been possessed by a surge of recklessness, and why should I measure my words to Mr. Sparrow? Not only did his composure remain intact but to my surprise it did not appear to have been dented. The communication he understood had little to do with language; motive talked to motive, instinct to instinct, emotion to emotion. He remained attuned, waiting for the sort of intelligibility that his practical experience had led him to expect, and I am sure he was considerably less astonished than I that before the day ended I had kept an appointment at the Statehouse. Mr. Sparrow's persuasiveness had nothing to do with this, however. My change of intention was brought about by the intervention of Henry Spinney.

Henry appeared within a half-hour or so of the time of Mr. Sparrow's leaving, and he carried a full rig for the city. He seemed to me impressively dated in costume, and I quickly formed a mental association with the advertisements in the *Fall River Line Journal* that used to be distributed aboard the *Priscilla, Commonwealth* and the others. I recalled illustrations of the Broadway Central Hotel, which bore the stamp of a period and I suppose of an old grandeur, naïve, or part of an old pretension. Henry Spinney with his winged collar, plain but overgenerous blue silk tie, double-breasted suit and ceremonial manner of handling his cigar, seemed to me an apotheosis of the Broadway Central.

"Sparrow was here, wasn't he?" Henry inquired after the shortest of greetings.

"I'm sorry to say he was."

"Mind telling me what he wanted?"

"For one thing, he seemed to want me to go over to the State-house to meet some politicians."

"But you didn't say you'd go?"

"I certainly didn't."

"That's good. That's very good. You sit tight, Gid. You let me handle this."

"Handle what?"

"Don't be a goddamn fool, Gid. Don't talk like our young friend Johnson—still wet behind the ears."

"Henry, I'm not talking like anybody. I just want to know what you're up to."

"I'm up to what practically everybody else is up to. I'm heading over to the Statehouse to talk roads. Expect to see Sparrow, too."

"Henry, you're not!"

"By God, I am!"

"What do you expect to gain by mixing with Sparrow's kind?"

"Except for his kind there wouldn't be much company in the so-called circles of government."

"Better no company at all."

"Highty-highty," said Henry.

"I suppose you think I'm not being practical in this. I'm being as practical as you are."

"Well," said Henry.

"Well, what?"

"I'll see you in Dinton, Gid. I'll give you a report."

"You'll see me sooner than that. If you're going over to the Statehouse, so am I."

"I think you'll be a handicap, Gid."

"If you want plain speaking, that's what I intend to be. I think you're likely to land us all in a hell of a mess."

"Maybe," said Henry.

He really didn't want me to go, I didn't want to go, but I went

because I didn't trust him. I thought his intentions were gran-
diose. I thought he was going to have himself a ball, as they say
nowadays. At that moment Henry Spinney was a dedicated man,
and his dedication was to raising hell and as much hell as possible. I did not doubt that he would do well in this direction, but
I doubted his ability to make any good come of it.

I don't know what the Massachusetts Statehouse may have
been before the pretentiousness of those marble wings was added
to the warm dignity of the Bulfinch brick, or, for that matter,
before the floodlights were set upon their nightly glare; but in
our day it had become an ironic entombment of history. Guides
would show you around and tell you about the patriotic past; you
could look at the archives; and if you were a stranger you might
not suspect that in its modern function the Statehouse was a mart
where everything had to be bought, by influence, money, trading,
deceit, or by some of the meaner coinages of flattery and emotion.

If you were not a stranger, you would be aware of this; and if
anyone was crude enough to mention it, you would point to the
new industry brought to Boston by Route 128.

I don't know whether Henry Spinney knew his way in the
Statehouse or whether he relied upon navigational instinct. I
couldn't possibly have retraced the course he followed, yet at the
end of it Henry overhauled, as if by precise foreknowledge, the
representative from our own district, the Honorable Rufus Handmore. Mention Rufus to anyone in Dinton and you would get the
reply, "Oh, Rufe is all right." This quality of being all right had
brought him out ahead in three elections, though the words were
usually spoken with easy tolerance and not with enthusiasm.

I half suspected that Henry had not met Rufus by appointment, perhaps from the very determination with which he
grabbed our legislator by the arm. The two quickly mingled with
the rather heavy pedestrian traffic in the corridor and vanished
around a corner that might have been contrived for the occasion.
Before I could subdue my chagrin I was observed by the watchful

eye of Mr. Sparrow. I judged that this particular corridor must be used as a rendezvous. Mr. Sparrow bore down on me with an expression that wasn't affable.

"Who was that with Rufe Handmore just now?" he demanded of me.

I don't know why I told him—the influence of habit, I suppose.

"That was Henry Spinney, up here from Dinton, and maybe you can guess what brought him." Then I made a declaration on my own behalf. "Mr. Sparrow, however it may be with Rufe Handmore and my friend Spinney, I am not here to meet you. I do not desire to have any conversation with you whatever."

He was not even dampened. "I wonder if I'm being crossed up. I wonder if Ellie Kempton is doing business with this Spinney character."

"Business?" I asked.

"Oh, for chrissake!" said Mr. Sparrow.

I took satisfaction in letting him know I felt his suspicions were well founded.

"By God, they'd better not cross me up. First thing you know, they won't get any goddamned road."

"Now you're talking," I said.

"There's things you do and things you don't do," said Mr. Sparrow, apparently stating a law of ethics.

"I thought the double cross was standard in Massachusetts," I said.

"It don't get by with me," said Mr. Sparrow.

"How did you happen to get in on this with Ellie Kempton in the first place?"

"He was referred to me by a friend in the D.P.W. I told you that already."

"I guess you did, at that."

"There's no mystery about it. He talked with the district engineer about this new road, and the district engineer took it from there. When it got through to me, I could see it was a big deal. It could mean what you call an arterial highway. What I want to know now is why your man Spinney didn't follow through with me. Where did Rufe Handmore take him?"

"The unexpected is what makes life interesting," I said.

Mr. Sparrow uttered a scatological epithet. I continued to stand there a few minutes longer, unaware that my being in Mr. Sparrow's presence would turn out to be a factor of some influence later on. I stayed because, after my first impulse had faded, staying seemed easier than going. In a short time, shorter probably than it seemed, Henry Spinney and Rufe Handmore came walking toward us.

"Tell him who I am," said Mr. Sparrow. "Tell your man Spinney who I am."

"Tell him yourself," I said.

He did, but the news affected Henry Spinney so lightly that Mr. Sparrow's mood continued to blacken.

"I'm the man you wanted to see," he protested. "That's why you're here. Mr. Lester has been telling me about you."

"No need to trouble yourself, Mister," said Henry. "See you later, Gid."

He made his departure on a straight course, Mr. Sparrow veering after him. I didn't have much that I wanted to say to Rufe Handmore, knowing he was incapable of telling a straight story about any controversial issue, but he had something to say to me.

"Gid, I wish you hadn't come here to see Sparrow."

"I didn't come here to see him. I didn't want to come here at all."

"You've been observed talking to him. Certain people up here are bound to attach a lot of importance to that. They'll draw conclusions."

"Rufe," said I, "I talk to dozens of people every day, and I'm not aware that one of them ever came away from a conversation with me with five cents' worth of prestige or significance of any kind."

"This is different. This is the Statehouse. You have to consider.

It may seem nothing to you, but it's the kind of thing a lot of influential people are likely to go by. You're in business, Gid, and when a businessman of your reputation shows up here under peculiar circumstances, an interpretation is sure to be put on it."

I overlooked the "peculiar circumstances," because even from my point of view they were peculiar. "By whom?" I asked.

"All right, Gid, we may as well name it. What we're talking about is politics."

"So I gathered. Now, Rufe, don't tell me you're in favor of this nightmare of a new main highway in Dinton?"

"I'm not for it, and I'm not against it—not yet. What I say is we've got to get our fair share of the gas-tax money, and if they build this road it's got to be built right. The property owners have got to be protected."

"I suppose that was on Henry Spinney's mind."

"Well, he's a property owner."

"I don't particularly want to fight you, Rufe, but I'm going to fight this road, and don't you forget it."

"Nobody who's seen you talking with Sparrow or hears about it is going to take much stock in that, Gid. Anyhow, the people around here who have influence don't talk for or against. They talk price."

"To hell with Sparrow," I said. "I'll be talking to people bigger than Sparrow before I'm through."

Rufe shrugged, and I left him. Of course, from now on his views about the proposed road would vary according to the opinion of those with whom he discussed the project. He'd be for it, and at almost the same time he'd be against it, and in the end he'd plump for what seemed likely to lose him fewest votes. Most people in Dinton wouldn't blame him; they'd go on saying, "Oh, Rufe is all right."

⤸

I didn't expect to see Henry Spinney again that day, at least not in Boston, but he arrived at my office in midafternoon to ask if I would give him a ride back to Dinton. I said that Barry was driv-

ing me back but I was sure Barry would be glad to have him as
another passenger. Henry said he would sit across the street in the
Common and feed squirrels until he saw me emerge, this signaling the time of departure.

As it turned out, Barry telephoned to ask me if I would mind
leaving the office early. He had experienced some sort of brain
wave about our protest movement and had decided to gain time
by interviewing a number of Dinton citizens. I didn't mind at all,
but Henry Spinney was not expecting me so soon and I had to
invade the Common to look for him. Sure enough, he had acquired a bag of peanuts and was sitting on a bench feeding not
only squirrels but a large concourse of dirty Boston pigeons.

"Your friend Sparrow was here," said Henry.

"Friend be damned."

"He tracked me down, though I guess he was really on his way
to see you."

"What would he want of me?"

"No idea, Gid. Here, hold this, will you."

He handed me a plain Manila envelope while he stood to
brush remnants of peanut shell from his clothing. He was so fas-
tidious about this that the performance took a little time, and we
walked along together. I expected him to reclaim the envelope,
but he demurred.

"You take the goddamned thing, Gid. It's for Ellie Kempton,
and you'll be seeing Ellie before I will."

This seemed natural enough at the moment. It's an ingrained
and ancient custom of Dinton to have one's friends and acquaint-
ances carry messages, do shopping errands, and dispatch and de-
liver articles to and from Boston and way stations. I suppose the
custom began when mails and transportation were infrequent,
and it probably continues because of Dinton's inherited independence. In this instance I assumed Henry Spinney had agreed
to do Ellie a favor. I put the Manila envelope in my pocket and
rather impatiently dismissed it from my mind.

Ten minutes later we were in Barry's car turning into the

Southeast Expressway, a horrible and marvelous example of a
modern highway, depending upon which way you looked at it. I
could see it from either viewpoint. If you wanted to get out of
Boston in a hurry, as I usually did, the expressway had to be cher-
ished. This was the selfish attitude, and I never yet have seen a
man in an automobile who was not selfish. On the other hand, all
that Boston had ever stood for, all that our civilization had as-
pired to in its finest flower, was violated and subordinated to gasoline fumes and speed.

As Barry put his foot on the accelerator we made a mockery of
the Adamses driving out to Quincy behind their clop-clopping
horses. But in our language and in our times who the hell were
the Adamses?

Overhead the sun shone, but on that band of asphalt the sun
and air and horizon were unimportant. The new law of motion—
Callahan's Law, I guess, since this was the name of the most cele-
brated highway builder in Massachusetts—erased the reality of
all the older verities by the quick superiority of concentrated forward motion. Caesar's roads were nothing compared with Callahan's. Caesar influenced history, but Callahan made history obsolete.

They say that Dinton pilots used to take ships out around Cape
Cod and safely into the port of Boston and then walk home, re-
quiring perhaps twenty hours for the return journey. I won't say
that Barry achieved new records at the wheel of his car, but he
made considerably better time than those pilots.

When we arrived at the mouth of our lane, we could see that
Gretchen was standing at the gateway in the citified picket fence
that she and Barry had put in front of their house. Dinton people
somehow never used pickets—they were addicted to simple
capped slats. And the notion of fences went in cycles; sometimes
almost all fences disappeared, opening surprising vistas, and the
people in the cycle were referred to as an unfenced generation. In
some discussion with Gretchen was Johnny Mason.

As Barry drew up, Gretchen remarked, after the barest greeting to us, "Mr. Mason says they're trying to raise money for a refrigerator in the fire station."

"What do they want of a refrigerator in the fire station?" Barry asked.

It was Johnny Mason who answered. "To keep the beer in."

Evidently Barry meant to say something, no doubt something ironic or withering, but Henry Spinney jabbed him in the back. Barry's expression remained, I should say, indignantly embattled, but he did not sound off.

"What are you selling chances on?" Henry asked Johnny.

"Three turkey dinners."

"Give me a couple tickets," said Henry.

"I'll take a couple," I said.

"All right," said Barry. "I'll go along."

I could tell from Johnny Mason's expression that "going along" wasn't quite up to the mark, but he didn't say anything; on the other hand, Barry considered that he was surpassing all reasonable expectations in putting up money for something in which he disbelieved on principle. I remarked upon this to Katie later on, and she said, "Well, what's principle?" I had to admit that in Dinton it seemed that you hardly ever knew, the nuances and exceptions were so continually besetting.

From the Johnson gateway Henry Spinney and I proceeded along the lane afoot, parting at the entrance to my own property. I had expected to treat Katie to a running account of the day's events, but she had a matter of greater import to our household on her mind. She said that when she got back from shopping about ten o'clock she had found the kitchen full of catbirds. She said some irresponsible idiot had opened an unscreened window in the buttery and neglected to close it afterward. When she spoke of the idiot, she meant me.

It was Katie's pleasure to supply raisins every summer to all the catbirds and robins in the neighborhood. The robins were never forward, but the catbirds showed great acumen and boldness in seeking out the source of supply.

"I wish you wouldn't talk about the buttery," I said. "You know it's an ordinary pantry."

"Pantry or buttery," she said, "some fool left the window open."

"It's one of your affectations, and unfortunately it's an obvious one. Everybody knows that people around here stopped talking about butteries long before you were brought up."

"I like catbirds and they like me," said Katie, "but I don't want them doing their jobs on the top of my range."

"You should have your mouth washed out with strong soap," I said.

"As to butteries, this house was built with one, and that's what it's still got. I don't give a hoot about genealogy, but I stand firm on periods." Then Katie glided into a different subject. "If Barry continues to make these unexpected early arrivals he's due for a surprise, and so is Gretchen. Beelzebub was here again."

"He was?"

"I don't guess he'd been gone more than five minutes when Barry drew up with you men in the car. What was all that palaver about?"

"There's a raffle to raise money for a refrigerator in the firehouse. To keep the beer in." Katie saw the reasonableness of this. "Henry Spinney and I were afraid Barry would make an indignant speech—you know—his reform temperament."

"His type all have it," said Katie. "Wonder is that he didn't blow up. He could have turned the firemen against us and we'd have had a highway in no time with pumpers and ladder trucks streaking past us on practice nights."

"Well, it turned out all right. We all bought chances. Gretchen didn't like it."

"She's politically pure," said Katie. "I suppose even modern women have to have a certain amount of purity in them somewhere."

Then at last I found an opportunity to recount what had happened in Boston during the day. Katie listened with appropriate interest while I described Mr. Sparrow and the behavior of Henry Spinney and Rufe Handmore. This was when I remembered about the Manila envelope in my pocket. It was properly addressed to Ellie Kempton, but I was surprised to find when I turned it over the return address of Lorenzo E. Sparrow on the back. So, it appeared, Henry Spinney had tricked me into doing an errand for Mr. Sparrow.

"What's in it?" Katie asked.

"How do I know?"

"Let's look at it."

She didn't wait for my permission; she took the envelope from my hand and held it up to the light.

"They always use plain Manila envelopes," Katie said. "You're always reading about plain Manila envelopes. They get produced before grand juries."

"What are you talking about?"

"The bribe money, of course. The sugar—or is that word for it out of date?"

"I don't know what you're getting at. Not sensibly, that is."

"How'd you get so innocent all of a sudden? This envelope is supposed to go to Ellie Kempton, isn't it?"

"Yes, but who would be fool enough to waste a bribe on Ellie Kempton, and why?"

Katie was testing the gummed flap of the plain Manila envelope. It had been sealed, but she coaxed it open without too much difficulty.

"Look!" she said, holding up four fifty-dollar bills that Mr. Sparrow had dispatched in this conventional manner for the apparent purpose of holding the fealty of Dinton's highway supervisor.

"Just Ellie's size," said Katie, waving the bills.

She said later that I turned purple and swelled up like a bullfrog. It is not unlikely that I did. Nobody enjoys being taken for a fool or used as a simpleton by the breed of which Mr. Sparrow stood as a detestable example. Moreover, I was angry with myself and Katie because I had missed the significance of the plain Manila envelope and she had seen the significance at once. Such envelopes are used for other purposes, but nobody can say offhand what they are. Even my profanity did not help much, for I couldn't swear a quarter as well as Henry Spinney.

"What are you going to do?" asked Katie. "Go to the police?"

"That would be bright, wouldn't it?" I asked, climbing back astride my masculine knowledge of the world. "What the hell could the police do about a thing like this? Nothing has happened yet."

"No, I suppose they couldn't. They have to go by law and not by common sense."

"I'd like to stuff the whole business down Henry Spinney's throat, but considering Henry's nature and disposition I'm more likely to take it back to Boston, put it in Sparrow's hands, and tell him to do his own dirty work."

"Yes, I guess that's the right thing," Katie said.

"What are you up to now?"

"Oh, just for the principle of the thing I'm noting down the numbers of the bills. And marking them. Bills in all bribery cases should be marked."

She was already resealing the envelope, which she now put behind the clock on the mantel.

I don't think people in general have clocks on their mantels any more. Barry and Gretchen wouldn't have been found dead with a clock on their mantel. The survival of the old Dinton custom in my own house was typical of the division that permeated the affairs of Katie and me. We were both loyal to the past and fretted by it, abreast of the times yet not free of tradition or prejudice.

Katie once said, "The real hell of it is, Gid, that you and I both have preferences."

"Doesn't everybody?"

"Not the way we do. Ours are sort of staggered."

We were condemned, it seemed, to be looking always in both directions, resisting the forces that pulled, tugging against the forces that held.

However it might have been about the clock on the mantel—a nondescript black-marble affair trimmed with bronze or what looked like bronze, and which might have been a wedding gift at some time in Katie's ancestry or mine—the custom of putting things behind it was entirely Katie's. I found the practice objectionable, perhaps because it harked back to unpleasant observances in my childhood, but my protests never influenced Katie in the slightest.

"If there's anything that makes a room look slack and untidy," I had told her more than once, "it's a clutter of papers behind a mantel clock."

"My mother always kept the milk bills there," Katie would say, or "There's nothing like having your household reminders in plain sight" or "That sounds funny coming from a man who always forgets to wipe his feet on the door mat."

There was more variety to Katie than there was to me. I felt the handicap but was powerless to overcome it.

So the plain Manila envelope and the at least prospectively tainted money were slipped behind our mantel clock and stayed there for about forty-eight hours. When Katie and I were comfortably in bed that night, our lagging conversation came around to further consideration of the whole matter.

"My," said Katie, "I'll never get used to your stomach being so big."

"It's not big," I said. "My measurements are pretty good for a man of my age."

"I'm glad you're able to stick to your own point of view. People who can do that are very fortunate. What I say is I ought to feed you nothing but salads for a couple of months."

"I wish you wouldn't harp on things the way you do."

"Lots of carrots," said Katie.

"You're already buying up most of the domestic carrot supply."

"No matter what I feed you I know you'll gorge on lunches in Boston."

"My lunches are one of your ridiculous fictions."

"Do you know, Gid, I wonder if you ought to take that plain Manila envelope back to what's-his-name, Sparrow, after all."

"Why?"

"Well, it's so unimaginative."

"I don't see why it's unimaginative. It happens to be the right thing to do. What would you suggest?"

"Oh, maybe advertise in the Dinton *Courier* that we have some bribe money for Ellie Kempton."

"Don't be preposterous."

"Or set a trap with it. Or give it to a minister to preach a sermon on. Or . . ."

"Or nothing," I said.

"You're such a conventional porpoise, Gid."

"I'm in my right mind, if that's what you mean."

"Not exactly. We might need a tape recorder and flash bulbs."

"You'd enjoy that sort of thing. I wouldn't."

"I wonder what Ellie is expected to do for the money."

"Presumably Sparrow thinks Ellie can swing things his way."

"Things?"

"Fees, land damages, construction contracts—all that."

"Let's change the subject. I don't want to dream about it. Are you really sleepy, Gid?"

"Not really."

"Neither am I. I'm sorry you felt insulted about your abdomen—which syllable do you pronounce it on? What does it rhyme with?"

"You know as well as I do."

"I really wouldn't want you to be skinny, Gid."

"I'm not insulted," I said. "I could be but I'm not. I know you too well."

The next morning while Katie and I were at breakfast the telephone rang. It was Gretchen passing along the message that Barry wouldn't be driving to Boston; he had to go to Pawtucket for two days on business. I reminded her that this was not one of my days to go to Boston, so I wouldn't be inconvenienced, and anyway it would have been my turn to drive Barry.

"Well, that's all right, then," said Gretchen.

"Yes, and tell Barry his transportation is all arranged for on Friday."

She hung up, and Katie said, "The Johnsons live only a song and a dance away from us and have to use the telephone as if they were on the far side of town."

"Why not? It's convenient."

"It's unneighborly. Would I call Gretchen up? I would not. I would walk over to her house in the nice spring sunshine, getting my feet all soaked with dew, and I would make sure of what you might call a conversation. Something solid and satisfying."

"You're being obstinately old-fashioned."

"Better than being suburban."

"If you put it that way."

Though I didn't have to go to Boston I did feel obliged to do a good deal of office work at home both that day and the next. Katie was always good about not disturbing me, yet I was aware of the aura of domesticity surrounding my affairs. Sometimes a smell of jelly or of old-fashioned soap, sometimes a humming or the smack of a broom. But also there was the reprise of something that used to be but had gradually faded out when businessmen stopped going home for lunch—or dinner as they always called it then—and adopted the universal custom of eating downtown. The separation between business and the home had widened into a gulf, but in our case it had narrowed again, so that Katie and I could step across it without too much strangeness.

Toward evening of the second day she and I were standing in the side yard second-guessing each other about whether some hollyhock plants would produce flowers of watermelon pink or perhaps of deepest red. I didn't really care and I don't think Katie did, but we made a discussion of it. Presently we were joined by Henry Spinney, who out of compliment to the fine weather wore nothing above the waist but a balbriggan undershirt with suspenders over the shoulders. The suspenders held up an overlarge pair of summer duck pants that were weathered rather than soiled.

"That Johnson fellow is getting back," Henry remarked. "Look out for trouble."

I didn't realize what he meant. All three of us stood watching the Johnson house, where Barry had halted his car in the driveway and was lifting out the inevitable briefcase and overnight bag.

Katie, with her acute perception, heard a window in the Johnson house go up or down, and I suppose it was on the evidence of this sound that she said, "Look! Something's going to happen!" Henry and I had heard the same sound, but our instincts were not as apt as hers. For a moment I doubted whether there was any real suspense.

Then, as we watched, a man leaped from a second-story window of the Johnson house and loped for the nearest cover, a lilac hedge at the rear of the grounds.

"Jack be nimble, Jack be quick," remarked Katie.

She reached inside the pantry window, the same unscreened window that she had accused me of leaving open, and grasped her bird-watching binoculars from the shelf where she kept them. Henry and I could see the escapee moving along in the cover of the hedge, and Katie could see him better. Her binoculars were quickly brought into focus.

"It's Beelzebub, of course," she informed us. "I knew something like this would happen. I told Gid that Barry had better stop arriving home early."

"Devilish fool!" said Henry Spinney. "First time I ever knew anyone in Dinton to get chased out a second-story window."

"He hasn't any pants on," said Katie. "My, he did leave in a hurry."

"I don't know what the Bible says we ought to do in a case like this," said Henry Spinney, "so I guess we'll have to take it into our own hands."

"Why do anything?" I said. "It's none of our business."

"Gid!" said Katie. "Of course we have to do something. You, Henry Spinney, go over and see if you can smuggle his pants out so we can be ready to get him dressed properly."

"I had that in mind," said Henry. "It's a queer sort of errand for a man of my habits and principles, but I'll have a go at it."

I didn't say so, but I was certain Henry would have an advantage, because whatever would appear outrageous or preposterous in anyone else would seem natural in him, especially to Barry or Gretchen. I realized later, too, that a man accustomed to the seas off Point Judith and the tide race of Hell Gate could be nonchalant under extreme circumstances ashore. Nonchalant was what he was as he left us.

I couldn't imagine what he would say when he reached the Johnson house, and I had no time to wonder about it, for Katie and I were closely occupied in watching the redheaded man, christened Beelzebub by Henry Spinney, work his way toward us, keeping whatever objects he could between him and the Johnsons.

"What's he coming here for?" I asked myself aloud.

But I saw quickly that he was not planning to include our house in his itinerary; he was intending to skirt the wild hedges that grew between us and the Henry Spinney place. Katie, to my annoyance and astonishment alike, put her fingers in her mouth and whistled sharply in the manner of a small boy. This was an accomplishment I had not known she possessed.

The redheaded man braked himself, looked around wildly and, as Katie repeated her unladylike whistle, came uncertainly toward us. He was as decently clad, or more so, as the underwear advertisements in the magazines, but to say this was not relevant to any of the circumstances. He wore shorts decorated with purple fleurs-de-lis, and I found myself wondering, as a childhood devotee of the romances and intrigues of Dumas, whether this would have meant fealty to the Cardinal or to the King in the age of Porthos, Aramis and various others. Certainly this was no D'Artagnan, at any rate.

Beelzebub's coloration was not of the brighter reds but on the dull, rusty side, even to the hairs on his legs. They were spindly legs. He was all stock and no flesh, yet his thin face held a degree of distinction that probably served him as well as or better than good looks could have done. I suppose he was in his late thirties. His occupation, clearly, had to be one of the intellectual pursuits, and I suspected him of being *avant-garde,* though it was impossible to tell for sure. A man can't successfully be embarrassed and *avant-garde* at the same time; he must accept a choice between the two, unless he is young enough to be a hipster, which is a different breed entirely.

I didn't like anything about this encounter, but since it had been brought about I would have waited for the redheaded stranger to say something. Katie, though, isn't the waiting kind.

"You came out of that window like the breakfast food that's shot from guns," she said. "Did you hurt yourself?"

"I expect so, a little. I believe I'm going to have trouble with my right ankle."

The man's voice was cultivated and under the circumstances surprisingly assured. This counted in his favor.

"You looked as if you had just shot Lincoln," said Katie.

"I was afraid of being misunderstood, you see. I had torn my slacks on the briers in that wild pasture over there, and Mrs. Johnson had very kindly offered to mend them when . . ."

"Pish!" said Katie. "It isn't likely, and anyway you can't very well tell such stuff to Barry Johnson now."

"No, I don't suppose I can—but I can't think of anything that will sound better."

"You can't ignore the basic fact that you are a man and Gretchen is a woman," said Katie.

"I haven't ignored it."

"I should think not," said Katie. "Gid, do you suppose you have some pants that will fit Mr. . . . Mr. . . ."

The stranger did not fill the gap.

I said, "No I haven't any that would remotely fit him. Anyway, you sent Henry Spinney next door to get his own pants."

"Yes, I did, and I don't doubt he'll be back with them directly. While you're waiting, won't you sit down, Mr. . . . ?"

The redheaded man still refrained from identifying himself, but he did sit down. We had, wisely, taken shelter, so to speak, in our house, and we were now an interesting and entirely conventional group in the living room except for the fact that our guest wore no trousers. His knees were held stiffly in front of his chair.

"I don't know why we're being so solemn," said Katie. "It's really funny, isn't it?"

"Not to me," said the redheaded man.

"If you don't tell us your name, we'll have to invent one," said Katie.

He remained silent.

"This will be something to tell your children," said Katie.

"Katie!" I said. "You're only making things worse."

"I should take you for a Harvard man from the waist up," she said, ignoring me. "Science, probably. Or would it be the School of Business Administration?"

"No, it wouldn't."

"By the way, did you ever read *Lady Chatterley's Lover?*"

"Goddamn it, yes," said our guest.

"I'm sorry," said Katie. "I didn't mean that the way it probably sounded. *Lady Chatterley's Lover* is really quite a deep book and has a lot to do with our present-day civilization. It's agreed everybody knows, or should know, about sex and the part it plays in the human dilemma. But not all fun, by a far cry. In my own childhood I began with barnyard things because we lived on a farm, and then I worked up through the various levels of culture. This right now is the highest I've been."

"Katie!" I said again.

The odd part was that our guest seemed to be looking at her with unwilling but genuine interest.

"I'd better be going," he said suddenly, but he made no movement, and I guessed that this was a way of reminding Katie that action ought to take the place of words.

She had stepped to the window and now announced that Henry Spinney had come into view carrying what looked like pants.

"Yes, they're pants all right," she reported as Henry came closer.

He entered a minute or two later, short of breath but in a state of high satisfaction.

"I asked permission to look out their upstairs window," he said. "I told them I wanted to get a sight along the rear line of my property with this highway business in mind. They were having a hell of a fight in the kitchen. Here, my friend, is what you're in want of."

"Those aren't my slacks," said our guest.

"They're Barry's," said Katie.

"Second best is better than none at all," said Henry Spinney.

Katie had not moved from her post at the window, and she now gave warning that Barry was heading toward our house. I don't think the redheaded man quite caught the import of this, for he had stepped through the doorway to the front hall while he put on Barry's pants. But Henry Spinney knew exactly what was up.

"The Johnson fellow is only about ninety per cent fool," Henry said. "He knows certain indications when he sees them, and he sure caught sight of our friend here. What's worse, it's hard to lose a redheaded man. He sticks out like a spar buoy at slack tide."

"What shall we do?" said Katie.

"Nothing at all," I said. "This is none of our affair."

"We could hide what's-his-name under the bed in the spare room."

"No good," said Henry Spinney. "So long as he's been seen, he's got to be explained, which means likewise that he's got to be produced; otherwise it's all too much like storytelling. Which it already is."

"There's only one explanation," I said, "except for adding to it how he happened to get into Barry's pants."

"There must be lots of explanations. We've only got to think of one," said Katie.

"You mean you're hell-bent to put together some preposterous lies," I said.

"Be quiet, Gid. When people need to be helped, they need to be helped."

"Let them help themselves."

If there had been any rational means of assistance, I wouldn't have opposed it. I was adamant simply because the situation was beyond any bailing out, and I didn't want Katie doing foolish things.

A couple of minutes later we were all in our sitting room together, Henry Spinney, the redheaded man, Barry, Katie and myself. This wasn't my idea of a happy gathering, but Katie's view was different. She became an actress.

Without acknowledging Barry's entrance by any word or expression, she faced the redheaded man and fairly shouted at him, "Then you demand that we give you the envelope?"

"What? Well, yes, certainly I do." He couldn't help responding to a cue thrown at him so boldly.

Katie stepped across to the mantel and took Mr. Sparrow's envelope from behind the clock.

"My God, Katie," I said, "don't give him that!"

So it was I, with my surprise and indignation, who clothed

Katie's improvisation with enough convincing realism to compensate for its defects. I realized this immediately, but I still wanted to prevent her from giving him that envelope.

She said to the redheaded man, "You know this is supposed to be given by hand to Ellie Kempton?"

"Yes, I know. It's what I'm here for."

"Go ahead, give it to him," said Henry Spinney.

"Katie, you can't go on with this," I said.

The whole exchange had occupied so little time that Barry was still inarticulate, his reactions confused and delayed further by a conflict of impulses. I thought that I, one sane person, should give him an explanation, though to mix truth with the stage effects of Katie and Henry Spinney would be a gamble.

"I told you about this man Sparrow," I said to Barry, "but I guess I didn't mention the plain Manila envelope he wanted delivered to Ellie Kempton. At the time I didn't know there was money in it."

"Money?" said Barry.

"Mr. Johnson," Katie said by way of introduction, "this is Mr. Pettigrew."

"Pettigrew?"

"He's mixed up in this road business."

"Damn it," I said, "this is all preposterous. Let's get things straight. Katie, for once I want you to keep still!"

Henry Spinney put his hand on my shoulder and said, "Steady does it, steady."

"You too," I said. "You and Katie have gone crazy. What do you expect . . . ?"

"A man never knows what to expect," said Henry Spinney. "Now take Pettigrew here . . ."

Barry said, "Evidently this road proposal goes much deeper than I realized. I've seen this man Pettigrew, if that's his name, skulking around here for weeks."

This was when Gretchen made her entrance, and it was the moment of my resignation. I was through. I left the situation to

Katie, Henry Spinney, and any other higher forces. Gretchen stared at the redheaded man with frozen concentration. I have read that in the great crises of life we are often taken up with trifles, and I felt certain that what really flabbergasted her was seeing this man in Barry's trousers. But she had heard his remark and followed the instinct of her kind for saying the right thing.

"We're not having any road here. We are definitely not."

Everyone looked at everyone else, surprised, and then—though I can't explain it—rather settled. I suppose this was because sides appeared to have been chosen or reaffirmed and the issue of the road had been brought to the fore. Except for unimportant reiterations, this was how the scene ended. I recall that the redheaded man waved the Manila envelope defiantly as he went out the door and that Gretchen treated Barry with icy reproof. He was in for a bad time. Whatever he might have said in the quarrel at their house that Henry Spinney had interrupted he would now regret.

And the road project now had to be a grab, or a steal, or a scandal that called for a probe. You could think about it only in headlines.

❧

"Why did you say his name was Pettigrew?" I asked Katie.

"I told him that if he wouldn't say who he was, we'd have to invent a name. When I was a girl, most of the books I read had Pettigrews for characters."

"What books?"

"Books that Frank Stockton wrote, or John Kendrick Bangs, or . . ."

"You're making that up. You never read them. You're not half old enough."

"Also *Rebecca of Sunnybrook Farm*," said Katie.

"If there was a Pettigrew in that book, I'll eat it," I said.

"Get stuffy with me and I'll spit in your eye," said Katie.

I knew the strength of my position, and it was exactly that which made me withdraw. I did not want to be responsible for the defeat at Katie's hands of so logical and correct a view of the outrage she had perpetrated. I was the custodian of a logically impregnable cause, and I would have felt disgraced if I had allowed it to be tarnished. So I walked out, defeated, but with my position intact.

I headed down the lane toward Henry Spinney's. He had tarried outside his house, fussing with his lilac and bridal-wreath bushes, and he evidently had anticipated my coming.

"Want a word with me?" he said.

In all my prior experience I couldn't remember that anyone had addressed me in this way, and I had not expected that anyone ever would; yet there was no one from whom the ancient form of inquiry could have come more naturally than from Henry Spinney.

"Goddamn it, yes," I said. "You and Katie have had your fun, but what happens next?"

"Ha," said Henry. "You've put your finger on something there."

His gratification was so high-spirited that I abandoned my sense of outrage. I realized later that Henry must have interpreted this change of attitude as my coming down from my high horse.

"How do you expect a man in my place to feel?" he asked. "A man who has to stand by and see noble steamers like the *Commonwealth,* the *Priscilla* and even the *Chester W. Chapin* broken up for scrap, and why? All because of these goddamned sons of bitches and their goddamned highways. We got along all right with the railroads. It wasn't the railroads that did in our coastwise steamship lines; it was these highway sons of bitches. You wouldn't think much of human nature if you doubted how I would feel when challenged in what you might call my own field of experience."

He went on in this vein, and I now understood Henry's deeper motive. I had assumed only a perverse preference for raising hell, but actually he was dedicated. Of course, a man of his sophistication would not seriously question the manifest destiny of the modern highway system or commit himself to any hopeful combat against it. Nevertheless, here was his rationale, and it was a good one and would serve him well. He would go on relishing it, coddling it, making as much of it as he could.

As I sat with him on his doorstep and listened, he told me that in his days as pilot on the Fall River Line he had filled the long hours with useful reflection. Inevitably I was reminded of the Gilbertian lines: "When all night long a chap remains on sentry go, to chase monotony, he exercises of his brains—that is, assuming that he's got any," and I pictured Henry Spinney in his uniform standing in the wheelhouse of the *Priscilla* as she took the rollers off Point Judith or passed between the distant lights of Long Island and Connecticut, exercising of his brains in the long night voyage.

Conclusions arrived at under such circumstances would be not only shipshape, but, considering the period of the *Priscilla,* they would have elegance as well. I had been a passenger in the grand saloon of that ornate side-wheeler often enough to feel the quality of Henry's philosophy. He was convinced that men usually act against their own interests, that they are not gifted with real imagination, and that their predictability exposes them to exploitation and circumvention.

"You've got to break out," said Henry. "In a sense, you've got to put to sea." And when I finally left him he called after me, *"Similia similibus curantur,"* which I not only took to mean "Treat the sons of bitches as they treat you" or "Fight fire with fire" but to have far greater learning of a sort and likewise elegance.

When I reached our house, Katie seemed unreasonably glad to see me. This, I learned quickly, was because she had carried off a postscript to our recent scene all by herself and wanted to tell about it.

"Professor Hamilton came back," she said. "That's his real name. I surprised it out of him and out of Gretchen. She was here, too, though only for a kind of surprised, anxious minute. I'm not sure it's Harvard he's a professor at, but he is one."

"He ought to be ashamed of himself."

"Do you think so? It may be he's specially gifted."

"Gifted or not, what did he want?"

"He wanted to give back the plain Manila envelope. 'Here it is,' he said. 'Shall I put it right here on the table?' 'You will not,' I said. 'You took it in the presence of witnesses, and you said it was what you had come to get. Don't try to back out now. You'll find yourself in a mess.' 'I seem to be in a mess anyway,' he said. 'You'll be in a worse one,' I said. 'Now take the plain Manila envelope and scram out of here in a hurry.' 'I don't know what to do,' he said. 'Then call up somebody at Harvard and get some classical advice,' I said. 'I know I'm indebted to you,' he said. 'Up to date you are, but from here on in, who knows?' 'What do you mean by that?' he asked. 'I mean you'd better take that plain Manila envelope and get going.' 'What's in it?' he wanted to know. 'Money,' I said. 'Really?' he said. And that's how the conversation kept going on for quite a while. Finally he put the plain Manila envelope in his pocket and off he went."

"Whose pants did he have on?"

"Barry's, of course. Where would he have had a chance to change them?"

I accepted Katie's account, although I was sure it was only vaguely accurate. I had had enough. My appetite for this sort of thing was considerably less than hers or Henry Spinney's, and I liked my facts ungarnished. With a long night's reflection in the privacy of the wheelhouse of a Long Island steamer I might have been able to form some idea of where we had got ourselves, but short of such an opportunity I preferred to drop the subject as completely as possible.

When we were in bed that night, Katie said, "I'd love to know what a grand jury will make of this."

"Will you please shut up?" I said.

The next day Ruth Ellen came home again, unexpectedly as before, and we saw her walking around in the newly lengthening green grass, her hands in the pockets of her blue slacks, the turtle neck of a lighter-blue sweater framing her throat. Simultaneously with her arrival Katie learned quickly, and I, being male, learned tardily, that Barry and Gretchen weren't speaking. When I met Ruth Ellen in the lane that afternoon, I thought I could learn why, but Ruth Ellen was detached and uncommunicative.

"Anything new about the through-way project?" she asked after a greeting that was friendly enough but crisply detached.

"Well, yes," I said. "There have been various developments."

"I suppose so. It's the modern tragedy. Every day our highly developed creatures of civilization ring the same old changes on the themes of Frankenstein and Faustus."

I didn't recall having heard those themes lumped together in this way, but I let the allusion pass. I wanted to find out what I could about what seemed to me more immediate matters.

"Your father's as dead against the road as ever."

"Is he?" she said, looking up at the sky.

"You don't seem surprised."

"What? No."

"Don't you remember what you said to me on your last visit home?"

"Yes, I do. It was straight talk. No man so typed as he is by breeding and business and social forces can escape the end product he represents—because it is an end product, you see."

"How about free will?"

"Some types escape all that. It's convenient. I suppose my father will have a half-life, maybe, of sixty-five years."

I responded to this staggering *non sequitur*. "How much of a full life?"

"Why, none at all," Ruth Ellen said. "That's the point. Don't you see?"

The fact that Katie called me in for dinner provided an unsatisfactory anticlimax and spoiled my appetite with a sense of defeat.

Ruth Ellen stayed only a day or two, and Barry and Gretchen

resumed speaking. Toward the middle of the week Barry and I drove to Boston together, but I learned nothing about any family affairs. The subject was the road.

"Did you know that a syndicate has taken an option on a tract of one hundred and sixty acres at the Point?" Barry asked me.

"I didn't know there was that much acreage at the Point; a lot of it must be under water."

"Very likely. Just the same, this group has the option. It smells as if this outfit is close to important people at the Statehouse, though I haven't any proof yet. You see what that will mean."

Of course I saw—pressure. Highways and land went together, and politics completed a devastating triumvirate of modern times. If Barry was right about the Statehouse tie-in, we were in trouble. Even at this moment of anxious concern, however, I realized how similar Barry was to the type his daughter had described, though in vague, unsatisfactory terms. Her generation indicated, not taking the trouble to fill out. Yet, I thought, even the stereotyped suburbanite can stick to his convictions, or at any rate to his interests.

"It was this funny business about the redheaded man that started me digging into the registry records," Barry said. "It didn't make sense to me that he had been hanging around Dinton for these weeks without some definite purpose. Obviously, he was no ordinary politician or speculator, and I couldn't picture him as working for a contractor. Well, then, what was he up to?

"I got a promising answer out of my head and then I looked for proof and found it. By the way, his name isn't Pettigrew. He imposed on Katie when he told her that—though I don't blame her for swallowing his story, whatever it was."

"Well, what's his real name?"

"Hamilton. But the option was taken by the Beloff-Driscoll Management Corporation, George R. Beloff, President, and Herman Driscoll, Secretary and Treasurer. Moreover, I have photostatic proof that both Beloff and Driscoll are on the state payroll."

"You mean they have D.P.W. contracts, or what?"

"They have contracts, engineering and construction."

As we discussed the outlook, it seemed to me that Barry had been astute in everything except his original premise about Professor Hamilton, and that was now of no importance. My foresight was limited.

"By the way, Gid," Barry said, "do you think Henry Spinney is really all right? I mean, do you think he's with us?"

"Don't worry about Henry's fighting convictions. He has no intention of letting the enemy into the quietude of our lane."

"Well, then, why is he always barging off? What's the reason for his antagonism toward me?"

"I wasn't aware of any antagonism. Henry's an odd bird, you must understand, and his orientation is different from ours. He wants to reopen the battle between Long Island Sound and Route 1."

Most of the overused modern words I don't like, but "orientation" I've always been fond of. It represents the space travel of ordinary conversation.

Late that afternoon, when I got home from Boston, I met Ellie Kempton strolling in the lane, his hands in his pockets. I wondered if the money from Mr. Sparrow had been delivered to him. He seemed smug enough. But this thought was quickly put out of my mind.

"Hello, Gid," Ellie said. "Here's something I bet you never thought of. If we get this new road, there's going to be a need for a rotary along about here, and you know what? We've got a first-rate chance of having the biggest rotary in this area of the state."

"Why not a clover leaf?"

"A rotary. A real big rotary."

"Is that good?"

"You don't seem to catch on, Gid. It would be bigger than anything around—bigger than the rotary at the Hyannis airport, bigger than the ones at the Cape Cod Canal."

"Oh, hell, Ellie," I said, more or less copying Henry Spinney, "then you wouldn't have any underpasses."

"No, I don't suppose we'd have any of those, but I'd rather have the biggest rotary in this part of Massachusetts."

I reported this encounter to Katie. "I don't know who's been pulling Ellie's leg. It's a sure thing he didn't get any such idea from official sources. Whatever other folly may be committed here, there won't be any rotary traffic circles."

"Only one person could have made up a yarn like that."

"I suppose you mean Henry Spinney."

"Of course. He knows how to spread the seeds of future discontent. Besides, he's unmarried, accustomed to large horizons, and as cussed as your Uncle Eben."

I have never had an Uncle Eben, but I let that go. I chose that moment to remark upon Ruth Ellen's attitude toward her father, particularly her characterization. The attitude of youth was strange and disturbing, I said.

"But not really new," said Katie. "I remember my brother saying my father was a barnacle-crusted old skinflint. He was real mad when he said it, but he wasn't entirely wrong. Ruth Ellen has more of a gift of language, but I doubt if it runs much deeper than that. As civilization advances, everything smoothens out."

⁓

On Sunday morning, early, Barry and Gretchen came over with the signs of sleepiness still upon them. Gretchen's face was blue under the eyes. They were both smoking cigarettes without enjoyment.

"As I get it," Barry said, "there's precious little hard-nosed opposition to this road."

"Even those who are against it seem so—so, oh, so complacent," said Gretchen.

Well, people in Dinton are complacent, like people everywhere else. Calamitous events in the future do not wholly dismay —they also fascinate; and, anyway, in this case the projected road could not be regarded as wholly calamitous since all it would do would be to destroy our particular outpost and defense against civilization. People enjoy being in on spectacles of this kind.

The four of us talked on for a while until finally Gretchen snubbed out her fourth or fifth cigarette in her teacup.

"Oh, well," she said, "we may as well forget it for now. Nobody's at his best this early in the morning."

"That's as stupid a remark as I've heard in a good while," said Katie.

"What? You mean you're at your best in the early morning?"

"Such as it is," said Katie. "I brim over at sunrise or earlier. I sparkle. I have what they call overtones of genius."

"I bet you have, at that," said Barry, looking at her with what I took to be a combination of curiosity and envy. Gretchen simply thought Katie was kidding.

We all walked out into the sunshine together, and it was then, while Barry and Katie lingered on the doorstep, that Gretchen found a chance to whisper at me.

"Come over when you can," she said. "Any time after ten—Barry's leaving to see some people. I must talk to you. I absolutely need your advice."

So this explained their dejected, desultory, otherwise useless early call. Of course, I whispered that I understood and would slip over as near ten as possible. I didn't tell Katie where I was going, but I wouldn't have bet that she didn't know.

I found Gretchen less blue under the eyes and otherwise improved in appearance, but in what is often called a state of nerves —or used to be so called by Dinton people. She asked me to come in, sat down, had me sit down, and then got up and walked a few times around the room, inhaling a cigarette.

"I don't know how to begin," she said. "Oh, well, here. Look at this."

She thrust at me a newspaper, folded quarter size, which I think she had stashed behind a couch cushion in readiness for my coming. The headlines she wanted me to see were something about space research, and the picture immediately below was a large one, an excellent likeness as I recognized at once, of Professor Jonathan Hamilton, the redheaded man of our lane. He had been appointed to a new presidential advisory commission and would be on leave of absence from M.I.T. on an assignment in Washington.

"You see," said Gretchen. "You see. It's fairly horrible. So far as I know, Barry hasn't noticed this—hasn't identified Jon as anyone he's seen lately. Barry never reads the papers closely, you see. But lots of people around here will catch on. They're bound to, and they'll be talking."

"You call him Jon?"

"Oh, don't make it difficult. You know perfectly well that he's a friend of mine. You know why he came here. You know he hasn't a thing to do with the lane."

"I guess I know."

"I guess you do. I'm not ashamed of my affair with Jon, if you want to call it that. There's not the least thing sordid about it. He's a remarkable man, an amazing man, entirely different from Barry. He has one of the truly great intellects."

"Gretchen, I'm no censor of morals, and you don't expect me to believe that a woman as young and attractive as you can be a purely intellectual companion of . . ."

"Don't be silly, Gid. You and I both know the elemental facts of life. Mind and body aren't partitioned off—they're all one. It isn't that I don't love Barry. I do. I'm married to him and I want to stay married to him, but a woman must have more than one phase of her personality. She can be pluralistic with as much right and reason as a man, and things happen to her that are right and natural, even though they may not fit in with middle-class conventions."

A moderate pause occurred here, during which I reflected that Gretchen and the professor seemed a perfect image, if not of middle-class conventions, then of suburban customs.

"Besides, he needs me," said Gretchen, taking another turn around the room.

I didn't think of anything to say.

"Call me a rebel, if you like."

This was an invitation I couldn't accept, since she had done and was doing exactly what she wanted to do with as much social sanction as most people have for their behavior.

"Jon Hamilton is a man I respect and admire so much that I should be proud to be the mother of children by him."

"Wouldn't Barry be bothered if you began to supply the household with redheaded babies?"

I hadn't meant this as Gretchen took it. The turn from romantic fantasy to cheap realism made her face pucker, and for a moment I thought she was going to cry.

"Gid, I didn't know you could be such a stinker!"

"You mustn't be so touchy, Gretchen. I'm really sympathetic. I'd like to help in any way I can."

"The trouble is, I don't see what can be done. Not actually, I mean."

"How about the crass details? Has everything been covered up or reconciled? I guess I mean mostly did you get Barry's trousers back?"

"Yes, I did, and Barry doesn't suspect anything. Jon told me he delivered that plain Manila envelope, too, so that was taken care of. His money was in his own trousers, and there wasn't any in Barry's, so he borrowed one of the bills from the envelope and replaced it later."

What I thought of right away was how Katie had marked the bills, though exactly how it was she had marked them I did not know. I didn't mention this possible complication to Gretchen; to have done so would have been pure inhumanity, and, after all, marks on bills are fairly common and usually impossible to trace. Gretchen continued to be occupied with what was obvious and irreparable.

"That picture in the paper is almost sure to attract somebody's attention around here."

"Maybe not," I said. "Let's hope not."

I had no useful advice to offer, and I was surprised later to learn that she had thought of something herself; it must have been soon after we had parted that she went downtown to Joe Bunker's store on Main Street and bought up the entire stock of the New York *Times* for the day. It didn't come to a great deal— something on the order of fifteen or twenty copies, I suppose.

I managed not to tell the whole story of this conversation to Katie, but she pumped a good deal. In any case, she would have found out about the buying of the newspapers at Joe Bunker's.

"At least," I said, "Gretchen has probably gained some time. It may be a while before the professor's picture gets into a newspaper again."

"You think she's gained time?"

"Don't you?"

"I've lived too long in Dinton to believe any such foolish thing."

She didn't care to explain, but on our way to the movies that evening I discovered what she meant. She led me into the paper store, where Joe Bunker was leaning across the counter looking for dirty passages in a new paperback; the book had a gay picture of a nude woman on its glossy cover, but evidently Joe hadn't found anything in the text to match this display. Usually you couldn't in a paperback, and Joe knew this better than most people, but I suppose he could always hope.

I don't remember whether Katie said anything at all to Joe, though perhaps she did. At any rate she gave him a sort of half-way wink, whereupon he produced from under the counter a large sheet of cardboard upon which he had pasted a clipping from the New York *Times* showing the portrait of Professor Hamilton and the story of his appointment. If Gretchen had not tried to corner the day's issue of the *Times,* relatively few inhabitants of Dinton would have paid the price for a copy; but now, partly because of Joe Bunker's sense of obligation to the principle of a free press and partly because he enjoyed satisfying public curiosity, everyone was viewing Professor Hamilton's picture without cost. I imagine that by bedtime the professor's features were as well known in Dinton as those of any man except, perhaps, Abraham Lincoln.

"That fellow was in here, that professor," Joe Bunker said. "He came right into the store and changed a bill—fifty bucks. I change bills like that a lot of times, even in the winter, but this one looked funny, so I kept it."

Joe turned to his cash register and produced a fifty-dollar bill marked in one corner with an outline of a red heart.

"Look," he said.

We had already looked.

When we went out, I said to Katie, "What possessed you to do a thing like that—make a red heart?"

"It seemed appropriate. You know, to a sweetheart deal. Isn't that one of the words?"

"I think the term is used only in a special sense, but that doesn't matter now. Where this will lead is more than I can guess."

"It certainly is interesting," said Katie.

"And how did you know Joe Bunker had that exhibit?"

"Gussie Tripp told me when he came to read the meter."

If it hadn't been Gussie it would have been someone else; for a town that some strangers considered sleepy, Dinton possessed remarkable powers of communication. Everything interesting always got around with the greatest dispatch. But nobody, absolutely nobody, would say a word to Gretchen. Her illusion of security remained unbroken.

～

The next morning I saw Henry Spinney using a rake in his yard. I thought I would feel more comfortable if I knew his present intentions.

"Our redheaded friend turns out to be important," I remarked.

"Quite a notable. If this professor hasn't left for Washington yet, maybe we can use him."

I said I didn't see how.

"We've got to get into the Governor's office, haven't we? Now that a bribe's been passed and an option taken on land at the Point, we're late already. This highway scheme can move fast—for all we know those fellows on the Executive Council have been bought up for days. Not that anyone can trust the bastards after they've taken his money."

"Now Henry, I hope you're not planning to talk to the Governor on your own."

"The thing is to see one of his secretaries first—pick out the one that's going to be appointed a judge later on."

"How the hell can you predict who's going to be appointed to what?"

"You go by the signs, more or less like navigating in a heavy snow or fog. You use your intuition."

"If you insist on going to the Governor, some of the rest of us will have to go with you."

"So long as I'm not kept waiting, Gid."

The imminence of Henry's intention disturbed me, especially since I knew that if Henry wanted transportation to Boston I would be bound to supply it.

I included these thoughts in my report to Katie, adding that I thought Henry was right in saying that someone should get to the Governor. I was chagrined that Henry's astuteness had run ahead of mine.

"You'll have to make another trip to the Statehouse yourself," said Katie. "Get in there ahead of Henry."

"I suppose so, though the idea doesn't appeal to me at all."

"Be sure to look irascible, the way you look now. It always makes an impression on a politician when a businessman appears irascible."

"I wish you wouldn't talk like Henry Spinney. I've been exposed to enough homespun sailing directions for one morning."

But that, always, was the atmosphere in which I lived, and I suppose at bottom I was envious of Henry and of Katie for the native uprush of their ideas and their separateness from the civilization of which Barry Johnson was so convenient and apt a symbol.

⁓

I had no difficulty in making an appointment through one of the Governor's secretaries, and I did not inquire about his horoscope. When I had penetrated the make-believe of the Statehouse once more, however, I couldn't help admitting Henry Spinney's wisdom; this man who greeted me with a confiding smile on his long, rather sharp face was easily imagined in judicial robes. His chin jutted suitably, and his gray eyes told you that they saw what they wanted to see, a sort of confidence much better for his purpose than actual seeing. His name was Walter Lanesboro.

"I can make a good guess why you are here," he said. "It's that new road down in Dinton."

"There isn't any new road."

"Not yet, of course. These things take time."

"Let's not have any misunderstanding," I said. "This whole road idea is the final word in idiocy. No one in his right mind would consider it."

"Oh? Well, Mr. Lester, you have to be aware that roads aren't built for the present but for the future. You have to look a good way ahead."

"I guess you don't understand plain English, Mr. Lanesboro. Idiocy was what I said—maybe imbecility would have been better."

This sounded irascible, as I had intended it to sound, and I'm sure I looked irascible.

"You feel strongly, sir, you certainly do. But we're both men of our time, and this is an administration with a strong commitment to a progressive highway program. . . ."

I uttered a single scatalogical four-letter word that I do not believe I had spoken since boyhood. Lanesboro's expression became a bit wry, and he shifted his ground.

"How do the people down your way feel about their share of the gas-tax money?"

"I don't give a damn how they feel."

"Oh, come, Mr. Lester. The taxpayers want some tangible return. You have to remember that the gas tax comes from all parts of the state, and people up around North Adams like to drive to the shore and see what the scenery is in an area such as Dinton. This adds up to roads."

I repeated that four-letter word because Lanesboro had irritated me beyond any other articulateness.

"You talk it over with Rufe Handmore."

"To hell with Rufe Handmore."

This wasn't proper Statehouse talk. You never disparaged your own representative, no matter how much of an ass or an ignoramus or sharper he might be; to do so went against the system, and the system is one of the unalterable ills and foundations of state government.

"Don't you worry, Mr. Lester. The Governor will be impressed with your point of view. If you can wait a couple of minutes I'll slip you in so that you can register your ideas right now."

I said all right, and he led me into a large anteroom with rugs and pomp and pretense and knots of people standing or sitting, each group evidently unrelated to any other. Lanesboro and I were halfway to the farther door when he was halted by another of the Governor's secretaries, who, it appeared, had been assigned to the drafting of a proclamation in honor of Greek Independence Day.

"Jeez," he said to Lanesboro, "you ought to have heard Senator Caggiano just now. He has this constituent, a Turk, an influential guy. He's afraid of this Greek Independence Day stuff. He wants us to just skip it."

"George, you know better than that. Who does Caggiano think

he is? It's nothing but a goddamn lot of words, anyway, so why should we skip it?"

"He's just worried about this one Turk. I don't know whether he can read or not, but he tunes in on TV."

"Mr. Lester," Lanesboro said, "this is George Wilcox. He does a lot of speech writing and so on."

"You must be here about that goddamned road down in Dinton," said George. "Can't you build it right up to the edge of a nice high cliff so we can send a lot of Statehouse traffic to hellangone over the brink?"

Lanesboro thought this was not funny, and even I could see that George Wilcox would never reach the Massachusetts judiciary.

"George, you tell Caggiano from me that the Greeks have got to have their proclamation," said Lanesboro.

"O.K. I've got it practically written—we'll go right back to Simonides. 'Tell them in Lacedaemon, passer-by, that here obedient to their words we lie.' "

"Wait a minute. Wasn't it the Turks who killed off those fellows?"

"It was the Persians. We don't have to worry about the Persians, or do we?"

"You go ahead and never mind the laughs."

Lanesboro and I were free to reach the doorway of the Governor's private domain, though the word "private" seemed hardly applicable. His Excellency was seated at an enormous desk flanked by the flags of state and nation, adorned with numerous trophies, and faced by a delegation of citizenry numbering a dozen or fifteen.

"These people are from Sackfield," Lanesboro whispered. "They want a community college. I think they are about through."

Since I was a reader of the newspapers, Governor Lemuel P. Ferrick's face was entirely familiar to me. He could be described as rugged or as intellectual or both; by this I suppose I mean he could either turn it on or off. His face was weathered by both statesmanship and the outdoors. You could think of him as Lincolnesque if you wanted to. Even sitting down he gave the impression of big-boned height, and I noticed his bony, hairy wrists as he held a document on the desk before him.

I judged that everything useful to the Sackfield contingent had been said, and possibly more. Governor Ferrick obviously took our entrance as a welcome end to the conference.

"Every consideration," he was saying. "I shall have a detailed report of your project on my desk tomorrow, and I want to say that you people in Sackfield are fortunate in being represented by so able and conscientious a legislator as Herbert Fowler. Herb has your welfare at heart, and he's an absolutely tireless worker."

According to the Boston papers, Herbert Fowler was making trouble for the Governor's tax bill, but the Statehouse code had to be observed.

Even before the last of the Sackfield delegation had reached the doorway Lanesboro had presented me to the Governor, and though I couldn't have asked for a more cordial greeting, I would have been more favorably impressed with one a lot less cordial.

"Mr. Lester thinks the Dinton highway project is getting out of hand," Mr. Lanesboro said. "I wanted him to have a chance to state his views to you personally."

"Let's see," said Governor Ferrick, "what's the proposed width of that road?"

"Twenty feet, I think," said Lanesboro. "I can check that."

"I wish you would," said the Governor. Then, to me, "I suppose we might widen it out, say to twenty-five or so, if that would help."

"Your Excellency," I said, "do you mean to tell me that the only question in your mind is how wide this so-called highway is going to be?"

"I wasn't aware of any other question."

"Through way isn't the word," said Lanesboro. "It's all secondary construction—unless Governor Ferrick thinks it ought to be upgraded."

"Mr. Lester, what phase of the matter do you think ought to have consideration?"

"Mr. Lester thinks, for instance, that if the state has money to spend in Dinton, why not spend it on something of absolutely first priority, like schools," said Lanesboro.

The thought was not one of mine, but I recognized it; after all, it wasn't so much a thought as a convenience. Anyone could use it, and almost everyone did.

"We have good roads and good schools, too, Mr. Lester," said the Governor. This was precisely what Lanesboro had given him the opportunity to say.

"Governor Ferrick," I said, "let's not play around. We don't want this goddamned road. We don't want *any* goddamned road. We don't need any, least of all where this is apparently going to be laid out in defiance of all common sense. Nobody needs it. Nobody has asked for it except two or three who stand to enrich themselves at the expense of the taxpayers."

"You surprise me, Mr. Lester. Of course, I'll have the whole situation looked into. I haven't prejudged the matter—don't think that for a moment. I've just been trying to establish a frame of reference, a perspective."

"Orientation," I said.

"Exactly."

"If you establish that, you'll protect the integrity of the road program, the public treasury, and the legitimate interests of Dinton," I said.

I must have said a lot more, too, and Governor Ferrick told me in kindly fashion that I had helped him, and he wished many more Massachusetts businessmen would come to him and put their cards on the table, and discuss things without evasion as man to man.

Lanesboro led me out through the anteroom where the knots

of people seemed to have acquired a kind of permanence, as if they were part of the installation, like the thick rugs and the statesmanlike furniture of expensive dark woods.

A few minutes later I was walking down the Park Street hill, and the clearing mists of my subconscious let me discern what had been false in my interview with the Governor and, in fact, with my entire Statehouse visit: it was that neither Governor Ferrick nor Lanesboro had believed a word I said, and neither had expected me to believe a word he said, either.

ᔕᔓ

"You went at it the wrong way," Henry Spinney said to me the next morning when I set out for a before-breakfast walk to regain, if possible, the peace that God had intended to be found in Dinton's countryside, now so delicately balanced on the coy margin of spring. Katie had wanted to get me out of the house, anyway. I wouldn't have chosen to meet Henry Spinney, but there he was, waiting for me.

"I don't know where your information came from," I said.

"Could have come from anywhere in Dinton. News travels fast."

"I suppose Rufe Handmore has been talking plenty."

"Nobody is supposed to see the Governor without fixing it through Rufe."

"So Rufe said I went at it the wrong way."

"No, I was the one said that. Who the hell cares what Rufe says, anyway?"

"I don't pretend I made much westing, but I'm not sure anyone else would have done any better."

"One trouble is, you were compromised, as they say."

"How?"

"Rufe says it's well known on the Hill that you're hand in glove with Lorenzo Sparrow."

"Who's Lorenzo Sparrow?" Incredibly, I had forgotten. The man's importance to me was as nothing. Then I remembered. "Henry, anybody who's half-bright can see the absurdity of that."

"It ain't brightness, Gid, it's politics. That's the hitch. You've been seen with Sparrow at the Statehouse. Anyhow, the thing now is to get up a delegation to see the Governor."

"Why on earth should we get up a delegation?"

"You were just the scout, Gid. We've got to make a landing in force. Also, we've got to draw out the enemy. Besides our own people we'll need someone from this outfit that has taken an option on land at the Point—let 'em show their hand—and, most important, we've got to have what's-his-name, the goddamn bedroom jumper, Professor Hamilton."

"Henry! You're mad, completely mad. . . ."

"That last is a very neat proposition. It's as close to genius as a man can generally hope to strike."

"It's a lot closer to sheer lunacy."

He didn't trouble to make any further comment. He simply stood there, studying me indulgently from the safe redoubt of his own satisfaction, much as he had looked so often from the pilothouse of the queenly *Priscilla*.

When I got back to the house I reported to Katie, who, to my surprise and irritation, did not share my view in the least.

"If Henry Spinney wants a delegation, he probably has his reasons. What's more, I think it's generous of him not to hold it against you that you deliberately made your trip to the Statehouse without telling him, when it was his idea to see the Governor in the first place."

"That's just what you advised me to do."

"Well, you didn't have to take my advice."

"Since when haven't I had to take your advice—or else?"

"So far as including Professor Hamilton, it will be a kindness to Gretchen—bringing him back into her life."

"And what do you think the professor will contribute to the matter of turning our lane into an expressway? How can he possibly appear as an expert, or even as one informed? There'll be reporters present, remember. And what about Barry?"

"Oh, Barry's all right. You can tell him one thing one day, and another thing another. He's realistic. Like all the others who are smooth and wear good clothes and say 'Hi, fellow!' he's aware of a need for accommodation. He's so anxious to face up to something that half the time he doesn't see what it is."

"I don't recognize the characterization."

"I know better."

She was right. I did recognize it. She couldn't have done much better if she had listened to the talks that Barry and I had on our drives together to Boston and back.

"Well," I said, "this is not going to be my kind of delegation, and I'm not going to have anything to do with it."

"You must act according to your dictates," Katie said. "Unlike Barry, you don't face up to things."

I had made a resolution, but of course I altered it when I met Ellie Kempton on his purposeful way to see me accidentally. That is, he hoped to establish the fiction that our meeting took place by chance.

"Hi, Gid," he said. "I would have expected you to be in Boston today."

"Well, I'm not."

"Not unless there's two of you." He could see I wasn't going to smile, so he didn't put himself to much trouble. "So long as you're here, I've a mind to say something that I hope you'll take the right way. When we see the Governor, all of us, I hope you won't come out flat-footed the way you did the first time."

"I'll damn well say what I think."

"There's times when it pays to keep something back, Gid. If you go ahead and shoot your bolt, then where are you? You ain't got another shot in the locker."

"This is not a case of horse trading, Ellie. Nobody's going to be in any doubt about how Katie and I feel about this idiotic road scheme."

"I realize you've got your ideas, but I wasn't thinking so much about the road, not at the moment. The thing is that Mr. Driscoll is coming along with us to see the Governor. He represents the people who are interested in the development at the Point, and they tell me he's a real nice man. Even if it was to turn out that the road was never to be built at all, we wouldn't want to discourage someone who's got money to invest in Dinton."

"I have no desire to make Mr. Driscoll's acquaintance," I said, choosing my idiom. "And I'll be damned if I'll tag along to the Governor's office with him and Lorenzo Sparrow and Professor Hamilton and God knows who else. You, for one more."

"What? Is the professor coming?"

"I understand he's going to be dragged in."

For a moment I did not understand Ellie's expression of delight, but then I remembered that no matter what Professor Hamilton might mean to the rest of us, to Ellie he was the bearer of a certain plain Manila envelope. That he would be present seemed to put things in a different light.

"Well, Gid, maybe you're right. If I was in your place, I figure maybe I wouldn't go either. I hadn't been thinking of the trouble it would put you to."

"I'm obliged for your interest," I said, but he was immune to such sarcasm.

I suppose it was partly to spite Ellie that I decided to join the delegation. Also, it was partly because I was invited to have lunch at Schrafft's with Gretchen, Ruth Ellen and Professor Hamilton prior to the appointment with Governor Ferrick. And there was the fact that Katie said if I didn't go, she'd kick me in the teeth.

Come to think of it, my luncheon invitation from Gretchen had not mentioned Ruth Ellen. I soon formed the impression that she had turned up entirely of her own notion and that her precocity (this was the only word I could think of, though I knew it wasn't the right one) found no welcome.

We were suddenly in a kind of stage setting, arranged at a small table in a restaurant that should have been interchangeable with any of countless establishments all over America but wasn't; the spirit of Boston defeated even the potent forces of standardization. Just by being in Boston and catering to Boston shoppers and suburbanites, inert objects assumed a difference that was Boston's.

My interest at first, obviously, was taken by Professor Hamilton, but his self-possession showed no vulnerability and allowed scant holding ground for inspection. In his lean, redheaded way he could be called handsome, and, anyway, Gretchen would have called him so; anyone could see that, except that Ruth Ellen didn't bother to see it.

"Why isn't Barry here?" she asked. "I'm damn sure he isn't working."

"Your father is tied up," said Gretchen. "Isn't that the right expression?"

"Tied up," said Professor Hamilton.

"That doesn't mean working," said Ruth Ellen.

"I don't see how you can be sure of anything about your father and the things he has to do."

"He's out to lunch. He would be. A couple of dry Martinis first, or maybe three. More than likely he's with some woman."

"We needn't concern ourselves," Gretchen said.

Professor Hamilton laughed. "Ruth Ellen is a version of a modern Sybil whose pronouncements draw their very authority from her irresponsibility—because she ignores the fictions by which we all choose to live."

Gretchen stared at him.

"Luncheon should be a perfectly safe meal," he said.

"I think all this is in poor taste," said Gretchen.

"As culture varies, so will behavior," said Ruth Ellen. "You can key the culture. Isn't that right, Professor Hamilton?"

"I seem to recognize the phrase."

"Autolytic activity," said Ruth Ellen.

"What's that?" asked Gretchen.

"It hasn't anything to do with physics," said Professor Hamilton.

"I'm not exactly sure what it is myself," said Ruth Ellen.

"I think we should get on with our meal. Aren't we all having a cocktail to start with?"

"It's indicated," said Professor Hamilton.

"Me, too?" said Ruth Ellen. "I guess yes—special occasion and all that."

"You can't be legally served," said Professor Hamilton.

"Well, there's no harm in trying. What route did you drive up, Gretchen, 3 or 28?"

"Three, of course."

"No 'of course,' really," said Ruth Ellen. "As a matter of fact, you may have lost some time. There's a lot of construction after you get across the Duxbury line."

"You seem to keep well informed," said Professor Hamilton. "I wouldn't have thought you did much driving."

"I don't, but route numbers and so on are a part of modern thinking."

"Not in Dinton," I said, and they were suddenly reminded of my presence, a fact that had apparently become almost less than a fact.

"Yes, I know. This meeting with the Governor," said Ruth Ellen. "That's reason enough for Barry to be somewhere else."

"I don't believe I understand," said Professor Hamilton. "I am sure your father is violently opposed to the Dinton highway."

"I hope so," said Ruth Ellen, "but you have to admit that in a crowd he would always look as if he favored it. He would have to look so."

"I wish you wouldn't be so silly, Ruth Ellen," said Gretchen.

"Do you think I'm being silly, Professor Hamilton?"

"Perhaps not completely."

"That'll be enough of that," said Gretchen, and since Ruth Ellen became occupied with olives and celery, the subject was dropped.

❧

I judged that we were the last arrivals of the group waiting to see Governor Ferrick. In the anteroom were Henry Spinney, Ellie

Kempton, Jared Bartlett, and Mrs. Bronson Alder. The only stranger was introduced to me as Herman Driscoll, whom I associated at once with the land deal at the Point and therefore took to be the most dangerous of our adversaries. Ellie and Jared were prepared to play the honest rustic game they knew so well, but I doubted if they could go much beyond it. Driscoll, who seemed to be about thirty, still carried a look of Harvard about him. His clothes, though expensive, were indifferently assembled, and I could imagine him lounging with his legs over the arm of a chair, smoking a pipe, and either discoursing about nothing much or looking quietly shrewd. There was plenty of intelligence in his blue eyes, coupled with an assured I-don't-give-a-damn look.

The Governor's appointments were running about on schedule, and we waited only briefly before Lanesboro led us into the executive office. The Honorable Rufus Handmore was already inside. A photographer slid out from somewhere and grouped us around the Governor, inviting us to smile.

"Hold it! Hold it!" he said. We held it. "Just one more." Flash, flash went the bulbs.

Governor Ferrick relaxed as automatically as he had smiled, and the Honorable Rufus Handmore exercised his prerogative as representative from our district by presenting us individually to His Excellency.

"I can tell you right now," said Governor Ferrick, "you people down in Dinton are fortunate in having a man like Rufe Handmore working for you at the Statehouse. He has your best interests at heart every hour of every day of every week."

If the Governor had known what was impending, he would not have paused. Yet how could he have done otherwise? Pausing is an indispensable trick of political communication.

Into that pool of silence a voice intruded with commanding distinctness. "I don't agree with you, Governor. In my opinion Rufe Handmore is a horse's behind."

The voice, of course, was Henry Spinney's, yet as Henry stood, broad-beamed and substantial in his double-breasted serge suit, it was difficult to believe he had used the expression we had all heard, or that he had spoken at all. His manner was factual rather than belligerent. There is only one image to describe Governor Ferrick's response, and I regret that it is a hackneyed one. He did a double take.

"Yes, we need more like Rufe. WHAT?"

"And always has been," said Henry Spinney.

The Governor's glance was hurt and reproving, but Henry, who had nothing on his conscience, returned the look with a complete absence of any acknowledgment.

Mrs. Alder, standing at my elbow, whispered to Ellie Kempton, "What did Mr. Spinney say?"

Ellie, probably in a state of shock, replied more audibly than he had intended, "He said Rufe Handmore is a horse's behind."

"There's always someone to stab you in the back," said Rufe.

None of the rest of us had anything to say. Handling the situation was up to the Governor—one of the things he had been elected for.

"Now, now," he said, drawing his eyebrows close in, "this isn't the way to approach a community problem. We don't want to begin this discussion with bad feeling."

"Who showed any bad feeling?" asked Henry Spinney. "I only said . . ."

"Never mind!" exclaimed Governor Ferrick sharply.

Mrs. Alder whispered to me, "Ellie Kempton just used an expression to me that no gentleman should use to a lady."

It was all right with me if she blamed Ellie rather than Henry Spinney. The Governor shuffled some papers on his desk.

"As I understand it," he said, "this is a matter that will in ordinary course come before the Department of Public Works. Nevertheless, I regard myself as a servant of you people in Dinton no less than of all the citizens of this great Commonwealth, and I can assure you that I am prepared to listen attentively to what you have to say."

Naturally, we had supposed that in the end Rufe Handmore

would plump for the road, as for anything that meant money, but it wasn't like him to commit himself irrevocably in public as long as continued avoidance was possible. Now, though, he was ardently in favor of anything Henry Spinney was against.

"This is more than a highway question," Rufe said. "It's a matter of building prosperity and values. We can handle the D.P.W. on the item of Chapter 90 money all right—Dinton is way behind the rest of the state in getting its fair share of the gas tax. We want to get moving, Governor, and we want your support."

"If I may be heard," said Professor Hamilton, "I think there are some more fundamental issues involved. Quite apart from the fact that the Dinton road project—to use that absurd phrase— would mean an entirely unnecessary expenditure, it would represent another step toward the destruction of our native environment. . . ."

In another atmosphere, before another group, Professor Hamilton's sensible presentation both of the principles and the common sense of the matter would have carried conviction, and I was sure the Governor could not avoid its force. How he would act, though, was a different thing. For the moment, he allowed a pause to follow Professor Hamilton's statement, then wheeled around to face Rufe Handmore and inquired, "What's your comment, Rufe?"

Ellie and Jared were looking their bafflement, for they had supposed Professor Hamilton to be on the side of the road builders.

Rufe said, "Well, we've got a Division of Tourism in our Department of Commerce, and it must be there for a reason. The people of our state aren't going to do much touring unless they have good roads."

"Our dear, lovely Dinton doesn't want to be tourized," said Mrs. Alder.

Herman Driscoll had taken out a strip of chewing gum. As he peeled off the paper, he remarked to Gretchen, "You couldn't guess how long it's been since I smoked a cigarette."

Gretchen remained icy.

"Ten o'clock this morning or a little after. It's quite a business, quitting the habit."

Meantime, Rufe Handmore had begun invoking the history of the republic and the spirit of progress.

"Trouble with Rufe's speeches," Henry Spinney announced, breaking into one of these flights of rhetoric, "is that he ain't loxodromic."

"No man has to stand for stuff like that," Rufe yelled. "More especially with ladies present. Either he goes out or I go out."

But Lanesboro had come in to break up the conference. The time of the Governor's next appointment had already gone by. Professor Hamilton stayed behind, though, while the rest of us walked out. I hoped that what the two said to each other might turn out to be helpful.

"What was that word you used just now?" Gretchen asked Henry Spinney.

"Loxodromic. There's nothing out of the way about that. It only means that a man don't know how to sail rum lines."

Herman Driscoll said to Gretchen, "Are you doing anything special tonight?"

"I'm going home with my husband."

"Oh," said Driscoll. "By the way, where is this place, Dinton?"

"You mean to say you don't know! I understand you've invested money there."

"In real estate. Real estate is everywhere, if you know what I mean. Dinton is a real place? People live there?"

"They most certainly do!"

"I'll give you a ring when I go down there sometime—or up there. You and your husband, I mean."

He walked off, hands in his pockets, chewing gum.

Before I had reached the corridor, trailing the others, Lanesboro called to me.

"This thing isn't as hopeless as you may think," he said. "I know the Governor has in mind quite an acceptable compromise.

I can't say much about it now, but I thought if I mentioned it you'd feel a little easier."

"I can't see any middle ground. Either it's a road or it isn't a road."

"But the whole matter will appear in a different light if the Governor can announce that the entire cost will come out of the federal antipoverty program."

"That's the compromise you're talking about?"

"Part of it. There's more."

"Don't let the Governor think for a minute that he can get away with any such outrage. What sort of idiots does he take us for?"

Lanesboro was sorry I hadn't been mollified, and I knew he thought me stubbornly unreasonable. I didn't mention the "compromise" to Henry Spinney or to Barry and Gretchen when we were all back in Dinton. It wouldn't have helped matters at the moment, and my feeling was grimly morose. The only original comment on the day's proceedings came from Henry Spinney.

"Governor Ferrick is a man of destiny in politics," he said.

"I wouldn't think so," said Barry.

"You didn't see the hairs in his ears and on his wrists. Heavy eyebrows, too. Things like that give a man a big advantage when he's in the public notice. Connects him up with history."

"You seem unusually well satisfied for a man who kicked everything apart," said Gretchen. "I don't see why you felt you had to turn Rufe Handmore against us."

"He was already against us, only he didn't plan to say so. We're better off now that he's in the open."

"From what Gretchen has told me, I'm afraid you've made Rufe a hero in Dinton," said Barry.

But he didn't know Dinton. It was Henry Spinney who became a hero around town for the next few days, not because of any malice against Rufe Handmore but because almost everyone appreciated the aptness of the phrase Henry had used. Rufe would, of course, be elected again and probably again, but it was agreeable all around to have him realistically characterized.

Rufe's wife, Lurana, thought Henry's remark had been spicily amusing. Politics is hard on wives, I have always thought.

∾

It turned out that Professor Hamilton's private words with Governor Ferrick were influential. I suppose that our redheaded advocate used the prestige of the Washington administration to tilt the Governor's position.

This effect became evident in the news that reached me when I joined Lurana Handmore and Henry Spinney in front of the post office soon after mail time.

"Heave to a minute, Gid," Henry said to me. "Lurana's just been telling me something you'll be interested to know."

Lurana Handmore must have been pretty once, and she still had good skin and coloring; but her features had become hard and her expression pettish. The space between her eyes had narrowed into grooves of permanent disappointment, presumably with the passage of years and the effects of her marriage to Rufe.

"Good morning, Lurana," I said. "So you're still on speaking terms with Mr. Spinney."

I am sorry to say that Lurana uttered an indecent word, which I suppose had become her best means of meeting the world head on. She did not derive from Dinton, and the report generally credited was that she had once had something to do with the stage.

"The thing is," said Henry Spinney, "that the Governor is coming to Dinton to look things over for himself. He's going to make a personal investigation."

"He wants to go fishing," said Lurana. "That's what he's coming for. Happy holiday. Show me a politician who don't like to go fishing."

"They always do, of course," said Henry Spinney. "In a sense we're still living in the time of Calvin Coolidge. Just the same, he'll look things over. He'll have to."

"Certainly he will," said Lurana. "He and Rufe will be photographed doing it, looking so goddamned important and satisfied that it will turn your stomach."

I had learned of Governor Ferrick's impending visit just ahead of a flurry of gossip in which all hard fact was lost without a trace. Ellie Kempton reported that the Governor's errand was to select the final route for the road; he had learned this on the best authority and therefore showed a natural jubilation. Rufe Handmore let it be known that the impending visit sprang directly from his personal ties with the Governor, and Rufe had the pleasure of reserving accommodations at the Central House for the official party. This confirmed the story that Governor Ferrick intended to stay long enough to go fishing, and of course it meant a lift for the winter economy of Dinton, with Rufe taking the credit.

There was also a report that Professor Hamilton would be arriving at the same time as the Governor, and Jared Bartlett was quoted as saying that we didn't need any help from the Washington bureaucracy and they had better keep their creeping socialism away from Dinton. I myself doubted that we would have the honor of the professor's company.

"Of course he'll come," said Katie.

"Why would he? Look what happened to him here. Besides, he has more important things on his mind."

"Tell me something more important than male and female."

"Roads," I said.

"Well, maybe," said Katie. "Sex can be a sideline, after all, but not highways."

"All else aside," I said, "I don't think Gretchen will want the professor showing himself around Dinton again."

"Why not?"

It seemed to me that the reason was obvious, but Gretchen's arrival at our door the same evening proved how right Katie had been, as usual in such matters.

"Hi!" said Katie. "At first glance I took you for Audrey Hepburn."

Gretchen only half laughed. She was intent on her errand, though obviously the compliment pleased her. She said, almost breathlessly, "Of course, with Governor Ferrick right here in town we can't afford to let our side slip behind. I'm absolutely determined to get Jon Hamilton. He's the only one we can count on with the right kind of influence."

"Have you thought this over carefully?" asked Katie.

"Yes, naturally."

"I supposed you had."

"My God!" said I.

Gretchen looked at me, and at once I became the defendant in the situation. "Whatever happened is in the past. I don't think there's any point now in giving it any attention."

"But will people in Dinton swallow that notion?"

"How can they help it? Anyway, things started fresh the other day at the Statehouse. Everyone around here knows now what Jon stands for."

"It's like the fable of the boy and the nettle," Katie said to me. "You grasp it firmly and it won't hurt you."

I said, "It seems to me, all the same, that Jon may not be anxious to visit Dinton again right away."

"I believe I can get him, and it will help if I can lure him with the idea of his staying in an authentically Dinton home—you know, one representing the maritime New England tradition with the old atmosphere."

"Such as this one?" Katie asked.

"Well, yes, your house is a lovely example of old Dinton, and you and Gid show such a feeling for authentic culture."

"You really want us to invite Professor Hamilton to stay here?" I asked.

"It would be nice for Jon, and I think it would be nice for you. You'd like him."

"We've met," said Katie.

"But not properly. I mean, not in the way you'd get to know one another."

"You want him to see the natives. Gid and I fit the description sure enough, but not the maritime part. Gid's been in the food business practically all his life."

"We could perfectly well have Jon with us, but you know how Barry is."

"How is he?" asked Katie. "In good health, I hope."

"Of course he's in good health. What I mean is—well, he's not really jealous—he's too intelligent for that, but all the same . . ."

"These things take a good deal of maturity," said Katie.

"They do, don't they?"

"Life was simpler when I was a girl."

"It isn't simple now. We're all so overcultivated and overbred. Our civilization is rushing at such a tempo."

"Everybody's on wheels or in bed," said Katie. "Well, you can trust us with Professor Hamilton. We can put him up here overnight."

So that was settled. But after Gretchen had gone, Katie boiled over.

"Imagine! That decorated little tart has been looking on us as freaks."

"Forget it," I said. "She has to keep her friend away from Barry. How else could she work it so smoothly? Anyway, if you go out of your way to prove how different you are from the suburban types, you can't complain when the pose is successful."

"Pose!"

"What else is it? You're always making yourself out a Dinton character."

This wasn't being subtle or exactly accurate. There was more to Katie's chosen role than I could sort out. The Declaration of Independence was mixed up in it, and the war between city and country, and the old philosophical conflict of popular experience with professional dogma.

"Gid," she said, "if you know what's good for you, you'll scram out of here. I intend to serve Professor Hamilton boiled dinner with enough cabbage to flavor his memory for the rest of his life. On top of that I'll give him rhubarb pie."

I didn't choose to scram, but I did keep my mouth shut. Katie was planning to give herself a ball, and I was in for a bad time.

Hardly anything evolves as you expect. Up to a point, though, we were on the set course—which is to say that Professor Hamilton arrived, drove his car into the bed of myrtle under the red maple, showed no inclination to move it when Katie hinted (hospitality restrained her from doing more at the moment), and was installed in our guest room, where Katie had festooned some gorgeously crocheted guest towels on the ancient walnut washstand. She had also brought down from the attic an enormous flowered pitcher and washbowl with matching soap dish, though the soap dish was badly chipped.

No smell of cabbage came from the kitchen, and I inferred that she was holding back the boiled dinner until later. I went for dry Martinis at the earliest possible moment. The professor wanted his on the rocks.

How he hoped to be at ease with us in our house I had not been able to imagine, but it appeared immediately that he intended to manage by disliking us intensely and dramatizing his dislike in small, irritating ways.

"We understand you're interested in the picturesque customs of small-town life in America," said Katie.

"Not at all," said the professor.

"Where, then?"

"Where what?"

"If you're not interested in small-town life in America, where are you interested in small-town life?"

"Whatever I'm interested in, I'm interested in it right here."

"We were told you wanted to see the natives in Dinton."

"I don't know anything about that." He turned in his chair

until he could see me quite clearly. "I could use another of these, but not so much ice this time."

When I came back from the kitchen with the second Martini and not so much ice, Katie had taken the offensive.

"You look more carroty than usual," she said to the professor.

"I don't care much for personal remarks."

"Beggars can't be choosers."

"What do you mean by that, please?"

"Don't look so sour. I was only quoting."

"Quoting what, Mrs. Lester?"

"Old proverb. You should know. Since we're doomed to be together for a while, I think you'd better call me Katie and I'll call you Jon."

"Familiarity is cheap when you get into it too soon."

"Anyway, I'm Katie and you're Jon."

"I suppose I have to accept that."

"After all, this is not the first time we've met—though I guess it is the first time when you've had your pants on—or maybe the first time and a half, because you did get yourself into that pair of Barry's. By the way, what became of them?"

"I had them pressed and returned," said the professor. "What did you think I'd do with them?"

"Hadn't any idea. I was curious."

"Now you know," said the professor.

"Gid told me what happened at the Statehouse when you delegates met the Governor. What did you think of that session, Jon?"

"I thought the man Spinney should have been kept at home. If he wanted to upset things, he did a first-rate job."

"Job," said Katie. "There it is again—job. Everybody uses that word for everything nowadays. You can't get away from it. I'm always reminded of when I was a girl and we had a dog named Plutarch and there was a red carpet in the hall. . . ."

"Katie," I said, "will you shut up?"

"I don't usually, but I will this time."

"What about Plutarch?" asked Jon, irritated.

"He was our dog when I was a girl. A Newfoundland—you know, big and black."

"I know he was your dog. You said so. I was listening. And you had a red carpet in the hall."

"Yes, we did, and Plutarch did his job on it. Such a big dog. You should have seen that carpet."

Jon looked something like Calvin Coolidge when he had forgotten his rubbers the last time out of the White House.

"You're a scientist," said Katie. "You're entitled to straight answers."

Jon sort of bubbled his lips.

"Don't forget your identity," said Katie. "To judge from all the new books it's a common thing nowadays. Though when I was a girl I can't recollect anyone who had doubts. If they did, we gave them nicknames, and that made everything all right. I can never forget a boy with a flat nose who put on airs. We called him Lord Pancake."

From somewhere in Jon's red-burned personality there emerged a sort of wolfish grin.

"Come to think of it," Katie said, "I almost lost my identity the other day. It was when Gretchen told us you wanted to see some real Dinton natives in their habitat—like us."

"You knew what she wanted," said Jon sharply.

"Oh, well. But all the same, losing my identity was like having a garter break. Then I got mad."

"Katie," I said, "let's change the subject."

"We should talk about this road thing. That's why I'm here," said Jon.

"Anyway, it's one reason why you're here."

"It's all pretty obvious," I said, trying to head her off. "Smalltime politicians and promoters—the craze for roads—the temptation of easy graft. You know yourself that this business had got to the stage of a pay-off that time you were . . . well, that time."

"A pay-off?"

"The plain Manila envelope and the bills."

"The marked bills," said Katie.

"I remember the envelope and the money, but who was being paid off?"

"You paid Ellie Kempton, the Dinton highway surveyor, to throw business to a Statehouse hanger-on named Lorenzo E. Sparrow."

"I did?"

"Well, you gave him the money."

"In marked bills," said Katie.

"I didn't know." The professor hadn't exactly dropped his dislike for us, but he had turned human.

"It was the price of getting you out of an embarrassing personal predicament," said Katie.

"I think you could have thought of something better than that."

"I couldn't. Not at the time."

The professor grinned sourly. In spite of everything, I guess he really was amused.

It turned out that Katie had made chicken chowder for dinner—I mean supper, of course—and this seemed the best possible promoter of tranquillity. Maybe hunger had been part of the professor's trouble.

Over the apple pie he inquired again about Henry Spinney.

"Oh, there's a lot about Henry Spinney," said Katie. "You can't really sum him up. He goes by dead reckoning. Moreover, he's the only gentleman of my acquaintance who wears a drop-seat union suit."

"Katie sees his laundry on the line," I said.

"Don't be so prudish," said Katie. "I know where Henry buys his underwear and what he buys. So does every woman in Dinton. This is a well-informed community."

"I suppose there's even been some gossip about me," said Jon.

He looked bleakly up from his pie as if the thought had struck him for the first time.

"If we all lived in the Southwest instead of New England," said Katie, "I'm sure ballads would have been written about you before this. They would probably have gone all over the country."

"I don't think that's very funny."

"It has its comical side," said Katie.

We were back in the sitting room when Barry arrived alone and walked right in. He seemed as disturbed as if he had been overcharged for something—the high mark in suburban anger.

"Whatever's happened, break it to us gently," said Katie. "We're having a high-strung evening, nervously. Anyway, the main thing about bad news is to get the most out of it."

"I don't know the meaning of this," said Barry. "It could be as serious for us as all hell. Governor Ferrick has changed his plans. He's ditched us. Lanesboro telephoned a few minutes ago—says Ferrick can't make the trip. He called our house because Gretchen is chairman of the committee. Remember the committee?"

Now that we were reminded of it I guess we all remembered the committee.

"Somebody got to Ferrick," said Barry. "That's plain enough. Somebody got to him."

"He's chicken," said Katie.

"Lanesboro says his arthritis is acting up," said Barry, but no one paid any attention.

"This may be a favorable sign," said Jon, and you could really appreciate the man when he turned analytical. "It may be that Ferrick doesn't want to expose himself to local pressures, after all. Some of the strongest ones would be in favor of the road. Your representative is in favor of it."

"Rufe Handmore," said Barry. "That's right."

"If he's going to turn the project down, maybe it's a smart thing for him to stand clear of Dinton."

"I hadn't thought of that," said Barry.

We talked along for a while, and then the subject came up of how long Jon would remain in Dinton.

"Gretchen thinks you should stay over a day or two, Professor Hamilton. . . ."

"Jon," said Katie.

"What?"

"That's his name. He wants to be called Jon."

"O. K., Jon."

"I ought to be getting back, but I guess I can spare another day in view of the importance of all this."

"Maybe the committee can have a meeting," said Katie.

"I doubt the value of a full-membership meeting," said Jon. "It will probably be better this time round if Gretchen and I go over the whole matter quietly and informally."

This was the trend of the conversation when Ruth Ellen appeared in the doorway, her pale-yellow hair glinting more than usual, a blue bow holding it just above the neck. She seemed almost prettier than her mother, her cheeks contoured with shadows that moved with the light, and bright lipstick giving a brag to her lips. But in any case she had the relaxed boldness of her generation.

"Hi, Professor!" she said. "How does it feel to be stood up by the Governor? Incidentally, if I'd known you were coming to Dinton we could have driven down together. You're not much on knowing the fast routes, remember?"

"I made good enough time."

"What route did you come?"

"I don't really recall. Is it important?"

"If it isn't important, what is? You don't want to be an illiterate in an era of sophisticated transportation."

Barry interrupted. "Ruth Ellen, are you here for some special purpose? If not . . ."

"I certainly am here for a special purpose, Father. Governor Ferrick's secretary is trying to get Gretchen on the telephone again, but she's not home."

"That's funny. I wonder where she went?"

"I think she hoped to meet someone," said Ruth Ellen, looking directly at Jon. Barry didn't notice.

He said, "All right, I'll go."

"There's going to be a new underpass just before you get to the big rotary where the Pickwick Grill is," said Ruth Ellen. "Remember?"

"No," said Jon.

"You should be up to date on these things. They're part of your life."

"I was in no hurry. I got here in ample time."

"Just the same, you've got to live in the age you live in, haven't you? Tell you what I'll do. I'll drive back with you and show you the way to work the routes."

"I'm not planning to go back tomorrow."

"When?"

"Probably the day after."

"Maybe tomorrow would be better. Have you got plenty of gas in your car?"

"Probably not."

"Well, let's get some. Come on. I'll show you a station that's open evenings. You'll need the gas no matter when you go back."

Jon sat motionless.

"Well, won't you?"

"I suppose so."

"Come on, for God's sake."

Jon rose from his chair, and the two went out together. They were gone quite a while, probably long enough to have refueled a battleship. When we saw them again, Ruth Ellen paused only a moment at the doorway. Jon came in alone.

"Something's troubling you," Katie said.

"As a matter of fact, something is. When I paid for the gasoline a little while ago, Ruth Ellen noticed that I gave the man a marked bill. It had a small red heart on it. She didn't say anything at the moment, because she didn't want to call attention to it, but she told me afterward. Do you think this could have something to do with what you were speaking about earlier? I mean the plain Manila envelope, the so-called pay-off. . . ."

"Well!" said Katie. "Well!" This was nothing put on; this was genuine Dinton brevity, under the circumstances a form of complete eloquence.

"But you recalled that I had given the envelope with the marked bills to somebody or other. . . ."

"Ellie Kempton, our highway surveyor," said Katie.

"Then how did I happen to have a marked bill left over?"

I was the one who answered. I suppose I thought that somewhat clarifying the situation was man's work, not woman's. "Your money was in your own pants pocket, and the pants you had on at the time were Barry's. So you took a bill out of the envelope and replaced it later."

"I see," said Jon. "And I didn't need to spend anything, after all, so I've evidently had that marked bill all this while."

"You hoarded," said Katie. "Maybe nothing will come of it, after all."

Jon didn't like her tone; she sounded too hopeful.

"I guess I'd best be leaving tomorrow instead of staying over."

"It'll be fun driving up with Ruth Ellen," said Katie.

"Will it?"

We couldn't tell whether Jon was nervous or just thoughtful. He decided he was tired, and went upstairs early; early for him, though not early for us with our Dinton tradition. It didn't matter, though, for Katie and I were to be kept up a while longer by Barry and Gretchen.

⟡

They arrived together while Katie was pulling down the shades, an almost useless rite since the evening was practically gone and the shades would have to be put up again the first thing in the morning.

"I would have been back here a lot sooner," said Barry, "but I couldn't find Gretchen. She was wandering around in the dark, God knows why."

"I wasn't wandering. I was looking at the stars."

"Same old stars. Funny time to be looking at them," said Barry.

"I don't think that remark is very clever," said Gretchen.

"Anyway," said Barry, "since Governor Ferrick can't come to Dinton—so he says—now he wants some of us to go up to his country place in Scituate and have a huddle there while he's recuperating. This may turn out to be a break for our side. Under his own roof he'll have to listen to us."

"Us? But, Barry, you said you couldn't go."

"I can't, but you can." He looked at me and Katie. "Gretchen can take along whatever committee members she wants. I hope you'll go, Gid."

"I don't think so."

"I do," said Katie. "Of course Gid will go. He wouldn't miss the trip for anything, and besides, he represents all the sound business principles of the republic."

"We'll have Jon. We'll need Jon," said Gretchen. "By the way, where is he?"

"He packed himself off to bed," Katie said.

"Already?"

"He's decided to leave tomorrow. He's driving up with Ruth Ellen so she can clear up his views about the main roads between here and Boston."

"Are you serious?"

"As much as ever."

"But he was going to stay over. We had arranged that I was to show him around Dinton so he would have the whole situation clearly in his mind."

"Oh, the hell with it, Gretchen," said Barry. "What does it matter?"

"It may matter a great deal."

"All right, but if he's decided to leave tomorrow, then he's leaving tomorrow."

"Sometimes you make such an effort to be obvious," Gretchen said.

There was, of course, an entire night intervening between this scene and that of next morning when we all stood at our front gateway awaiting the departure of Jon and Ruth Ellen, but in my recollection the continuity seems unbroken. Jon's departure was the common theme. He had agreed to make the Scituate conference, no matter what. And Katie had agreed that I would make it.

"All right," I said, "but only under duress."

"You may enjoy it," said Barry. "You and Gretchen on a kind of house party at the Governor's estate." I'm sure he intended to say this lightly, and he managed not too badly in his suburban idiom. He turned to Professor Hamilton. "Jon, I may as well tell you that Gid and Gretchen sometimes aren't above having a bit of romance. If I were the he-man Tarzan type, I'd probably be as jealous as hell—but I'm as modern as anybody when it comes to a broad viewpoint, and I don't get jealous."

Nothing said in Jon's presence during his stay in Dinton had astonished him so much as this. I was somewhat astonished myself at Barry's broad-minded misinterpretation of the facts, for I hadn't thought much recently about the walk that Gretchen and I had taken to the Point and back.

"I wouldn't have brought it up," said Barry, "but I thought maybe I'd better ask you, Jon, to stick close to Gretchen while you're all at the Governor's. I wouldn't want to frustrate my old friend Gid, but after all a husband is a husband."

"It would be ungallant for me to make any comment at all," I said.

"Oh, that's all right, Gid. Just a gag," Barry said.

"I'll be happy to look after Gretchen," said Jon.

I judged that this was why Gretchen could look charming and not miserable as Ruth Ellen took Jon by the arm and pulled him toward his car. Then we were waving them off as they gathered speed along the lane toward the town road. Dinton had always waved, but I'm not sure it always will. When country evolves into suburb, nothing is safe.

Barry and Gretchen started for their house, and to my surprise I saw they were walking hand in hand. Katie went indoors, and I walked downtown to get the morning paper from Boston.

Across the front page streamed a headline: CONGRESS OKAYS $10 BILLION MORE FOR PRESIDENT'S HIGHWAY PROGRAM.

I wondered more and more what Governor Ferrick might be up to, and how long Jon Hamilton would stick with us. Again in the tranquillity of our lane I wondered, and it seemed to me that the lane, with all its innocence, might be engaged in the same speculation.

⌣

"Which side is Ruth Ellen on?" Katie asked when we were sitting at lunch, which we still called dinner. "On the concrete proposal she seems so reasonable, but she's always gabbing about route numbers, overpasses, and so forth."

"I know. Youth nowadays is unpredictable. She's generally on the opposite side, whichever it happens to be, but even that can't be counted on."

"Do you think she was making sense when she said her father was really on the side of the new road whether he knew it or not?"

"No, I don't. Do you?"

"Maybe she had a point. I've always said Barry Johnson was implausible. He does look like a man who would be in favor of roads—along with God, motherhood, and—what college is he out of?"

"I don't remember. If you're going to be doubting people, how about the professor?"

"Jon? How can anybody tell? There's the central drive of our modern civilization, every foot of which has got to be hard black-top, and beyond that there's the temptation of Faustus and what happened to Adam and Eve, and there's the cult of alienation, and there's the search to find out who you are, as if the information weren't right on your birth certificate."

"Aren't you getting pretty far off the subject of roads?"

"No, Gid, I'm not. Roads lead everywhere except to answers. Read any novel nowadays and you can see how important answers are—especially since nobody ever finds any."

"I only want one answer," I said. "I want to get the future of our lane settled."

"It may be far off. We may have to retrace the whole history of the human mind first."

"My God, Katie," I said.

"I wish we knew at how many miles an hour or how many revolutions a minute," Katie said. "Then we could calculate. As things stand, we're on our way but going it blind."

Then she went back to her alchemy in the kitchen, and I went for a walk.

⟡

Later that afternoon I became aware of two figures in the lane not far from Henry Spinney's house, apparently engrossed in a large sheet of paper they were holding before them. The one who was doing the most talking and pointing with his finger was Ellie Kempton.

"Go find out what they're up to," Katie said.

I was already on my way. Ellie's companion, I soon saw, was the egregious Lorenzo E. Sparrow, manipulator of highway politics. He said something that I supposed was a greeting. I ignored him.

"Oh, hello, Gid. I guess you remember Mr. Sparrow. He's been appointed to do the appraising for the new road."

"What new road?"

"I told you it was bound to come, Gid. You can't hold back progress that's for the good of the entire Commonwealth, not to mention the township of Dinton. I guess we ought to include the whole United States—we're liable to have cars here from Texas."

"Ellie, it's a fact, and you know it's a fact, that the Governor will have something to say about this crazy scheme. He hasn't given a go-ahead, and there's been no official action by the town. This man Sparrow is without any authority whatever."

"I'm named by the Department of Public Works," Mr. Sparrow informed me. "The D.P.W. And you can say that to the Governor or anyone else."

"We asked for Mr. Sparrow. Of course we did," said Ellie. "The town highway department, I mean. That's all regular. We needed the best man we could get. You're going to see property values jumping around here. I shouldn't wonder, Gid, if you could sell your place right now for ten times what it cost. Maybe twenty times."

"My place has been in the family for a couple of hundred years, Ellie, and nobody knows that better than you. Once a main road goes through here with cars from as far away as Texas only a born fool would be willing to live on it."

"Well, we need motels. This would be a first-rate site for a motel, wouldn't it, Mr. Sparrow?"

"Why, it certainly would, Mr. Kempton. Anybody can see that. You'd have high bidding from a lot of operators."

"What's that important sheet of paper you're looking at so damned diligently?" I asked.

"It's a copy of the town plan," said Ellie. "This will help Mr. Sparrow arrive at figures as to the value of the property."

I couldn't think of anything effective to say, and I had no intention of retreating. The alternative that occurred to me was to go for reinforcements, and the best thing in that line would be Henry Spinney. He had been watching us, and he met me at the door. He wanted to know what was happening, but he interrupted my explanation several times with bursts of enthusiastic profanity.

"The sons of bitches have delivered themselves," he declared. "They've delivered themselves into our hands."

I would have been interested to know how, but there was no

use asking Henry. He reached into the hall for an old pea jacket, obviously unnecessary, but I supposed it clothed him with some added importance. We started out together, but by the time we had reached the enemy outpost Henry Spinney was several paces ahead.

After what was for him a merely routine burst of profanity he demanded to see Mr. Sparrow's credentials. Mr. Sparrow need not have responded at all, I thought—any credentials under the circumstances would have been absurd—but he did respond. He produced an ordinary business card. I recognized it easily, having seen the like of it before. Instead of dismissing this piece of cardboard as the meaningless thing it was, Henry Spinney seized it with a snort of triumph.

"Appraiser! I thought so. Appraiser—you know what that means in Massachusetts?"

"Same as it does anywhere," protested Mr. Sparrow.

"Goddamn your fat head and your stupid intelligence," said Henry Spinney. "Now I'll show you a different kind of credential. Look at that—ever see that before?"

In Henry's hand, to my astonishment, was a ten-dollar bill marked with a small red heart. He exhibited the bill first to Mr. Sparrow and then to Ellie. Ellie's confusion and self-consciousness were apparent, but Mr. Sparrow did not change his attitude or his expression.

"Know what that is?" demanded Henry Spinney.

"What is it?" asked Mr. Sparrow.

"It's a marked bill, as you can goddamn well see for yourself. What's more, it's hot money that was used in a pay-off on this goddamn road deal."

"I don't know anything about any marked bills," said Mr. Sparrow. "Do you, Ellie?"

"No," said Ellie, his negative answer failing to conceal in least degree the fact of guilty knowledge.

"I don't get this. I don't get it at all. Where did this here so-called marked bill come from?" Mr. Sparrow really wanted to know.

"It was passed here in Dinton," said Henry Spinney. "I've had my lines out for a long time, waiting for this to happen. The bill was passed last night at a gas station right here in Dinton."

"You been passing any marked bills, Ellie?" asked Mr. Sparrow.

"Not that I know of. I don't recollect getting any gas last night. Seems to me I would remember."

"Seems to you?" asked Mr. Sparrow.

"Well, yes. You know how it is."

Everybody was looking at Ellie. He didn't do well under the combined examination.

"The thing for the present is to cut off short on this goddamn so-called appraisal," said Henry Spinney. "That's the first thing. Get the hell out of the lane, Ellie. Get the hell out, Sparrow."

"You can't pull any bluff on me, whoever you are," said Mr. Sparrow, but when he glanced again at Ellie, he weakened.

"Oh, let's leave it lay for the present, Mr. Sparrow," Ellie said. "But . . ."

"Let's leave it lay for the time being."

"If you say so, Ellie."

I stood with Henry Spinney and watched them retreat from the lane, engaged in a bitter sort of dialogue I was sorry we couldn't hear.

"We got the sons of bitches," said Henry Spinney. "One of those bills was bound to turn up. We got the sons of bitches cold."

"I don't know, Henry," I said. "Do you know who passed that bill at the gas station last night?"

"Who passed it, Gid?"

"Professor Jon Hamilton."

"Beelzebub. For God's sake, why didn't you say so?"

"For God's sake, I didn't have a chance, and I wasn't fool

enough to let Ellie off the hook. He's noticed the marks on the bills—of course he has—and he's wondering if he could have got mixed up and passed one without realizing." I hadn't intended an analysis of the situation, but the thoughts came right out.

Henry Spinney, without a pause for reflection, laughed so loudly that his pea jacket spread apart like flapping sails in the wind. He kept on laughing.

"We took 'em broad in the beam that time," he said at last. "We took 'em right between wind and water."

"I don't know how funny it will be tomorrow," I said. "Or next week."

"Goddamn it, Gid," said Henry, "there's no danger getting things mixed up—the only risk is in letting 'em stand out clear. Dealing with scum like Ellie and that sculpin Sparrow is the opposite of navigation."

But Professor Hamilton, I thought, belonged in a different category. I didn't mention this to Henry—he was entitled to his triumph—but my feelings bordered on the morose as I walked home to report to Katie.

⟡

I drove Gretchen to Scituate on the day of the rendezvous at Governor Ferrick's country home. She looked as pretty as ever, or even prettier, but she talked of roads and politics and strategy. Out of sheer irritation I was tempted to tell her about Jon and the marked bill, but there are limits to what any man, or at least any man of my age, build and tradition, may do for revenge upon a desirably turned-out young woman who ignores the fact that her attractiveness could have any meaning for him. I couldn't gain anything, no matter what I said, and if she knew about her husband's delusion concerning me and her, she didn't take it seriously.

We might have been driving through beautiful countryside—very likely we were—but roads and countryside in the modern age have no affinity or agreement. The aim of roads is to get past—past the car ahead, past the curve, past the knoll or the copse or the refreshment stand. Figuratively speaking, civilization finds itself on the Southeast Expressway—some Southeast Expressway of its own—always. The only exception is on shorter roads and streets, when the uncontrollable impulse is to get to the intersection. The intersection is the true national goal.

Finally, Gretchen said, "Thank goodness Henry Spinney isn't invited on this trip."

"He isn't?"

"Well, I don't think so. Anyway, he's not coming."

"Did he say so?"

"Well, practically. He didn't seem interested, even."

"That's not like Henry," I said. "Sounds funny to me. Of course, he wouldn't need to be invited. You'd only have to let him know the address and he'd get there."

"I know what you mean, but I'm sure we're quite safe."

"Unless we happen to need him."

"This isn't going to be the kind of a conference at which we could possibly need Henry Spinney."

"I'm just as well satisfied in a way," I said, "but on the other hand it sounds ominous. Too slick. Too political."

"I think we can function as intelligent human beings."

I've conceded time and again how old-fashioned I am, but looking at Gretchen's legs and hearing her talk about intelligence seemed a strange inversion of our weapons and resources.

There was no difficulty in finding Governor Ferrick's country place, sitting on a rise of ground comfortably distant from an old stone wall and a hedge of blooming lilacs. The forefathers must have had a part in building the house as they had in putting up the wall, but I thought most of their spirit must have been exorcised by suburban contagion—not that the lines of the house had been ruined exactly, but the wings were too modern and coy, the shutters screamed of affectation, the chimney tops had been contrived beyond all taste in contriving. Anybody but an architect would have known—and maybe even some architects would have known. Katie could have told them; her gaze automatically separated the genuine antique from the instructed adaptation or imitation. Aside from the rampant lilac hedge the neatness was too considered and perfect. Too expensive, too, but that's an element in any owner's pride.

Gretchen and I left the car in the driveway and proceeded to the front door. We were admitted at once. Governor Ferrick and Mrs. Ferrick emerged from a room at the right of the wide lofty hall, which, I noticed, was papered in a block design of sailing ships and raging seas. The feeling of the house assured us that, though we were modern, we were expected to slip some generations backward into a period. Katie hated "periods" but I didn't give a damn.

Mrs. Ferrick greeted us cordially and, I thought, with good nature, even humor, that was unaffected. But how can you tell? There may be layers and layers of externals that need to be penetrated before you know the reality, if you ever do. Mrs. Ferrick was almost as tall as her husband. A good deal of gray showed in her hair, adding to the distinction of a slender, handsome face, contributing also to the poise of a governor's wife.

"Come in and have a cup of tea," said the Governor.

"Yes, please do," said Mrs. Ferrick. "You must be tired after your long drive. Your things will be put in your rooms, and I will show you up directly."

"What a nice idea!" said Gretchen. "Tea is exactly right."

I guess it was, too, so long as I could feel sure of a drink later on.

"You're the first, and I'm glad, because I've heard so many complimentary things about you," said Mrs. Ferrick.

The room into which we went was still sunny, though of course the afternoon had been wearing on. I had noticed crutches leaning against the hall doorway, but Governor Ferrick did not use them. He settled without too much apparent difficulty into a chair near the tea table.

"How cheerful—and snug—and aloof!" said Gretchen.

"Aloof?" asked Mrs. Ferrick.

"In a nice sense. Where you can be yourselves—and complete."

"I like that," said Governor Ferrick. "Privacy isn't an escape or a retreat, you know. It's strengthening and rehabilitating."

"It's nice, anyway," said Mrs. Ferrick.

"You've probably wondered why I'm having you come here, no doubt at some inconvenience to yourselves," said the Governor. "Well, I'll tell you. My motive is partly selfish. The day of a governor is full of pressing decisions that need to be made. If the decisions themselves don't press, plenty of people do. You have to make up your mind, pleasing some, angering some, and no doubt hurting and disappointing others. That's life—and government. It's also duty and responsibility.

"But I do have a special feeling about you people down there on the coast. I can see the conflict of cultures, and I can see that this road question involves more than transportation. Well, we'll be going into that later. What I started to say was that, since I'm in a manner of speaking laid up for a few days—though my arthritis comes and goes—I thought I might treat myself to a really adequate consideration of this microcosm—this small-scale instance of a universal modern problem—with a rather remarkable group of people.

"I mean to say, you're the treat—you people. A modern, civic-minded young housewife who is, if I may refer to the obvious, also perfectly lovely; a Boston businessman who represents not only an old firm but a magnificent mercantile tradition dating from the early days of the republic; a distinguished scientist who will be interpreting his science to leaders in government at Washington; a young intellectual from the new Harvard—you see what I mean? It's almost as if the author of a novel had chosen the group."

Gretchen made some conventionally unassuming remark that I don't recall, and maybe didn't hear, but I remember my own question, which was blunt. "Who's the young intellectual?"

"Oh, the Driscoll boy."

"I'd hardly call him a boy," said Gretchen, rallying.

"You don't look out from my altitude of years," said the Governor.

"I'd hardly call him an intellectual," I said.

"The fact that he cuts his hair shouldn't be held against him," said the Governor. "I know a number of promising young men who keep their hair cut."

"Dear me, yes," said Mrs. Ferrick.

Our tea was finished and we were shown to our rooms, both in the same wing, the windows overlooking open fields and copses, with not a highway in sight.

Of course, we had drinks before dinner. Our entire group had assembled by then, and I wondered what sort of novelist would have chosen us as characters, and for what purpose. In real fact, it seemed to me, a half-bright modern novelist would have discarded us in favor of employing Mr. Sparrow, Ellie Kempton, Henry Spinney and maybe Rufe Handmore. We were too much sicklied over with a gloss of social compromise; we could fall so readily into the habit of being unreal. The one exception was Herman Driscoll.

Mrs. Ferrick offered him a cigarette, which he declined, saying he would be happy to smoke one of his own brand. He took a pack from his coat pocket—he was wearing a relatively subdued sport coat, the fabric of which suggested exploding pine needles —and extracted a cigarette.

"First one I've smoked out of this pack since morning," he remarked to his hostess.

"Well, that's what I call cutting down," she said.

"Well," he remarked producing another pack from another pocket, "of course, I've smoked a few out of this one." He then took a pack from his breast pocket, examining it carefully. "Only a couple out of this."

"I'm afraid I don't see the point," Gretchen said.

Herman grinned, and the grin proved that his face could light up if the occasion warranted. "It goes easier this way," he said. "Come the end of the year I'm liable to be off the habit altogether."

"I don't see how. No matter how many packs you may take a few out of, what counts is the total number of cigarettes you smoke in a day."

"You think so?"

"Don't you?"

"Mathematically, yes, but there's the little matter of psychology. It carries you along."

"What carries you along?"

"Psychology," said Herman.

The Governor and Mrs. Ferrick seemed gently amused.

A youth in a white coat entered with Martinis for everyone else and Scotch for me. I moved over to sit beside Gretchen, who seemed rather isolated, and Mrs. Ferrick sat beside Herman. The Governor said something of no importance that took my attention for a moment, and then I heard Gretchen whisper, "Look at the Young Intellectual."

Herman, his head back, had decanted an entire Martini into his gullet, apparently bypassing his mouth as completely as physiology permitted. The awareness of a great experience drifted in ghostlike fashion across his face.

"Nothing happened to him. He didn't even wince," Gretchen whispered.

But something had certainly happened. Herman had achieved a degree of tranquillity, and maybe even of identity, which would be further heightened by his second and third Martinis administered in the same way.

"It must take practice, the way you do that," remarked Professor Hamilton.

"Straight to the heart of the matter," said Herman.

"Young men nowadays like to shock you," observed Mrs. Ferrick.

"Young men nowadays like to shock young men," said Herman. "They get so they take a lot of slugging."

"I've heard that thought expressed much less cogently at some learned professional conferences," said Jon.

"What's 'cogently'?" asked Herman. "No, don't tell me. It's beautiful all by itself—'cogently.' I'm just going to let it sit on a shelf in my brain, and when I get up in the morning it will be looking at me."

Dinner was announced a minute or so later. None too soon, I thought; yet we were, including Herman, still a polite, controlled group who had taken a great deal of comfort, as Katie would say, without perceptible ill consequence.

Of dinner there is nothing to be said except that it was well planned, delicious, and served with the perfection of dinners in motion pictures or on the stage, and with just a bit of the artificiality. The food was real, but as much could not be said for some of the conversation.

The gin that Herman had consumed did not throw him off, but his role of Young Intellectual did a little.

I heard him say, "Your name is Gretchen, if I'm correct."

"Yes."

"Did you tell me or did I look it up?"

"I've no idea."

"I believe I looked it up, and if so, it's a compliment."

"Thank you."

"You're a socialite, to use an obsolete expression."

"Not at all!"

"Then why do you look so much like one? Junior League?"

"Well, yes."

"I thought so. Perceptions like that come to me naturally."

"I'm trying to think of a good phrase for you," said Gretchen.

"No difficulty about that—I'm a highly placed person. Well, at least I'm in line. My old man is one. You can read it any day in the newspapers—'according to a highly placed person, the whangus industry is due for a going-over.'"

"What industry?"

"Actually, it's heavy machinery. Like building roads."

"I'm not surprised. Roads!"

"Listen, Gretchen, what's so queer about that? You have to have roads, and somebody has to build them, or look what would happen to the population."

"What would happen?"

"It would be a hell of a situation—everybody all in one place all the time."

"There's not the slightest danger of that."

"You aren't promoting the aircraft industry are you? Not that my old man would care—he builds runways, too."

"He builds them?"

"His machinery does. It's all the same."

"I see," said Gretchen.

"No wonder, with those eyes of yours. They couldn't be purely ornamental."

"I think I want to hear what Governor Ferrick is saying," Gretchen said, turning away abruptly. The gesture was a little marred, because she moved so quickly that she knocked a fork off the table.

What Governor Ferrick was saying concerned Henry Spinney.

"This fellow citizen of yours down there in Dinton—I should say he must be quite a character. In all my experience in government I have never heard anything more pat than his epithet for Rufe Handmore. I'm speaking privately now."

"But, Governor Ferrick," said Gretchen, "you paid Rufe Handmore quite a compliment."

"I know—political realism. It's the usual thing. Under our system of government it's necessary. You have to keep your own party together and at the same time work on the opposition. Do I sound cynical?"

"Yes," said Gretchen.

Mrs. Ferrick said, "I'm afraid I agree with you. There's a side of politics I've never been able to get used to. Flattery is one thing, but when it gets too far away from the truth . . ."

"You must recognize that there is more than one kind of truth," said Jon Hamilton.

"It's semantics," remarked Herman without looking up from his plate.

"In part, yes," said the professor. "Tell me, Mr. Driscoll, what was your major at Harvard?"

"I forget. Oh, I guess it was English or history. Seems to me history was more like it."

This stopped the conversation dead in its tracks. The Young Intellectual seemed entirely oblivious.

When dinner was over and we were heading for the Governor's study to begin a serious conference on the issue that had brought us here, I found young Driscoll at my side.

"You know what this son-of-a-bitch professor is going to do?" he asked me. "He's going to lay it on the line that Ferrick can't get to be a Senator unless this road is killed dead, period."

"I doubt if he can be planning to do just that."

"You know Ferrick is itching to be a Senator?"

"I understand he is well up front."

"He could be. What the hell business has a professor got mixing up in politics? Why can't he stick to the computers like all the rest of them? What bugs me is how you people can go against roads. Look at today's civilization. It's all roads."

"No, it isn't. We still need homes and libraries and churches. And baseball diamonds and football fields."

"Oh, well, if you're going to be like that."

❧

In the pine-paneled study we sat comfortably, all provided with highballs and some of us with cigarettes. The Governor leaned back behind his desk, swiveling occasionally.

"I think there's one common ground we can all agree upon at

the outset," he said. "We can have both good schools and good roads—there's no incompatibility there."

"I'll have to differ with you, Governor," said the professor, and this was a new side of his character, incisive, authoritative.

"Oh, come on! Our standard of living, our prosperity as a Commonwealth . . ."

"Tut!" said the professor. "Governor Ferrick, are you aware of the proportion of the gross national product that is now going into highways?"

"I guess I've missed that particular figure, Jon."

"That particular figure, as you call it, is perhaps the most significant and frightening in any statistical analysis of the American condition."

"Go ahead and name it," said the Young Intellectual, but the professor continued to stare at the Governor.

"Thirty per cent of our gross national product goes into transportation, construction and maintenance."

"Highways?" asked the Governor.

"Practically speaking, highways."

My estimate of Professor Jon Hamilton, which had joggled about since the beginning of our acquaintance, always at the lower end of the scale, suddenly improved. I began to sense some of his positive qualities. Anyone who can come up with the gross national product offhand in any situation has the power of command. From here on in, I felt, the professor and the gross national product would be formidable allies.

"Well, I must say that's impressive," said the Governor. "Thirty per cent!"

"So what?" inquired the Young Intellectual, but even he could not dent the gross national product.

Then the professor relaxed and spoke in a different vein. He deliberately turned human.

"If you'll allow me, I'm going to tell you what I saw in Dinton the other night. I made a sort of excursion under the stars, though for the commonplace purpose of filling the gas tank of my car. It's true that I had a charming companion, Mrs. Johnson's college-age daughter, as a guide, but I saw with my own eyes and heard with my own ears."

"God, what a man!" said the Young Intellectual, and I guess I was thinking the same thing.

The professor's description of pastoral, unspoiled Dinton verged on poetry. He spoke lovingly of our gentle lane. He evoked the nostalgia of a time and way of life in which the gross national product and the automobile played no part that anyone could be aware of. He argued for the preservation of such regions of innocence and sanctuary. He held the Governor's attention, he held my attention, and I saw that he was holding Gretchen's attention in a different way.

She was learning for the first time that Jon had been off with Ruth Ellen, thinking romantic thoughts during an interval under the stars when she herself had expected him. I could understand her emotion. Her expression froze only slightly, however, and I don't suppose anyone else could have suspected what an effort her composure represented.

When Jon had finished his pastoral, the Governor accepted it helplessly. He was stuck again, as he had been with the gross national product. The best he could do was to drag in the word "functional" by way of demurrer; it was, of course, a good word, though overmatched in the present instance. Surprisingly, the Young Intellectual did better; he almost bailed the Governor out.

"Look, Professor, how come you were out with that pretty girl? Where were you heading?"

"I've told you—I went to get my gas tank filled."

"I heard you. Gas tank. You must have been on a road. You got to have a road."

"I'm not disputing that," said Jon. "It's a question of . . ."

But this hortatory conclusion, sound as it was, I shall not attempt to record or even to summarize. I don't think it affected the general balance one way or another. As a matter of fact, Jon's subject matter had become dull and I thought he talked too long, though his authority was as strong at the end as at the beginning.

"Do you have anything more to say, Herman?" Governor Ferrick inquired of the Young Intellectual.

"It struck me," said Herman, "nowadays you hardly ever see a woman with her front hair down over one eye. You used to see them all the time, young ones especially. I wonder why that is."

"Individual taste. Fashion, partly," said Gretchen.

"I suppose. I suppose it is. Just the same, it strikes you funny the more you think of it."

The digression gave the professor an opening.

"Mr. Driscoll," he said, "I am given to understand that your people have acquired quite an acreage at the Point down there in Dinton. What are you planning to do with it?"

"Sell it to the middle class," said Herman without the slightest hesitation. "One thing you've got to remember these days. The middle class has got money."

I said, "There's already a good road to the Point—more than adequate."

"There is!" said Gretchen. "And you ought to see the Crying Swamp that this proposed road would have to cross. The cost would be perfectly fabulous."

We were again embarked on a discussion that was at least relevant, though it wasn't going to have any effect upon the purposes or convictions of anyone. I guess I was relieved when the Young Intellectual interrupted again.

"Governor, it said in the *Globe* today that you intended to take a hard-nosed look at all the state appropriations."

"Yes, I think I saw that," said Governor Ferrick.

"What I want to know is how do you take a hard-nosed look? There must be quite a trick to it."

The Governor said he guessed he shouldn't be held responsible for newspaper English, and what was apparently meant was that he would give all the appropriations a careful scrutiny.

The conference broke up after that in a matter of minutes. It seemed to me that our side had scored, and I was pleased that the professor remained behind with the Governor after the rest of us left. I guessed that one subject between them would be Ferrick's senatorial ambitions, a matter in which Jon Hamilton's influence might be of importance.

Gretchen and I said good night to our hostess and went upstairs together, followed by the Young Intellectual, who was vacillating about which pack to take a cigarette from.

I entered my room with a feeling of relief. The air was on the chilly side now that the sun had gone down, and there had been no heat on this side of the house all day or perhaps for weeks. A guest room ought to be cool, and I had no complaint. On the contrary, I found an atmosphere comfortably resembling that of old Dinton. I settled in a relaxing chair, drawing solace from the neat, unlived-in surroundings and from a bright seascape over the bed.

I reached for one of the bedside books, which I discovered to be a volume of Somerset Maugham's short stories—something you could really read. I expected to enjoy myself.

Of course, I didn't keep track of time but I suppose as much as an hour may have passed when a soft knock announced someone at the door. It was Jon Hamilton, not unnaturally wanting to talk things over.

"Mind if I come in? I saw the light under your door."

"Come ahead."

"Gid," he began, settling down in the chair from which I had just arisen, and lighting a dark-brown miniature cigar, "this Governor of ours is a hard man to do business with."

"So you really got down to business."

"To all intents, yes, though our language was pretty indirect. I wish you had been there. I'd like to know what you, as a businessman with your background and point of view, would have made of it."

"Ferrick didn't want me there."

"No, he didn't. No third parties. I wondered at first if he had his study bugged. I'm not sure yet. Anyway, I handled my side of the talk discreetly. I suggested that no matter what one thought of the Dinton road it should have a very low priority. So low that it wouldn't logically be reached for years.

"He said he agreed up to a certain question of realty values. He said Dinton stood to gain through a development at the Point, and if that were deferred it might easily go down the drain altogether—especially if he, who was so warmly interested in the welfare of Dinton, should be moved on from Boston to Washington. The possibility was a strong one, he believed, and he wanted to have some definite decision arrived at before the change overtook him. Obviously, he wanted me to ask about his prospects for the senatorship, so I did. He came right out and said that with a little more support in the proper quarters he would have it made.

"There I was with the proposition pointed right at me. I said I hoped his optimism was justified, but from what I had learned firsthand recently, the administration was fidgety and you couldn't safely count on anything."

"Then what?" I asked.

"Then we circled right back to the beginning. Hang it, Gid, how could I promise anything, even if I wanted to?"

"I suspect it would take a lot of promising to detach him from a commitment he's willing to make to the Driscolls. What they've got that he wants is money."

"Financing. You can't run a campaign without it, and nowadays there's no better *quid pro quo* than a main artery—especially one in Dinton where no one is likely to notice what goes on. I taxed him with encouraging Handmore and that fellow of yours who has charge of the streets. He seemed genuinely surprised that there was any action in Dinton and said right off that we needn't necessarily take it seriously."

Jon looked at his watch, but he didn't make a move to go. Up to now it had seemed natural that he should drop in on me to discuss what had occurred, and our man-to-man exchange was candid and friendly, even though surprising. He hadn't addressed me as "Gid" before, that I could remember, anyway, and now we were equals and also old friends. From here on, though, he made me wonder if he might be establishing some sort of alibi. Gretchen was close by, and the time he spent with me could lead indistinguishably into time he might be expecting to spend with her.

"That's the wind whistling, isn't it?" he said.

"It's a fairly biting northwester."

He snubbed out his third miniature cigar, or maybe it was only his second.

"I'd better be turning in," he said, adding as a final comment, "It's funny, Gid, that so much should seem to hang on so little."

He could have stated the proposition the other way around, I thought. As soon as he went out, I opened the windows, partly to get rid of the cigar smoke and partly because I was accustomed to sleeping in a room with plenty of fresh country air. So was Katie. I got into bed and prepared to let slumber overtake me.

⌒

Before I was fairly settled, however, another knock sounded, and this one seemed imperious. Moreover, the door opened at once and someone came in. I groped for the switch on the bedside lamp, but I knew already that my visitor was Gretchen. She brought a good deal of atmosphere with her.

As the light came on, I saw her standing just inside the door wrapped in a pale-pink robe with a fluffy collar, the legs of her pajamas showing just above her bare ankles, and a pair of quilted red slippers that had sprouts of fluff on the toes. Before she uttered a word her eyes had explored every corner and detail of the room.

"Gid," she said, "have you got a cigarette? I can't think what I did with mine."

"Look, Gretchen, you know damn well you haven't come here for a cigarette."

"Of course, I have. That's just what I've come for."

She made me think of the joke that had seemed funny to me when I was a boy, something about a man surprised in a bedroom who told the husband he was waiting for a streetcar. I considered telling this to Gretchen, but streetcars had long disappeared, and I didn't think the story would be funny if it were told about a bus.

"You're looking for Jon Hamilton," I said.

"Oh, has he been here?"

"You know he has."

"Whatever you're thinking, Gid, I wish you wouldn't."

"How the hell can I help it?"

"I don't know. I suppose you can't really. Have you any idea where Jon went after he left you?"

"I suppose he was going to bed. The way he looked at his watch I thought it likely that he intended to proceed on some schedule."

"Oh!"

"Neither of us is blind," I said.

"Gid, please don't be stupid. I hope you don't mind if I stay here just a minute or two. That awful Driscoll man is standing in the hall."

"If he saw you come in, he'd better see you go out."

"But he didn't see me, I'm perfectly sure. Please don't be disagreeable, Gid. It'll only be for a minute or two."

She found a cigarette in the pocket of her robe, lighted it with a match from the bureau top, and sat down where so short a time before the professor had been sitting. I thought this was funny, but not funny enough for a laugh.

"Why do you have it so damn cold in here, Gid?" she asked.

"I was nurtured on cold bedrooms. A cold bedroom is my strength and my salvation."

I slammed the windows shut.

"Don't be sarcastic. You know it's absolutely, totally frigid." She drew her feet up under her on the chair. "Gid, do me a favor. Peek out and see if the Driscoll man is still there."

I lumbered out of bed again, put on my unpretentious robe, and went to the door. Instead of opening it a crack, I threw it wide open and stepped into the hall.

"Hi, Gid," said the Young Intellectual, using the familiar name without a shred of warrant. He was sitting in an ornamental chair at the end of the hall, his legs stretched straight out. He was fully dressed, as if sleep meant nothing to him, at least in the nighttime.

"Was that you making a noise?" I asked.

"Strictly no. Honest."

"Well, don't make any," I said, stepping back into my room.

Just before the door closed I heard him say, "Maybe what you heard was the Governor talking about roads."

Gretchen wanted a detailed account of what I had seen and heard. I gave her what she wanted.

"If the Governor is talking roads, I ought to be there," she said.

"At this time of night?"

"They settle things at night, these politicians. What'll I do?"

"So far as I see, you have two choices—stay or go."

"I can't go out and have that insufferable Driscoll see me. Do you suppose he knows I'm here—or suspects? Is that why he's persistent about hanging around?"

"I've no idea."

"It's practically zero in here. I don't know how long I can endure it."

I considered wrapping her in a blanket, but I wasn't keen about stripping the only blanket from the bed. It would be more sensible for her to get in where I had been, and I advised her to do that. She hesitated, obviously weighing both the realities and the conventions.

"Go ahead," I told her. "I'll sit up for a while."

She kicked off her slippers and got into bed, pink robe and all.

"You *are* being kind to me, Gid. I realize that."

"I'm no Sir Walter Raleigh," I said. "I'm stuck—as you very well know."

"That's not a gallant thing to say."

"I thought it might reassure you."

"Well, it does in a way. I see what you mean."

"Not that you need that kind of reassurance."

"I guess it always helps a woman."

She had been right about the temperature of the room. It was hellishly cold, and my liking for chilled bedrooms did not extend to keeping vigil in them while inadequately clad.

"You might look again and see if he's still there."

"I can't keep sticking my head out every few minutes."

"This will only be the second time."

I went to the door, opened it, and made another survey. The Young Intellectual's eyes were closed, and I didn't know whether he saw me or not. I closed the door gently, glanced sadly at Gretchen, and shrugged.

"I'll bet he's watching for Jon. That's what it is—he's checking on Jon's movements."

It could be, I thought. The only catch was that if the professor had turned in for the night, the Young Intellectual would have turned in also. I remarked upon this.

"Well," said Gretchen, "he probably knows Jon isn't in his own room."

"Then where is Jon?" I asked, but the question answered itself. "I suppose he's in your room."

"I suppose he is—damn it!"

"I have a sense of order. I inherited it, and Katie has cultivated it all these years. I hate situations like this."

"You're turning blue," said Gretchen. "Aren't you getting chilled?"

"No matter. Pneumonia yields readily to modern antibiotics."

"Oh, get in here under the covers."

"I don't intend to do any such thing."

"You *will* come down with pneumonia."

"Probably."

"Your physical condition isn't too good, you know. For one thing, you're so overweight."

"The hell I am!"

"Stop talking and get in. If you should catch pneumonia and if you should be allergic to antibiotics, I'd be responsible. After all, Gid, we're not strangers. Get under the covers, stay on your own side, and don't you dare touch me."

"It isn't even a double bed."

"It's a three-quarters, and I'm way over on my side."

I got in, and as soon as the covers were over me I felt much better physically, though my psychic wounds were raw. I expressed my irritation.

"There's a hell of a lot the matter with sex in our civilization," I said.

"I don't know what you mean."

"I mean that here we are in bed, and nothing can come of it—good, or evil, or fun."

She giggled. "You wouldn't attack me. I'd scream."

"The hell you'd scream. I shouldn't have to attack you—things ought to happen automatically. I suppose sex isn't to blame, at that. It's a case of country custom against suburban custom, and all the superhighways in the budget will never tie them together."

"Gid, don't touch me!"

My feet had touched hers. She was near enough so that I could feel her warmth. But I wasn't a type like Barry. I was Dinton-born-and-bred, with the finishing done by Katie. So I moved nearer to my own edge of the bed.

"Come to think of it," I said, "maybe the professor isn't in your room. Maybe the Governor sent for him."

"It could be."

"If so, as soon as he's free he's likely to come barging in here to report what happened. You know he was here earlier."

"Oh, Gid! I can't have him find me like this!"

She whisked out of bed, pulling the covers away from me, and in another moment had slipped into her slippers. She half skipped, half sprinted to the door, opened it and departed.

I was curious enough to make another inspection of the hall. The Young Intellectual had passed out, half in the ornamental chair, half-sagging on the floor. Certain things I have noticed emancipated youth hasn't been able to overcome, even now: one, up to a certain age, is adolescent acne, and the other is the narcotizing effect of alcohol.

⤳

The breakfast room was sunny warm. But Mrs. Ferrick, although no less gracious than before, presented a subtly changed attitude. She informed us at once that the Governor hadn't slept well. He wouldn't be down. Why this simple statement should have sounded so significant I don't know, but it did. The Governor had entrusted her with a political errand, that of getting rid of us. She wrapped the anticlimax in disingenuous charm. We had come to Scituate; we had talked mostly in circles; we had been entertained—and nothing had happened. Nothing. And now we were being packed off.

Gretchen, her crisp societified self, projected a fresh, cleanly modeled profile and betrayed no emotion. The professor appeared to be in his Beelzebub personality: he looked sour; he grumped; he was good only for short words or single syllables.

And so we entered upon breakfast like characters in a play until the Young Intellectual asked for Tabasco to put on his grapefruit. The professor turned on him a look of diabolical hatred, but our hostess smiled as if this were the most natural request in the world.

"Do you always do that?" Gretchen asked.

"What's 'always'? Whatever you do at any old time is 'always' as long as it lasts."

"Must you be like that so early in the morning?"

"I didn't want to wait. You lose thoughts like that if you wait. Professor, you must have had a bad night. You look hung over."

"I do not look hung over, and moreover I am not hung over," said the professor, moved at last to a real speech.

"You mean you had plenty of rockaby?"

"If you are asking if I slept adequately, the answer is that I certainly did. In my own bed."

"We're not interested in confessions, are we, Mrs. Ferrick?" said the Young Intellectual. Our hostess merely smiled. "Well, I'll tell you what I thought, Professor. I thought that probably you had been with the Governor in a coffee-filled smoke room and the two of you had come to some big decision."

"Why did you think that?"

"I can kind of smell it."

"Has there been some big decision?" asked the professor.

"Oh, I doubt it very much," said Mrs. Ferrick.

We dropped back into flat silence, and I suppose we were all thinking that something must have happened to bring about this postbreakfast dismissal. Mrs. Ferrick certainly knew what that something was, but she had no intention of telling.

"Professor," said the Young Intellectual, "are you always grim like this in the morning or is your superego under pressure?"

Jon ignored him, or maybe I missed some short and possibly profane or scatalogical reply. A maid announced that I was wanted on the telephone, and I followed her into the living room and picked up the instrument.

"Gid," said Katie's voice, and it was like her to bother with no preliminaries, "I thought I'd better call you in case any stories have reached Governor Ferrick. It's not true that Henry Spinney's in jail. He's not in jail."

"For heaven's sake, Katie, tell me what this is about."

"It's too much to go into over the telephone, and anyway you'll hear the whole story as soon as you get home. I just thought you should know, in case the Governor says something, that Henry is positively not in jail."

"Why should anybody suppose he was in jail?"

"If they don't, it's all right anyway. In that case you don't have to tell the Governor anything."

"I don't want to tell him anything. He's supposed to be sound asleep. We're all dismissed—nobody knows why."

"See you soon, then. Don't worry about anything, Gid." And Katie hung up.

When I went back into the breakfast room, Gretchen's curiosity fastened itself on me, and I must say that the others were, to say the least, attentive.

"Henry Spinney is not in jail," I announced.

"Wha—a—a—t?" exclaimed Gretchen.

"No," I said, "he's not in jail."

"Isn't Mr. Spinney the one who applied the rude epithet to Representative Handmore?" asked Mrs. Ferrick. "I hope they wouldn't put him in jail for that. Just something nominal would do."

"Look," said the Young Intellectual, "tell me again the name of this place where you people live."

"Dinton."

"That's it, Dinton. Well, look, if your wife were to call you up about everybody down there who isn't in jail, it would be a pretty good thing for the telephone company, wouldn't it? Or take New York City, even more so, if your wife happened to be in New York City."

"This is stupid talk," said the professor. "Why speculate on something you know nothing about?"

"You don't have a hell of a lot of charm, do you?" said the Young Intellectual. "How are you with women?"

Jon almost choked into his napkin.

Mrs. Ferrick interjected enough charm and inconsequence to get us over this hump, but we were no longer a recognizable cast of characters. We were badly fragmented.

Somewhat later, Gretchen and I were briefly alone in the hall with Mrs. Ferrick as we prepared for our departure.

"I hope you haven't minded Herman Driscoll too much," she said. "Apparently he's going through a phase. There's nothing one can do until the phase passes—I discovered that long ago. Actually, Herman's a very nice young man. He did surprisingly well at Harvard. He got excellent marks and was on the chess team."

"Oh, you know the family?" said Gretchen.

"Yes, we know the Driscolls quite well. You'll come again, I hope, but not on one of these political missions. I'm sure you shouldn't consider this trip wasted, though, not in any sense. The Governor is very much involved. I know that."

"Involved in what way?" I asked.

"He wants to come up with the right answer."

The Young Intellectual had joined us. "That's what the right answer is—it's what you come up with. So I hope the Governor doesn't stay down too long."

Mrs. Ferrick smiled lightly, and a moment later we were on the porch, then the steps, then the neat path.

"Level with me, Gid," said Herman Driscoll. "Do you know why we're getting the bum's rush out of here? Last night everything was slick as Hocus-Pocus Margarine."

"No, I don't know. Do you?"

He shook his head. "I think the professor knows—or has a pretty good idea. I can't make that guy out."

"If you can't, who can?" asked Gretchen maliciously.

"Exactly," said Herman, the Young Intellectual.

The sun had risen beautifully, and every mile we proceeded over the road the more beguiling the morning became. The chill of the night before—like all else about the night before—had become as incredible as fantasy.

"It's good to be going home," said Gretchen.

"There's just one thing. I'd rather have been told Henry Spinney was in jail than that he wasn't in jail. The news would have been a hell of a lot less disturbing."

I dropped Gretchen off at her house. As she got out of the car she touched me on the wrist and said, "Gid, I do appreciate your tact—and everything."

As far as I could recall, there hadn't been anything but tact, and too much of that. One trouble with tact is that it has to lug around so many inhibitions.

Katie met me at the door, and I was surprised at how much I seemed to have needed her affectionate greeting. Kissing her could still be an event.

"Tell me what happened with the Governor."

"Nothing, take it as a whole. He and the professor jockeyed around. Gretchen spoke her civic duty, and Herman Driscoll was underfoot. Now what's this about Henry Spinney?"

"You can hear all about it this afternoon. Judge Holley is going to hold court."

"But you said Henry wasn't in jail."

"He isn't—they only summonsed him. But to hear the stories around town last night you'd think he was on his way to state's prison."

"What's he been up to?"

"He says he's going to be his own lawyer. Wouldn't you know? I used to hear a good deal about sea lawyers in my younger days, and I guess he's true to the breed."

"I'm still trying to find out what kind of crime he's being accused of."

"Didn't I tell you? They say he pulled up the stakes put down by the state surveyor. They charge conspiracy and malicious mischief."

"What stakes? Where?"

"No, of course you wouldn't know. It was soon after you left that a surveyor in a blue shirt and a pimply boy with hair down over his face, wearing a red sweater, showed up and started to put little stakes in the ground to mark where they want to put the new road. While the two of them were off somewhere eating lunch, or more likely getting a glass of beer, the stakes disappeared. Some of them turned up in Henry's yard. They were in plain sight."

"Why did he have to be so careless?"

"Not careless. Spunky. You know Henry Spinney. Now he's happy as Jamaica rum—he's got a good fight on his hands."

I was surprised at the speed with which preliminaries for the theoretical new road were being pushed. I judged that the Honorable Rufus Handmore was hot after his revenge on Henry.

Judge Holley's court came in at two o'clock, and I made it a point to arrive early at the courthouse, realizing that there would be a crowd. There already was one, and I had to squeeze in at the end of one of the golden-oak benches, glistening in its high varnish. There was nothing that our county commissioners thought more highly of than spar varnish. Perhaps this was a carry-over from nautical times; at any rate, the courtroom, year by year, received more varnish than use.

A court officer, with a single bob of his crinkly Adam's apple, yelled, "Court!" In Dinton, through the centuries, we have retained not only our full store of dignity but our full complement of petty officials as well; the two go together, for dignity and a few brass buttons are the chief reward of the officials. After all, the demand on their time is small.

We all stood, and Judge Holley entered in his black robes and settled almost out of sight behind the massive golden-oak bench. He was a gifted man but a small one. The fact that he had been paid fifteen dollars for drawing up the petition against the road would not occur to him to be a conflict of interest, and certainly it did not dim his blue-eyed judicial curiosity.

The complainant in the case was the surveyor, Blossom by name, but Henry Spinney would be prosecuted by the Commonwealth of Massachusetts in the person of Orilla Birdsley, Dinton's police chief, a first cousin of Ellie Kempton and related also in some way to Rufe Handmore's wife.

The clerk—old, whiskered Hanford McRobbin—who wore the only trifocal glasses in Dinton, read the complaint. Nothing was said about conspiracy, but it bore down heavily on malicious mischief and larceny.

Henry, standing at one of the tables within the railing that separated justice from the populace, looked unusually bluff and foursquare. He announced that he was not guilty.

Orilla Birdsley called Mr. Blossom to the stand; his ruddy, weathered face went with his profession, but otherwise he seemed to be no one in particular. He answered questions in a low voice while Orilla established the nature of his employment and the fact that in performance of his duties he had caused a considerable number of stakes to be placed in the ground not far from the home of the defendant.

Consulting an untidy sheet of paper, which he held in one hand, Orilla proceeded with his line of questioning. Probably Rufe Handmore had written the questions out for him.

"Do you happen to know, Mr. Blossom, if this defendant is in favor of having this modern highway constructed, or is he against it?"

"He don't know a goddamn thing as to what I'm for and what I'm against," declared Henry Spinney.

Judge Holley banged with his gavel. "Mr. Spinney," he said, "when you have objections to offer, you will address the court and make them in proper form."

"I object in proper form," said Henry.

"Sustained," said Judge Holley.

Mr. Blossom volunteered his five cents' worth from the witness stand. "When the district engineer gave me my instructions, he warned me to watch out for this man Spinney. He said . . ."

"Goddamn it, I object in proper form," said Henry.

"I want no profanity in this courtroom," said Judge Holley. "I will, however, sustain the objection. The witness may not lug in any hearsay."

Henry, obviously, was unaware of having used any profanity.

Orilla, though frustrated in his attempt to show hostile motivation, easily established the removal of the stakes and their reappearance on Henry's premises. He then called Mr. Blossom's pimply assistant for corroboration.

"Now, Mr. Spinney," said Judge Holley, "you may summon witnesses if you wish, and you may take the stand yourself, if you desire to do so. In that case the Commonwealth, that is, Chief Birdsley—will have the right to cross-examine you on your testimony."

"I don't need any goddamn witnesses," said Henry. "Who's testified that I took the stakes? Nobody. Who's testified as to who those stakes belong to? Nobody."

Judge Holley warned Henry that if he wished to be heard, he must first be sworn and take the witness stand. Henry obediently stepped forward and listened to Hanford McRobbin repeat the ritual of the truth, the whole truth, and nothing but the truth, which he in turn recited.

"So help you God," said the clerk.

"I thought there wasn't to be any profanity in this courtroom," said Henry. "Anyhow, so help me God."

He then told the court that the stakes were his and had his name on them. So they did, as an examination immediately showed. Observers in the courtroom, including myself, would have been interested in learning how Henry had acquired the stakes and when and how his name had been inscribed on them, but these were matters which went beyond immediate relevance. Judge Holley craned his neck above the bench and dismissed the case for lack of evidence.

⌒

When I reported these proceedings to Katie, she ruminated for a few moments and then observed, "It's all right for Henry to have his fun, but where does this get us, for heaven's sake? Seems to me we're more and more in the hands of the professor. I mean he's our hope. Who else has any important influence?"

I had no answer then or later. Katie wanted to pursue the matter. Did I think Jon Hamilton had made any impression on the Governor? Did the two of them talk together much during the overnight stay in Scituate? My answers had to be vague and un-satisfactory. In short, I didn't know.

"Considering what you went for, you might have been a little bit more noticing. I suppose you had to concentrate on Gretchen Johnson."

"Not exactly, though we were in bed together for a little while."

"You're getting smart all of a sudden," Katie said. "In the old days it would have taken you twelve hours to think of a remark like that."

I walked downtown, and wherever I went I was aware of a change in the climate of public opinion. The general impression was that Rufe Handmore had obtained approval of the road project under Chapter 90, which meant that the state would pay half the cost, the county a quarter, and the town of Dinton a quarter. It was hard to argue against a bargain of this sort.

We didn't see Henry Spinney again for two days. Then he called at our house early in the morning, greeting me heartily. I was short with him.

"The whole town has gone over in favor of the road," I said. "I suppose you know that."

"It don't surprise me in the least." He added a number of ex-pletives I shall not repeat.

"I heard you, Henry Spinney," said Katie. "Doesn't your lan-guage make you feel a little backward?"

"You know me and how I talk."

"Just the same," said Katie.

"Half the time I don't speak strong enough."

"Then the other half more than makes up."

"Getting back to the road," I said, "Katie and I can't see much hope unless we get real help from our professor friend in Wash-ington."

"Oh, him! Beelzebub—what's he done?"

"What have you done," said Katie, "besides stirring everybody up and having some fun?"

"My plans are just beginning. That's what I'm here for, Gid. I need to raise five hundred dollars right off. It's a campaign fund."

"Are you going to bribe somebody?" Katie asked.

"Hadn't thought of it."

"I'm afraid I can't help you out with any money," I said.

Then Katie said something that surprised me greatly. "Give him fifty dollars, Gid."

"Why?"

"Better to do something crazy than nothing at all."

"That's it exactly," said Henry.

"No," I said. "Not a cent."

"Gid!" said Katie.

I went upstairs and made out a check to Henry's order for fifty dollars. When I came down again, Henry received the check with complete satisfaction. I watched him from the window as he forged solidly along toward his own house like some kind of manor lord. If he had been shipwrecked on some far island, he would have made an imposing monarch.

But to Katie I said, "That was the wildest thing I ever did. Have you lost your mind?"

"Probably. Who knows?"

Not much happened during the day, but along about the cocktail hour Barry and Gretchen came over, and we all sat around in our living room with Martinis. Barry wanted to know if Henry Spinney had asked me for a contribution.

"To what?" asked Katie.

"Some fund he's getting up. He wouldn't say exactly what. Of course, I didn't give him anything."

"Of course. Barry couldn't," said Gretchen. "You don't simply hand around money like that without knowing a thing."

Barry must have experienced a hunch. "Did you give him something, Gid?"

"Well," I said.

"You did," said Gretchen. "You must know something Mr. Spinney didn't tell us."

"I don't think so."

The uncomfortable moment passed.

"Tell them about the letter," Gretchen said.

"We heard from Jon Hamilton—he really wrote to Gretchen, as a matter of fact. It was hard to tell whether he was encouraged or not encouraged. The pace in Washington must be terrific."

"Jon's hardly been there long enough to make the most important contacts," Gretchen said.

Barry took it from there. "I happen to know some people in the N.A.M.—you know, the National Association of Manufacturers. I'm getting in touch with one man tomorrow. The N.A.M. is all against wasting the taxpayers' money."

There was a little more conversation, an interlude sufficient for Gretchen to smoke another cigarette, and then she and Barry left.

After they had gone I remarked to Katie, "Everybody is against wasting the taxpayers' money. Nobody is more against it than Rufe Handmore. Barry can ask him."

"I wonder," Katie said, "which is more foolish—you giving fifty dollars to Henry Spinney or Barry Johnson talking to the National Association of Manufacturers."

"The two are on different levels."

"Still and all, I favor Henry Spinney."

On my next day in Boston I tried to find out something from Lanesboro in the Governor's office, but he would tell me nothing except that Governor Ferrick had been pressed with other matters and had not come to any decision about our road. I formed the opinion that Lanesboro was lying like a diplomat, but, like a diplomat or anyway like a politician, he made his answer stick. There wasn't any way around it. When I tried to question him about the Scituate conference, he said simply, "You were there and I wasn't." This was true but not in any spirit of candor.

Meantime in Dinton the surveying languished through a succession of rainy days. Stakes were put down again and remained where they were put.

The situation seemed to be hanging in a state of balance, but both Katie and I suspected that it really wasn't. You can't trust a calm in such matters any more than you can in the weather. This axiom, as I take it to be, was demonstrated when Herman Driscoll, the Young Intellectual, paid his first visit to Dinton. We saw him first from our sitting-room window, accompanied by a girl who turned out to be Ruth Ellen Johnson. How they had come together we didn't even wonder—their orbits had been bound to meet sooner or later.

"Go out and see what's going on," Katie said to me.

I didn't want to see, and I didn't recognize the importance of seeing, but I knew I had to. Henry Spinney must have started from his house at about the same time, and we all came together in the lane.

The Young Intellectual greeted Henry Spinney first.

"Hi, old-timer. Somebody was telling me that you're an old steamboat man."

"Who the hell are you?" inquired Henry.

"How long have you been on the beach?" asked the Young Intellectual.

"Jesus Christ!" said Henry Spinney.

"Long Island Sound steamers, I hear. Never rode on them myself—they were before my time."

Henry didn't say anything to that, but he spat on the Young Intellectual's shoes.

"I see you're the whimsical type," said the Young Intellectual.

Ruth Ellen had said nothing, and it seemed to me that her sympathies were divided. All along in this matter she had been a sort of referee, making the strange decisions that youth makes—and the stranger they are, the more attention you feel constrained to pay them.

Now she said, "There's going to be a meeting. Another meeting."

"We're all going to sit down together as friends and talk this over in neighborly fashion," said Herman Driscoll. He moved smartly away from Henry Spinney, half hiding in the protection of Ruth Ellen, and added, "Don't blame me, for God's sake. I was only quoting."

"Whose idea is this?" I asked.

Ruth Ellen said, "Hard to tell. It's something everybody's bound to go for—like apple pie and Mother. Sit down together and talk things over. How could it miss? Sitting down together is the main preoccupation of modern civilization, and I may write my thesis on it."

"I don't think we are very far apart from you folks," said the Young Intellectual. "Only a few points to settle."

"You," said Henry Spinney, "are the goddamnedest foolish young son of a bitch that ever showed up in the town of Dinton."

"Of course, I get the direction of your thinking, but I believe you exaggerate," said the Young Intellectual. "In my book all small towns have a high percentage of eccentric characters. Statistics tend to show . . ."

But Henry Spinney had turned sharply away and was striding off, spitting a few times as he did so.

"I wonder what troubles him," said the Young Intellectual. "Do you suppose he's really against this road?"

"You can't tell," said Ruth Ellen. "Behavior tends to be institutionalized, and so do attitudes. I've been observing this in my own family for a good many years. You have to wait for a moment of truth, often brought about by complex factors, and offhand judgments about people and attitudes must be constantly revised."

"You see?" said the Young Intellectual to me. "That's why this babe and I are so congenial. We have important understandings in common."

"If so, it's a very minor reason," said Ruth Ellen. "You were attracted by my blue eyes and blond hair."

"I don't know. Maybe."

"Jesus Christ," said Ruth Ellen.

"All razzmatazz aside," said the Young Intellectual, "what do you think of the idea of this meeting? Get everybody together and sit down together and talk things over."

"Together," said Ruth Ellen.

"Together. What's the matter with that?"

"I wish all meetings were in hell," I said.

"I guess hell is mostly meetings, at that," said Ruth Ellen, apparently with real thoughtfulness.

"Well, I don't know about hell," said the Young Intellectual. "We'll have to settle for Dinton for the time being. It's all set up."

"That's what you do with meetings—set them up," said Ruth Ellen. "It's the trouble with them, too. They ought to just bust out."

"Who set this one up?" I asked.

"The Honorable Rufus Handmore," said the Young Intellectual.

I don't know quite why I have reported this incident at such length; it seemed insubstantial enough at the time. I think perhaps the reason is that Ruth Ellen, despite her oddball remarks—deliberately thrown to our small gallery—seemed to me to be, as her generation always says, *with it*. I don't quite know how I got this impression so strongly. I think I must have had it before, in a way, but it had lurked below the level of consciousness.

The only report I gave to Katie, though, was literal and as objective as possible.

"Of course," she said, "with Henry Spinney antagonizing everyone in town, Rufe Handmore would naturally call a meeting."

"Set one up," I said, but she ignored me.

"Why wouldn't he call a meeting? Get everybody together to say publicly in one place what they've been saying separately on corners and drugstores and even at home. Henry Spinney!"

"Yet you made me give him fifty dollars!"

"I know I did. You can never have things both ways, but you can always try."

Like hedging bets, I thought. She and Ruth Ellen were both women, and as intelligent women they were both in their separate ways profound; but Ruth Ellen, being offhand and doubtfully coherent, was the one who was really *with it*. Whatever this might mean or portend.

~◦~

Katie and I walked to the courthouse on the night of the meeting, and Katie remarked on the coincidence that a full moon was shining. It has always been believed in Dinton that the full moon exerts a strange influence upon the thoughts and actions of our people. The tides of lifeblood within the human skull are not more removed from the influence of the earth's satellite in the heavens than the tides of the sea. So said Katie, and God knows she could produce plenty of Dinton evidence.

We met again in the jury room. The attendance was excellent, augmented by a residue at the back of the room of town loafers, street-corner statesmen, and one or two drunks. Aside from these recruits we were almost the same gathering that had responded to Gretchen's call way back at the outset of the road controversy.

Rufe Handmore sat at a table at the front of the room with Herman Driscoll on his right. In my short acquaintance with Herman I had never seen him look so organized and serious. He had even dressed for the occasion in a tweedy, expensive and relatively subdued sport coat, and tannish slacks, all in the manner of those who like to bring country life to the country.

Rufe looked at his watch, rose from his chair, rapped a couple of times with a ruler—since there was no gavel—and turned on the professional manner he had acquired in years at the Statehouse.

"I'm glad to see so many of you here tonight. We're all citizens of Dinton, and I presume we all know why we are gathered here tonight in this room of reason and justice. It is a privilege for me to call this meeting to order tonight."

At least it was clear that we were meeting on this particular night and not on some other night. Statesmen have peculiar ways.

The redundancy of their "night's" and "here's," "today's," and so on is a distinguishing mark of their eloquence.

"To my mind this ought to be a meeting of celebration," Rufe went on, "considering the great step forward that is about to be taken toward the prosperity that the township of Dinton is entitled to under the provisions legislated into law by the Congress of the United States and the General Court of the Commonwealth of Massachusetts. Our children and grandchildren will be grateful for the support we will be giving to the magnificent enterprise now within our grasp.

"But you folks don't want to hear from me. We have a guest here, a young man of vision and—well, of enterprise—who is going to tell you some of the details of the plans developed by his company and the capital improvements that will be reaped by the township and county of Dinton. Part of this is a road, but the road is only a beginning, my friends here tonight. The road has been pretty well settled in talks I have been able to have with my friend Governor Ferrick at the Statehouse. I don't need to remind you that I and others have labored long and hard to bring this modern highway to Dinton along with the development that will most certainly follow in its wake. I know there's some who still don't realize the advantage of the many as opposed to the selfishness of the few, and there's some who don't like progress and set their hearts against it. We hold no ill will against them, but we don't believe the unborn future generations want us to lay back in the traces and let the forces of reaction prevail."

He said more, but it was much the same, and in any case I don't remember it. Finally he got around to introducing Herman Driscoll, who scraped his chair away from the table and stood up.

"Hello," he said. "I guess that's the way to begin, though I don't want to sound like one of these guys on the radio. You know, too folksy. We're here to talk road, mostly. The rest comes later, like the night after day. The subject tonight is the road to the Point. It has to be, because without that road the land at the

Point can't be developed, and without the development of that land you folks can't have the prosperity the Honorable Rufus Handmore was telling you about tonight, just now.

"My friend and senior partner, Mr. George Beloff, reminded me that I was to come down here close to the grass roots. That sounds like radio talk, too. You'd think that nothing but grass had roots. Fact is that dandelions have roots. Asparagus has roots. Parsnips have roots. You people know better than I. Leaving the grass roots and malarkey about prosperity aside, I am most probably going to surprise you. You don't hear John Bunyan quoted much these days, so I'm going to quote him. I joined up with John Bunyan at Harvard one time.

"He said: 'The way to the Celestial City lies through this town where this lusty Fair is kept; and he that will go to the City, and yet not go through this Town, must needs go out of the world.'

"The more you think of that, the more it hits you, the more you look around and realize that's how things are, whether you like it or not. So this road has to be built—by somebody, I mean—with the help of Boston and Washington. Everybody gets taxed, so I suppose we're all going to build it. That's the way things are.

"You know something? Just one thing more. Dinton wasn't even a name to me until I came down here just a little while ago. I mean I couldn't even remember the name half the time, like you forget about what you've never seen. But this is quite a place. I like it. It impresses me. I'm right with you people. Maybe some of you, so far, think you're against a road, but remember that the way to the Celestial City lies just through this town, and vice versa, and that's how it is and in our modern era has to be, and we live in an age of roads. Let's face it, friends—an age of roads.

"Now one more thing. I sure am glad to see Captain Spinney here tonight. This highway is going to delight him as much or more as it pleases everyone else."

"Who the hell is Captain Spinney?" Henry inquired audibly from the back of the room. Titles on the old Fall River Line were exact.

Katie whispered to me, "You didn't tell me that young man was as bright as that. What he said didn't amount to a Hannah Cook, but it was sensible-sounding in a figurative kind of way."

"I did tell you. He's a Young Intellectual. The Governor says so."

"What did you think of his talk?"

"It was a soft sell, and that's what Dinton likes, even though he spoke in a foreign language."

At that moment I wouldn't have given one small sour crab apple for our chances in the road matter, even with the professor supposedly working for us in Washington. My pessimism deepened, if possible, when I looked around and saw Barry Johnson vigorously trying to obtain recognition from the chair. All that was needed to bury our hopes even deeper was one of Barry's suburban Kiwanis speeches. But Rufe Handmore, altogether too prideful of his political know-how as a moderator, persistently refused to notice Barry. He called on Mrs. Herbert Clifford instead.

I don't believe any of us had thought of her in relation to the road since that first meeting; few of us, probably, had thought of her at all. We saw her at church, or at the post office, or on Main Street, and she was part of the Dinton blend, but we didn't think of her; there were always women like that who didn't say much and wore the same spring hat and winter coat for a lifetime.

She only half rose from her chair and said in her quavery voice, "Anyone would lay out as much as fifty cents on that lane ought to be put away for good. The taxpayers have got enough to contend with."

These words, as nearly as I could recall, were exactly the same ones she had spoken at the first road meeting. But this time, after she had sunk into her chair, she bounced up again quickly to her tentative, shy, half-standing position.

"And another thing. I've never seen Rufe Handmore hankering after anything as hard as he hankers after this road, not in all the years he's been going up to the Statehouse. I'd like to know what he's going to get out of it. I don't see why the rest of us should sit back and pay taxes while he feathers his nest."

She settled into her chair again, and you could tell that she had scored. Nothing is more credible in Dinton, or has been since the town was settled centuries ago, than the idea of avarice. Rufe Handmore's promptly expressed indignation held things pretty steady, though; and following the indignation he mentioned his hurt feelings, the ingratitude of some of the electorate, and the general martyrdom of all who serve the public.

Barry Johnson waved for recognition and didn't get it. Gretchen sat beside him, composed and coldly beautiful, and for a moment I thought she had tried to pull Barry down. Rufe's favor attached itself to the bosomy Mrs. Bronson Alder as the next to speak.

She rustled and fluttered upward and said, "I'm opposed to this road and always will be, but I think the world of Rufus Handmore. I realize he's doing his very, very best for us."

Rufe acknowledged his gratitude, but Mrs. Alder had more to say. "What I think we should all be told right here tonight is why they're going to put this road, if they do go ahead and build it, to the east of the Crying Swamp. I've lived here all my life, and I know it can't be done."

"Who said they're going to the east?" said Rufe Handmore. "Nothing has been decided about the route except for what surveying has been done in the lane, just for a starter."

"I beg your pardon," said Mrs. Alder, "I happen to know the road will go to the east."

"Nobody would be fool enough to put any road to the east of that swamp. Where would there be any dry land to the eastward—I mean in case of a rainy spring or fall? On the far side of the Atlantic Ocean, I guess." This was Jared Bartlett, who yelled out his judgment without having been recognized by the moderator.

"Rufe Handmore," said Mrs. Alder, "do I have the floor or do I not have the floor?"

"Go right ahead, Mrs. Alder."

"All right. If the state isn't planning to put that road to the east, then why is it all staked out on that side? As far as you can see, I mean. I didn't care to follow out the whole distance."

"There's been no staking done that I know of—not beyond the end of the lane," said Rufe.

"You'd better sharpen your eyes," said Mrs. Alder.

"I imagine the state engineers have looked into it," said the Young Intellectual, without recognition from the chair. "You can depend on them for proper engineering—you know, all qualified, like M.I.T. and all that stuff."

"They don't know any more about engineering in Dinton than my beagle dog," said Jared Bartlett.

"Now, now, please, all of you," said Rufe, "this has got to be a properly conducted meeting."

"You'd like to shut us up, wouldn't you?" said Ella Clifford. "We don't shut up as easy as you think. We wasn't born and bred in Dinton for nothing."

"As for me, I'd say . . ." began the Young Intellectual, obviously intending to promote harmony, but he got no further.

"You keep your trap shut, young man," said Ella Clifford.

"Sit down, you goddamned fool," yelled Henry Spinney.

Rufe Handmore rapped with his ruler. Barry Johnson stood waving his hand and saying, "Mr. Chairman, Mr. Chairman!" Rufe paid no attention to him.

"Order, order!" someone said, whereat the jumble of noise and excitement became greater.

Henry Spinney made himself heard above all. "What I want to know is why hasn't anybody said anything about those two oil trucks lately. The two oil trucks that has got to pass each other in the lane. It won't be very suitable if the town's two oil trucks get stuck in the Crying Swamp."

"This town hasn't got two oil trucks," said Rufe, momentarily forgetting which side he was on.

"If they go east, they'll never be seen again. We'll have to convert back to coal," said Charlotte Bartlett, her words distinct because they happened to fall into a trough in the confusion.

"Those oil trucks don't have to be in town. They can come from out of town," said Ella Clifford. "Or we might have a procession of elephants, four abreast."

"This has got to stop," said Rufe Handmore. "Anyone wants to talk has got to be recognized by the chair."

"Talk is cheap," said Mrs. Jared Bartlett. "The way to tell if that road has been staked out east of the Crying Swamp is to go and see."

Katie and I had thought of that, of course, and I suppose others had, but the meeting was too much fun to miss. Now that a signal had been given, people couldn't get through the door fast enough. Over Main Street hung that full moon, more palely luminous than earlier, but spreading a clearer glow over Dinton, the past of its narrow streets and gentle houses, its people, and the omens for its future. From the other side of the earth the sun was shining upon us still, but only by reflection, thoughtfully, judging us in our loud words and anger.

Some started the engines of their automobiles, but most of Dinton proceeded on foot toward the lane and the shadows of the native hedges that stood so much higher in the moonlight than by day. Katie and I went along, not the first by any means, but not far back in the procession, either. The march gained recruits as it proceeded, though the newcomers didn't know the reason for this outpouring in one unaccountable direction. No one had time to explain to them.

Soon Katie and I were where we could see the leaders pause at a rise of ground quite a bit beyond what we had always considered the ending of the lane. Apparently they had reached a spot where they could see enough to answer the immediate urgency of the question that had brought them this far. No one but a fool would push on and on into the Crying Swamp even under the full moon—or to the eastward or westward, either.

We walked swiftly and soon we were elbowing our way

through the leaders, and I remember that Jared Bartlett was one, for he was swearing under his breath. I must have noticed others, but I have no memory of them. What took my attention, and Katie's, was the succession of white stakes leading off into the distance, plain in the moonlight, even casting their engineering shadows upon rough ground, not upon the remnant of that ancient trodden path. For the stakes led unmistakably and with firm intention not only eastward of the Crying Swamp but several degrees eastward.

In retrospect it may seem odd that no violence of talk exploded as one group of arrivals after another took in the moonlit prospect and understood its meaning, or what one was compelled to accept as its meaning; but at the time a somewhat awed silence seemed the only natural thing. What Dinton beheld was both incredible and real; its consequence was not immediate explosion —though Jared Bartlett swore under his breath—but the nurturing of moods. I suppose some were stunned, and all found their thoughts casting ahead to consequences.

"In such a night," said Katie softly, "did Galileo take his telescope and point it aloft until he saw . . ."

She didn't finish, because she had no idea what it was that Galileo saw. But it was just such a night in Dinton.

And then I remember the Young Intellectual, arm in arm with Ruth Ellen Johnson, their young faces alive not only with the moonlight palely loitering, but with some kindling from within. As a young man I would have identified that inner flame, but in modern times the fuel has changed so greatly that I looked on as an uninitiated beholder. As with atomic energy new elements had been introduced, new joining of new elements, a puzzle to all the world that had lived before.

"Hi," said Ruth Ellen. "If you see those parents of mine, you might tell them not to worry. Driscoll and I have decided to walk to the Point. How about it, Driscoll?"

"O.K.," said the Young Intellectual. "We might as well find out all about this now Celestial City."

"Oh, for God's sake," said Ruth Ellen.

"If you must do such a foolish thing," said Katie, "don't follow those stakes. You'd get mired sure after last month's rains."

"This female says she knows the way. Come on, kid, let's go."

They drifted off, hand in hand now, Ruth Ellen and the Young Intellectual, and we watched them as they disappeared behind the silhouetted copses and reappeared again from interlude to interlude until they were out of sight for good.

"I know we should have stopped them," said Katie.

"How?"

"That's the question. How? They know what they want. They know what they're going to do."

"No," I said, "but they're going to do it anyway when the moment comes, whatever it is. They act things out and think about them afterward."

"They think plenty about what you and I should do—and all the rest of the people past the age of thirty."

"That's different."

"The differences are interesting, but the samenesses are much more comfortable."

I wasn't sure what she meant, for I guess I was more intent on what she didn't mean—and on the leap ahead of my own thoughts. I said, "Even if I could have stopped them, I wouldn't have dared take the responsibility. Who am I to interfere with the course of one as old and wise and knowing as Ruth Ellen Johnson?"

"I don't know about that," said Katie, "but I do know that if you get in the way of the future you're likely to get hurt."

We took our time about walking home, pausing now and then along the way to look up at the moon in the great sky or across some newly revealed familiar vista. By the time we had reached the house the lane had cleared. It was late, and we both felt like going directly to bed.

As she put out the light Katie said, "I guess that fifty dollars I made you give Henry Spinney was a pretty good investment. I wouldn't have thought you could buy that many stakes for fifty dollars."

"If he did buy them."

"Who else?"

That was impossible to answer. Yet there had been something so plausible, so finally convincing about that procession of moonlit symbols, the engineering design, the "fearful symmetry"—the phrase came into my mind—that one felt tempted to believe in some truth, even if it had to be occult, beyond the possible work of a Henry Spinney.

⁓

I suppose I could say that Katie and I from here on were prepared for anything, but the fact is that we were not. We were, for instance, wholly astonished when we looked from our bedroom window the next morning, through the leaf-filtered sunshine along the wild hedgerow, and saw Lorenzo E. Sparrow taking a swing at Ellie Kempton. His aim and timing were poor, Ellie ducked the blow, and Mr. Sparrow's old-fashioned stiff straw hat fell off. When he stooped to pick it up, Ellie kicked him in the behind. There are other words for that part of Mr. Sparrow's anatomy, but I use the idiom of my own generation in Dinton.

Mr. Sparrow barely saved himself from going flat on the ground, his hands flew outward as he sought to regain his balance, and Ellie put a vigorous foot through the crown of the straw hat. The two men stood in the grassy reach of the lane, facing each other warily. Nearby, the arching branches of elderberry bushes in the hedge were clustered with ripe fruit, and several of Katie's catbirds hopped about, taking their pick, paying no attention to the combatants. After a few moments of vituperation, which Katie and I could not hear, Ellie walked off along the lane to the place where he had parked his car. Mr. Sparrow, leaving the smashed hat on the ground, took his departure in the opposite direction and was lost to our view beyond Henry Spinney's house.

"What do you make of all that?" Katie asked me.

"I think they must have disagreed about something."

"They must have . . . oh, Lord!"

"Well, what do you make of it?"

"Shut up, Gid. Hurry and get your clothes on."

"Why do I have to hurry?"

"For one reason, you can tell this is going to be a big day—unusual. For another, we'd better go over to the Johnsons' as soon as we can."

"Why must we go there?"

"Because if we don't, they'll come over here."

I could see the force of that. We might as well drink their coffee for a change and sit in their kitchen and let Gretchen mess her own saucers with cigarette ashes and butts. We didn't need to rush, though; there was a lag between the country time that we kept and the suburban time of the Johnsons. From nine to five we were agreed, but other hours couldn't be expected to jibe.

I had been in the kitchen of the Johnson house before, but I hadn't noticed it as particularly as I did now. To reach this change of scene Katie and I might well have traveled a much longer distance than across the open ground and past the hedges of our lane. The room was composed around a refectory table that had nothing to say of Dinton. The chairs struck a chord of domestic antiquity but seemed to me a bit arch in their effect. The counters and cupboards were assembled out of pine, plastic, cracks and white paint—enough of the latter so that no one could say the place was too ornate or nonutilitarian. Katie always said that white paint needed so much scrubbing that anybody had to admit it was practical. The Johnson kitchen smelled of early apples, coffee, a swept strangeness different from ours in Dinton—and of Gretchen's morning fragrance. Bath bubbles, I guess.

Rather than a description of a room, this may be a disclosure of my own prejudices, but in this instance they were modified by the sight of Gretchen's bare legs, so nicely visible above the knees as she sat on a corner of the refectory table and dangled them in unconscious accompaniment to her thoughts. Almost immediately they crossed, recrossed, and swung back and forth and sidewise.

She and Barry had been surprised to see us, and they remarked upon the coincidence that they had been planning to walk across to our house. We were quickly supplied with coffee—the real thing, not the powder that Katie used; you would have expected the custom to be the reverse, and this was one of the interchanges among the civilizations adding piquancy to an observer's life.

"You have such a nice kitchen," Katie said, "but aren't these chairs lonely without a cuckoo clock on the wall?"

"I see what you mean. Maybe we should get one," said Barry.

"Katie's only fooling, Barry," said Gretchen.

"Even so, one of those cuckoo clocks would add to the room."

"Add what?"

"Well, you know. Anyway, I was on the point of saying something important. Gid—Katie, too—did you know that Rufe Handmore caught the first bus for Boston? Ellie Kempton told me."

"I'm astonished," said Katie. "Rufe needs to be here to do some explaining—a lot of explaining. The kind he enjoys, too."

"When did you see Ellie?" I asked.

"Oh, first thing this morning. As a matter of fact, I wasn't even up. I had gone to the back door to look for Ruth Ellen."

In the greater interest of a different matter we let this pass.

"Did you see Ellie kick Lorenzo Sparrow?" I asked.

"In the behind?" Katie added.

"No, I didn't. I don't understand this at all," said Barry. "Why would Ellie Kempton kick Sparrow—they've been in cahoots all along?"

"All the more," said Katie.

Barry looked at her.

"She means that conspirators fall out. There's this business of all those stakes suddenly showing up where either Ellie or Sparrow, one or the other, didn't want them," I said. "It's my guess, anyway."

"We might as well tell Katie and Gid about Ruth Ellen," said Gretchen. Barry pouted, but she went on. "Did either of you see Ruth Ellen last night?"

"Did we see her?" I asked Katie.

"Did we?" she said.

"I know we did earlier in the evening," I said.

"Earlier than what?"

"Earlier than what happened afterward," I said. "It's hard to keep things straight around here nowadays. Everything looks simple, but we have the most tormented complications. What is all this about Ruth Ellen?"

"She didn't come home last night," said Gretchen. "She hasn't come home yet."

"I suppose up-to-date young people, even girls, are irregular about coming home," said Katie.

"No!" said Gretchen. "I can't think where Ruth Ellen could have gone. Of course, she can look after herself—she's mature for her years, and she really is levelheaded in spite of the way she talks. I can understand why she walked out, but . . ."

Barry said, "What Gretchen is leading up to is that Ruth Ellen and her father had words last night. It wasn't the first time, and it won't be the last. Children like her can grab a lot of freedom but . . ."

"Barry, Ruth Ellen is not a child!"

"She damn well is. Anyway, when a girl like that begins to read her father's mind and put words into his mouth, a certain point has been reached."

"Oh, Barry, must you?" said Gretchen.

"Yes, my dear, I must."

"What did Ruth Ellen read in Barry's mind?" asked Katie. "Was it as good as using tea leaves?"

"Oh, let's not drag it out any more, and let's not be funny, Katie, if you don't insist. She wanted to put me in a false position, that's all. Just because my friend in the N.A.M. wouldn't help us out—wouldn't go along with our point of view at all—Ruth

Ellen chose to say I had been influenced. Brainwashed, I think, was one term she used."

"She said Barry was changing sides on the road business," said Gretchen. "Without any reason, she said it. She's bright and all that, but even Ruth Ellen can't tell people's opinions just by looking at them. She really was rude, and I told her she should apologize to her father."

"I'm pretty sick of this nonsense," Barry said.

"Ruth Ellen was being contrary, independent and silly. Also self-willed. I suppose she pretended to stay out all night in order to teach us a lesson. She probably found some perfectly comfortable bed."

"It's all right to suppose anything, but what the hell do we do now?"

"Why don't we all go over to Henry Spinney's?" said Katie. "It'll be a nice change, anyway."

My own curiosity had already tempted me in that direction, and I guess Barry's and Gretchen's had, too. We all walked out into the sweet morning air and the eternal softness, still blended so casually of night and day that it has always seemed to me a more refined distillation than any perfume. A couple of Katie's catbirds followed us, keeping us closely in view.

We knew before we reached his house that Henry was at home, for we heard an odd sort of forgotten music from behind his closed front door. It turned out that he was sitting in that embellished living room of his in his shirt sleeves, suspenders laid off his shoulders for comfort, smoking his first morning cigar and listening to his favorite record on an obsolete type of phonograph.

"Trumpeter, what are you calling now?" came the emotion-packed voice of a baritone soloist. "Is it the call I'm seeking?"

Henry didn't wait longer for that particular call. He got up, stopped the machine in mid-course, and looked us over as if to form a judgment about how things stood.

"You want a word with me?" he inquired, and without waiting

for a reply asked us to sit down. We sat, or, more accurately, sank into the cushiony seats of his age of elegance.

"Things have been happening, Henry," I said. "Rufe Handmore caught the first bus to Boston."

"Is that so? Well, did you see Ellie Kempton kick our friend Sparrow in the ass?"

"Why did he do that?" Barry asked.

"It was quite a natural thing. I had thought of it myself."

"Yes, but . . ."

"More to it, of course," said Henry. "In my own mind I concluded it was the direction of those goddamned stakes. Questions of politics and morality mixed up in it, too—Ellie's sensitive on the matter of being double-crossed. His own goddamned disposition is such that he recognizes the symptoms. When he looked over the prospects this morning and saw the stakes pointing out to the west of the Crying Swamp . . ."

"You mean to the east," said Barry.

"Goddamn it, don't tell me what I mean. Those stakes, give or take a mite, are heading a couple points west of west by south."

"That's not the way they headed last night," I said.

"I was coming to that," said Henry. "Ellie took notice of that very circumstance when he called around to do some crowing this morning. He became disturbed in his mind."

"You mean those stakes were moved after we looked at them last night?" asked Gretchen.

"Must have been. They ain't self-propelled like your goddamned automobiles. Question is—who moved them?"

I guess we all looked at Henry, and he looked back at us.

"You can have any suspicions you like," he said. "I was more goddamned surprised than anyone."

"People will remember how you said at the very beginning that the road ought to go to the east—if it was built," said Katie.

"If it was built. I said that to dispute Jared Bartlett, and I would have said the opposite if there was any disputation needed on that side."

None of us could doubt this factual declaration.

"Where does it leave us?" asked Katie.

"It leaves us in a muddle," said Gretchen. "Mr. Spinney, did you see anything of Ruth Ellen last night or this morning?"

"Don't recall. Pretty near everybody was here one time or another—except our friend Beelzebub. I suppose he's in Washington advising the President, but by rights he ought to be here."

"What do you mean, exactly?" asked Barry.

"Hell, what do I mean! With things busting loose the way they are now, he ought to be on deck same as everybody else."

I hadn't thought of this, and the aptness of Henry's perception did not impress me at the moment; my feeling was one of annoyance, a feeling that continued as Katie and I extricated ourselves and walked home. But an old mariner like Henry Spinney has the gift of what is, what should be, and what is ahead, even though not yet glimpsed through the bank of fog.

I say this with the benefit of hindsight, which is more peculiarly my own gift. We hadn't been home long before the telephone rang. I answered.

"Mr. Lester? I've been trying to get you. This is Lanesboro in the Governor's office." His voice was agitated. "Can you answer one simple, straightforward question?"

"I doubt it."

"Well, for God's sake try."

"What is it?"

"I want to know what the hell goes on down there in Dinton. Can you tell me that? What the hell goes on?"

"That's not a simple, straightforward question," I said. "If you want to know what goes on, why don't you come down and see if it looks simple to you."

"No, no, Mr. Lester. I'm not unreasonable. Let's be perfectly calm. In the first place, have you seen Professor Hamilton down there lately?"

"No."

"You haven't? That's damn funny."

"I don't see why. The last I knew, Professor Hamilton was giving important advice in Washington."

"Yes, yes. He's supposed to be there, but if he shows up in Dinton, will you let me know? I suppose people down there would recognize him."

"A little sooner than they would Dick Nixon."

"What? Never mind. Let me tell you, Mr. Lester, Rufe Handmore has been up here today talking to the Governor. Does that mean anything to you?"

"Should it?"

"I would think it should, but if it doesn't, O.K. In that case you can do me a favor if you don't mention this call. Just forget it, will you?"

"I won't go around talking about it, if that's what you mean. A reputation for eccentricity is all too easy to get in Dinton, and there's no point in asking for it."

"Then that's understood. There's one thing more, Mr. Lester. I can tell you it's practically a certainty that you're going to get your road."

"Whose road?"

"Yours. Dinton's. Things look better for it now than at any time. But don't quote me."

"Can we keep our schools, too?"

"What?"

"Oh, to hell with it. How often do I have to tell you that we don't want a road, we don't need a road, and we damn well won't have a road."

"Oh, Mr. Lester, everybody wants roads."

I swore oaths that would compare well with Henry Spinney's, but Lanesboro had hung up.

"What was that all about?" Katie asked.

"I don't know what it was about. I want a drink."

"You don't ordinarily use such drastic and ornamental profanity about something you don't know what the something is about."

So I repeated the conversation to Katie as well as I could, and that is why I am able to give so complete a report of it here.

"He ought to know the professor is in Washington," Katie said. "Everybody knows that."

Hardly had she spoken the words when we both looked out the window moodily, expecting to see the grass, innocence, catbirds and elderberries—such natural, immemorial things—and to smell the scent and tang of them even from a distance and through solid walls or window glass. We did see them, though obliquely, for the principal sight upon which our fascinated attention became focused was Jon Hamilton, hands in his pockets, walking along the lane.

"This," said Katie, "is exactly where we came in. I know the expression is old-fashioned, but there's no better. Don't you suppose that redheaded Romeo can find any outlet for his love life in Washington? What's this nation coming to if the President's advisers have to come all the way to Dinton for a pretty woman to go to bed with?"

She wasn't stating the case fairly, but I didn't argue. I supposed, as she did, that the professor was about to keep a tryst with Gretchen. I suppose, in my masculine way, I rather envied him. No man can see why another man, least of all a professor, is entitled to such indulgences.

Katie was watching me, and I tried to turn my mind to matters more suitable for a man of my age and my build—though what Katie had said about my figure was grotesquely exaggerated. As usual, she seemed to know what I was thinking.

"One thing this business has done, Gid. It's made a great change in you. You've lost weight. Your pants will be falling off any minute if you don't take up the slack in that belt."

"Katie, be quiet."

For the sake of my own tranquillity—not Katie's, certainly—I went out of doors and, giving Henry Spinney's house a wide berth, headed for the first rise of ground beyond the lane that would show me whether the stakes had been moved, and if so, how much. Though I knew Henry's word was to be depended upon, I felt inclined to see for myself. Deviating a little from the course of the onetime road, or path, or cow track—whatever it was—I came to a boulder on the rise of ground that the winter gales had kept bare except for thickets of bayberry and huckleberry.

The line of stakes stretched plainly in view until it mounted the next knoll, but it did not stretch with any geometrical accuracy. It staggered, and I formed the opinion that the stakes had been moved in a hurry and that whoever had moved them had had little opportunity to line them up correctly. All the same, the line indicated a route opposite to that previously laid out.

I leaned against the boulder and looked, as if further concentration might add to the evidence in view. It didn't, of course. Concentration rarely succeeds. Any true revelation must be taken by surprise and not by intent.

While I turned this great thought over in my mind, it seemed to me that a sound from some nearby source could hardly be caused by insects, or birds, or any known mammal other than a human being. I investigated fruitlessly until a sudden turn of common sense prompted me to walk around and see what was on the far side of the boulder. What was on the far side proved to be Ruth Ellen Johnson, rumpled by her night out, soggy with dew, sitting with her knees peaked and her wet shoes discarded beside her. She was sobbing, but only intermittently; between sobs her expression seemed to me intently defiant. Whatever she wanted to cry about was something to which the next instant she felt determinedly superior.

"Ruth Ellen," I said, "your parents have been worrying about you."

"Barry and Gretchen? Well, they ought."

"Why don't you go home, then?"

"I'm not ready. I don't feel like it. I don't suppose you have heard anything about the whereabouts of the Herman creature?"

"Young Driscoll? No, I haven't. Where did you leave him?"

"How did you know I was with him? Oh, you must have seen us start off last night. Just the same, I'm not responsible for anything except pushing him off the cliff. That certainly could not have hurt him much."

"My God, Ruth Ellen! What cliff did you push him off of?"

"A teeny-weeny one over at the Point. That's where we went last night. He wanted to see the Point. Natch. Well, he saw it."

"Where is he now?"

"How should I know? I don't suppose he's perishing. He's bound to find his way back to town eventually. Even he must know the sun rises in the east."

"Yes, but does he know Dinton is southwest of the Point?"

"I never thought of that. He might be plowing around in the Crying Swamp all day—making circles the way they do when they're lost in the wilderness."

She seemed so pleased with the idea that I couldn't help commenting.

"I'm not exactly pleased. I'm kind of excited. Aren't you?"

"No," I said. "Besides, I don't know why you pushed him off the cliff. Self-defense?"

"I didn't like him. He was running off at the mouth about his old development at the Point. If it was only a matter of his making passes, I could have handled that all right. A girl has to cope, and most times there wouldn't happen to be any old cliff around to push a boy off of."

Her interest in sobbing, or crying, had entirely evaporated. She rose from the ground, picked up her shoes, and shook her blue cotton dress into somewhat better order.

"What time is it?" she asked.

"Almost nine. Don't you think Herman Driscoll ought to have found his way back by this time?"

"It's a subject that doesn't interest me. Who's that shambling around our house?"

I turned to look. Just as the site of the boulder offered a view of the stakes straggling toward the Crying Swamp, so also it commanded a wide prospect in the other direction. Our lane shimmered a bit in the still-early sunlight. Its tranquillity gave me a sudden impulse of nostalgia, for it seemed to me that I was gazing into that sentimental past before Barry Johnson had been moved to put up his NO THRU WAY sign.

In answer to Ruth Ellen's question I said, "Jon Hamilton was wandering around a little while ago, and from that man's gait I think it's probably Jon."

"Let's go see."

We were suddenly businesslike. It had not occurred to me or to Katie to investigate the professor's errand; we assumed his intentions were of a secret order, but now I realized that this was not necessarily so. Of course the thing to do was to investigate. Ruth Ellen started down the slope, still barefooted and holding her shoes. I followed, admiring the grace with which she walked.

⤙⤚

By the time we had reached the Johnson house, the professor had entered by the front door, hidden from our sight. We were prepared, however, to find him with Barry and Gretchen, though not, of all places, in the kitchen. This was the logical place for them to be, we discovered, because they were discussing the lane, and its course toward the Crying Swamp was commanded from the kitchen windows.

I had noticed already that the professor, more than most men I knew, could change his personality to suit an occasion or a purpose. He had been more or less revealed to me, despite my limited acuity of observation, as a modern savant suiting his manner to the big phrases that come out every year like the titles of new, world-shaking books, which don't, it turns out, shake any worlds; as the discomfited lover lacking the propriety of pants (in my fancy I could see again the forced composure of his thin face); in his Statehouse image, somewhat condescending, assured, keen.

At the moment he was being keen but not formal. I couldn't at once tell exactly what was characterizing his manner, but whatever it was, I didn't like it. I didn't trust him; and to my surprise I realized the issue of trusting him or not trusting him had not risen in my mind before. I longed to ask Katie what her instinct had been, but, regrettably—for I knew my inadequacy in circumstances such as these promised to be—I should have to do without her.

The professor drummed on the refectory table with the knuckles of one hand. The gesture, I felt, was one of authority. He intended to speak, as the tired phrase went, "without fear of contradiction."

"For God's sake, what are you doing that for?" said Ruth Ellen, entering the kitchen with me directly behind her. The professor, startled, left off drumming and stared at Ruth Ellen with annoyance.

"Ruth Ellen, I want to know where you were last night. Don't you owe any consideration to your mother?"

I noted the fact that suburbia is not entirely sophisticated. It falls back upon the old attitudes and words. When you so deliberately try to break with the past, the part you break away from is usually the solid part, no matter how much it may be despised by those who are, without being aware, fugitives from it, and you are left with the infantile and trivial.

"I was out with Herman Driscoll, if I remember the name correctly. He wanted to see the Point. There was plenty of moonlight, so we walked the way I used to go when I was a little girl."

"My God!" said Barry.

"Oh, Ruth Ellen, you didn't!" said Gretchen.

"I'm still intact, still a virgin. Not, I suppose, that a girl should brag about such things when others are so much more important."

I had been looking at Barry and Gretchen, but their expressions were entirely conventional, as I suppose their thoughts must have been. They were surprised backward in time and in outlook. So I glanced at the professor, and it was clear that he was scandalized, resentful both of the interruption, its nature, and the breaking off of the scene he and his authority had begun.

"You don't happen to have seen the Herman this morning?" asked Ruth Ellen, not hopefully, I thought.

"No," said Barry. Gretchen shook her head slowly from side to side, staring at her daughter with wonder. "Where is he? Where did you leave him?"

"I suppose he's in the Crying Swamp somewhere. Probably mired."

"My God!" said Barry.

"I think you must tell us exactly what happened," said Gretchen.

"Nothing much. I've told you the important part. The Herman . . ."

"Stop calling him 'the Herman,' " said her father.

"I kind of like to call him that. But all right. It's just that there wasn't so much moonlight coming back, and I suppose he got mixed up, what with the cow paths, potholes and all. Things look so different in a dark night. You'd think they wouldn't look at all, but they do. There's always some 'look' to them. Did you ever notice that, Jon?"

"I don't believe I ever did."

"You're not the noticing kind, I guess."

"Where did you leave Herman Driscoll?" asked Gretchen.

"Oh, didn't I tell you? I sort of took it for granted you knew. Mr. Lester knew, didn't you?"

"Not at the time," I said. "You told me a few minutes ago."

"Yes, I did, didn't I? Well, I suppose, looking back, it was quite an important part, though it didn't seem so at the time. I pushed him off a cliff."

"Ruth Ellen!" This, of course, was Gretchen. Barry would

have said "My God!" again, but even to him a point of diminishing returns—or diminishing emotion—must have been apparent.

"I don't really like the Herman—I mean the man. You know. He can talk a lot, and sometimes he says cute things, but essentially he's ignorant, and of course he's on the other side from us. He was telling me where the new streets would go and where he thought the new hotel would look nice. He had walked right up to a high part, so it was quite easy to push him off."

"Then what did you do?" asked Barry.

"I came along home. I don't need much moonlight. I have night eyes. I found that out when I was quite a little girl."

"You've behaved very badly, Ruth Ellen," said Gretchen.

"I don't think so, Mother. You do things differently nowadays. I expect you've lost touch, somehow. The Herman might have made passes and then, when I poked him in the eye, as I surely would of, he might have proceeded on his own, the way they do, leaving me to find a hitch or to walk. It's only fair sometimes for a girl to do the opposite."

"You just walked off and left him?" asked Barry.

"Yup. Walking is nothing to me, day or night. I expect it is to him, especially when he's lost."

Barry said, "I'm sorry for all this, Professor Hamilton. I realize you came to see us because what you had to say was important enough to take you away from Washington at a very busy time."

"Don't apologize," said the professor. "But I should really like to get on with this. It is, as you say, important."

Utterly deadpan. He wanted something. He was hard as old Dinton nails underneath.

"I think I'll get myself some coffee and maybe lie down for a while," said Ruth Ellen.

"You must eat something. After being out all *night!*" said Gretchen.

"Orange juice, maybe. Night walking doesn't necessarily make you hungry."

Ruth Ellen took her coffee (the pot was on the stove) and a glass of orange juice, and went out, soggy, her hair wispy about her face, and, I thought, in her way entirely lovely.

"The nymph of the Crying Swamp," I said.

"Gid, this is serious," said Barry.

"I feel so *helpless*," said Gretchen.

"Let's get on with our talk," said the professor.

"You sit down, Gid," said Barry. "This concerns you and Katie, too."

I sat, though I noticed that none of them was really sitting; they were leaning or lounging or sort of hanging on table corners.

"The gist of it is," said Professor Hamilton—at the moment you could think of him as Beelzebub but not by any stretch of the imagination as Jon—"in this civilization of ours, whether we like it or not, we've got to relate."

There's nothing like an eloquent platitude to prepare the way for treachery or retreat, I thought.

"Of course, I can see that," said Barry, being led. "It's something we've had to face up to at board meetings at the bank lately. . . ."

"The reason we've been wrong about this road project is that it *relates*, and we don't."

"Wrong? You think we've been wrong?" asked Gretchen, lovely and open-eyed.

"Not altogether. Not emotionally, certainly. But we haven't measured the consequences in terms of where we stand relevant to the major themes of the times in which we live."

I thought this was sheer flapdoodle, but Barry was ready for it. He keened in his country-club way.

I said, "A road here would serve no purpose except the major themes of destruction and pollution, and to hell with the times in which we live. I've known better ones by a damn sight!"

"Hold it, Gid! Hold it!" said Barry. "Let's hear what the professor has to say. Remember, he's just come from the firing line down in Washington. No matter what we may feel here in Dinton, you've got to admit that Professor Hamilton is *with it.*"

"You're right, I'm *with it,* and in a few minutes I can translate these words into relevance and identification. . . ."

Somebody said "My God!" again, and I realized it was I. At the same moment I saw Barry as his daughter had seen him a good while ago. He had the very look of a modern man who would favor roads. But that wasn't all. The professor and the professor's tone impressed him. The authority of Washington, of modern times, of resonant platitudes, impressed him. More important than all else, though, he was what he was, as Ruth Ellen had so cogently realized.

Gretchen stared at him, only half listening to the professor's continuing talk of manifest destiny, the gross national product, and, again and again, relating. The gross national product never leaned to one side or another of any argument; it was always on both sides or all sides at the same time.

"Barry," said Gretchen, "Barry." He didn't look at her. Although she hadn't spoken loudly, her tone seemed commanding.

"BARRY!" said Gretchen. He slid off the corner of the refectory table and said, "What?"

"Are you going to look me in the eye and say you've changed sides on the road after all . . . after all . . ."

"Oh, Gretchen," said the professor, "this isn't a time for emotionalism."

He hadn't expected to have any trouble with her. I could see that. And why should he have had trouble now, after all those tender occasions in bed during Barry's absences? One reason occurred to me instantly: he shouldn't have accused an intellectual of emotionalism. You don't do that. There's a particular rule in the suburbs against it. Moreover, women, so often blamed for inconsistency, can have a tenacity of conviction that no rationalizing or opportunism or logic, even, can shake.

"I'm not changing my mind on anything," said Barry. "I'm just listening."

But he had changed. I knew, and Gretchen knew. Or, as I have said, what he had been all along was showing through. The occasion anticipated by Ruth Ellen had come. He who had put up the sign and agitated for the preservation of our lane was about to abandon all we had stood for. And, again, why? Because the ancient human impulse in him was overcast by a cult more commanding than any superstition of ancient times. Not his mind but his instinct for conformity, his herd craving, his addiction, compelled him to believe—in roads. And if in roads, how avoid believing in a particular instance?

"Barry," said Gretchen, "you must know this means I'll leave you."

"Don't be dramatic, Gretchen," said Barry.

And the professor, who all along must have wanted Gretchen to leave Barry—though maybe not; maybe his convenience was best served when he could be a back-window, second-story lover —said, "Don't be absurd, Gretchen."

"Dramatic? Absurd? What do you think of this, Gid?"

I didn't have a chance to answer, because at that moment Ruth Ellen came into the kitchen with an easy swing of her legs and arms. She had changed into a clean frock, unless my habitual use of an old-fashioned word puts me here in the wrong; anyway, she looked pink and neatly young instead of untidily so, and her face shone under tightly brushed hair held with a pink ribbon.

"Is there any more coffee in that pot?" she inquired.

"I think so," said Gretchen.

"What goes on? Who's been killed? Has the Herman's corpse showed up?"

"Don't be like that, Ruth Ellen," said her father sharply.

"Your father has decided we must have a road where the lane is," said Gretchen.

"I haven't decided any such thing. I've seen what the situation is going to demand. I've been reviewing the whole problem in . . ."

"In depth," suggested Ruth Ellen.

"I didn't say that."

"You were going to. I can see why you all look filled with hate."

"It's because we are. At least, I am," said Gretchen.

"I told you all along that Daddy would come out for the road. Anybody could tell by looking at him and his bankbook and his evil companions. . . ."

Professor Hamilton tried his authoritative tone. "Ruth Ellen, when you're older some of this will make better sense to you. I would suggest that for the present you pass no immature judgments on your father."

"Oh, for chrissake," said Ruth Ellen.

"The modern Sybil has spoken, Professor," I said. "As I recall, you put a good deal of stock in the nonconformities of the young, Ruth Ellen in particular, as the source of—well, what was it?— wisdom? Authority?"

"I don't know what the hell it was," said the professor.

"Whatever Professor Hamilton may have said, it didn't apply to . . . to . . ." Barry floundered.

"Roads," said Ruth Ellen briskly. "Of course not. Would you have expected it to? Don't be so alienated, Jon, old dear. Tell us again about the gross national product."

"Suppose you tell us."

"Look at the ratio represented by highway construction and maintenance. . . ."

"Exactly. How can we, how can anyone, fool around with so basic a fact in our economy? We're facing what amounts to a national commitment."

"But you're arguing the opposite of what you argued before," said Gretchen.

"I am perfectly able to explain myself, and I don't care to be explained."

"The hell with it," said Ruth Ellen. "After all, this is only what was due to happen all along. Look at our country; look at our people; look at money; look at the gross national product; look at our stuffy friend Jon—no, I'll leave that one off. Strike it. That's a phrase I like—'strike it'!"

All this had been generally frightening and offensive, though entertaining at moments, and I did not care to remain longer. I suppose instinct told me the situation was no longer fluid; everyone but Ruth Ellen had dug in. As the others settled into their entrenched positions, they looked upon her with outrage, for she was assuming to understand them—even to encircle or outreach them. She, at her age.

"My God!" said Barry.

"That's it exactly," said Ruth Ellen. "That's your generation in a capsule we could shoot into space."

"Don't be rude to your father," said Gretchen.

"And good riddance," said Ruth Ellen, "only I'd be sorry for space."

"You'll apologize to your mother," said Barry.

Ruth Ellen shrugged as she took up the coffeepot. "My God," she said, "it's almost empty."

As I found the kitchen door, opened it and stepped out, I could have wagered anybody that nothing could now astonish me—nothing. Not on this morning of escalated drama. Small-scale drama it might be, but it was the real thing and, for us, in dead earnest. But my wager would have been lost.

Only a few yards from the kitchen door of the Johnson house I encountered Henry Spinney, and as soon as I saw him I knew he was on fire with one of his characteristic announcements. I didn't much want to hear it. I had heard enough, and I supposed anything he had to say would be as absurd and unhelpful as most of his byplay since the road matter was first brought up by Barry Johnson. But Henry provided another turn of the screw for the morning's excitement. He outdid himself.

"Gid," he said, "this is the best yet. You know what I just did? I took the Fifth Amendment."

"You did what?"

He nodded grandly. "I took the Fifth."

"Listen, Henry, let's not have any more horsing around. Why don't you tell me in a few simple words exactly what has happened?"

"It's the F.B.I. One of J. Edgar Hoover's men got into town last night and has been trying to scare up information about those stakes and who moved them. The feller came to see me a half-hour ago, and I told him I had no notion of talking to him or anybody. Goddamn it, I said, I've got a right to the protection of the Constitution of the United States and, goddamn it, that's what I'm going to wrap myself in. You go back to Washington and tell Hoover that Henry Spinney takes the Fifth Amendment."

I could see that Henry's jubilation would be hard to penetrate with as feeble a weapon as ordinary good sense, but I had to make an attempt.

"You know as well as I do, Henry, that the monkey business with those surveyors' stakes is not a federal matter. All this about the F.B.I. is plain nonsense. . . ."

"You'd be surprised what turns out to be federal, Gid. This road fight leads right from Dinton through the Statehouse and all the way to Washington. Damn it to hell, Gid, I saw the feller's badge. I saw his official identification card, and it was no doubt genu-wine."

Of course, I still didn't believe Henry's story. There was obviously some hitch somewhere, but I had no desire to question or argue or dispute with Henry. Whatever lay behind this latest eccentricity of his could be of no help to our side, and more likely it would lead to some additional defeat.

Katie was waiting for me.

"What did Henry Spinney just do to you? I happened to be looking out the window when you two met, and it was as if he had fired a torpedo."

"Something like that, but not exactly. Henry's taken the Fifth Amendment."

"Gid, you come down to earth. Try to make sense, will you?"

I told her what Henry Spinney had said, and I could see that she wasn't as incredulous or displeased as I had been. But then she asked about the professor, and my report of the conversation in the Johnson kitchen reduced her to concern and then to discouragement.

"To sum up," I said, "the professor and Barry Johnson have joined the enemy. They're going to advocate the road from here on in. If there was any doubt about it, Ruth Ellen closed off the final possibility—she stiffened their attitudes. Even if they wanted to slack off now, they wouldn't do it on account of her. As men claiming to be reasonable, they've got to vindicate their logical position, which in this case is superimposed upon a lot of other stuff."

"Logical position! About as solid as a Dinton fog."

"But try to tell them."

"A person does what he likes and then makes up his logic."

"That's partly what Ruth Ellen says. She thinks a person does what he is."

"She should wait until she's older. Girls did in my day."

"Now you're agreeing with Barry and the professor."

"Am I? Well, then, I'll back water. Go on. There must be more. You haven't told me everything."

So then I finished by repeating what Ruth Ellen had told me about her walk to the Point with Herman Driscoll and how she had pushed him off a cliff and left him.

"Any hope of getting help from him has gone by the board," I said. "At one time I thought we might appeal to his sympathy or sense, or more likely to his eccentricity."

"Where is he? Hasn't anybody seen him?"

"I expect he's still wandering around in the Crying Swamp or circling in the wilderness, the way the books say."

"The devilish fool could come back to town if he chose to."

"How would he find the way, once he got his directions twisted?"

"Some things are born in a man. Any man."

"Not any longer. In Dinton, maybe, but not much of anyplace else."

"Why doesn't somebody go look for this lost sheep? Why doesn't somebody do something?"

"Because he's just as well off where he is as he would be somewhere else. I mean, from the point of view of anybody in Dinton. I don't imagine even Ellie Kempton has any present use for him, and I haven't heard that Rufe Handmore has got home from Boston."

"How about the F.B.I.?"

"Katie, all of a sudden a lot of things are beyond me, and the F.B.I. is one of them. If they want to find young Driscoll, why don't they go find him?"

"Do they know he's lost?"

"Do we know the F.B.I. exists? I mean here in Dinton. We've only Henry Spinney's word for it."

Katie had made some fresh coffee, and we sat down and began to have a more reasonable discussion. It was she who pointed out that the professor's change of sides needed more clarification than Ruth Ellen had provided in the case of her father. Katie said she had never liked or trusted the man, but Ruth Ellen's idea that he had been turned out in a mold and was, so to speak, predetermined like a plastic radiator grille must be a considerable oversimplification. Upon reflection, I thought so too, although without differing too much with Ruth Ellen as to the fundamentals.

"The professor is a man of words," said Katie, "but there must be some accountability in the background. . . ."

"Motive," I said.

"Yes, motive. Like I said, accountable."

"Have it your own way."

We had used up our compatibility along with our reasonableness for the time being, and Katie tactfully suggested that I walk over and console Gretchen, who, she said, was probably in a miserable state.

Katie was only partly right. Gretchen wasn't in her kitchen, and she didn't answer my knock, so I walked through to the living room, announcing my arrival along the way, and found her sprawled in a big imitation colonial chair smoking cigarette after cigarette. As I had expected, Barry and Jon had absented themselves. It was their only possible move under the circumstances.

"If you're looking for the hatchet boys, Gid, they're not here," Gretchen said.

"I thought they wouldn't be. Katie said I was to console you."

"I'm in a foul mood, but sit down anyway."

Miserable she might be, and certainly she was in a temper that amounted to fury. She used language that I had never heard from a beautiful woman—or any woman, for that matter—in my life up to then. Gretchen's fury was near enough to the Dinton tradition, but not her language. Dinton women when enraged would employ masculine talk, preferably with nautical idiom, but they wouldn't slip into dirtiness or more than mild profanity. I reflected that here was another expression of our suburban culture.

I reflected, too, on the change that had come into our lives because of a cultural commitment to roads; not the open road of romance, but the hot, stinking bituminous through ways for people with a lost sense of home, an addiction to speed and distance. I glanced at Gretchen, not wanting to peer too directly at her hot, strained face or the fist that clenched a handkerchief on the false-maple arm of her chair.

I remembered her as she and Barry had first discussed, so dispassionately yet so earnestly, the threat of the road, and how smooth and clubwomanish she had been presiding at the first committee meeting. Poor Gretchen, I thought; poor all of us.

"This isn't where we came in," I said. "How did we get so far astray? How can we get back?"

"I don't really know," she said, and began to sob.

This was plainly a time for me to leave her alone and for me to be alone. How had we, the resolved defenders of our peace, the united opponents of the fanaticism of highways and unease, fallen upon this division and subdivision into personal seeking? More anxious still, was this the doom—as it so often seemed when one read the newspapers and listened to the radio—of almost all causes such as ours?

I carefully avoided my own house, though aware that Katie would probably see me from a window, and headed downtown to get a morning paper.

In front of the paper store I ran into Rufe Handmore engaged in conversation with a stranger whom I took to be a cigar or liquor salesman. The old-time drummers didn't come to Dinton any more, but some firms in the modern prosperous industries did send sales representatives once or twice a year. This man was thinner than most of the tribe, and younger, and he wore a wash-and-wear, double-breasted suit of dark gray, another variation from type.

Rufe detached himself and began talking to me without the convention of a greeting.

"Gid," he said, "the road is all wrapped up and tied with a double knot. We've got it."

"So I hear. Did you cinch it with the Governor?"

It was an effort for him not to say "yes," but he played safe with a second thought. "Only in part, Gid, though Ferrick always listens to me. You know that. In this case Professor Hamilton swung some weight, too. We swung it together, you might say."

"I know about the professor. I heard him explain that he had changed sides, but I still don't know why. His explanation seemed to me a mess of words."

"Oh, Gid, he was always with us, really. You know that."

"No, Rufe, I don't know that, and you don't know it either. Something came up that buttered the professor's bread on the other side. Or he was scared into a flop."

"Why would he be scared? A big shot, with White House backing?"

"I have a notion that kind scares more easily than any other."

"Oh, now, Gid!"

And from this one expression, obviously disingenuous, I became suddenly sure that Rufe knew damned well what had caused the professor's changeabout.

"Rufe," I said, "you're a slick liar but a damned poor one."

I brushed past him into the store and picked up my paper from the reserved pile. As I walked out again, Rufe and the stranger were still in conversation.

⤛⤜

I must have hurried home, though without intention; your steps quicken when your mind teems as mine was teeming then. I suppose the entire organism accelerates. So here I was, almost at my own door, and I didn't quite want to be; this was another time when I felt it would be more comfortable to avoid Katie's further interrogation.

Yet I would have gone into the house and faced her if, as I swept my gaze over and across and around the familiar prospect in more leisurely and closer fashion than usual, I had not seen someone waving from an upstairs window in the Johnson house. I walked across the grassy space with expectancy and perhaps with some eagerness. Entering into unusual situations, at first a relief, may become an addiction, but in this instance I was undoubtedly susceptible because I guessed Gretchen was doing the waving.

It was she, although she quickly drew back from the window as I approached, first calling out that she would let me in at the front door directly. Why not the kitchen door, as usual, I wondered. The briefest glimpse informed me that she was in her underwear; but this is Dinton talk. The one garment I saw, and only in a glimpse, was her bra. I supposed she had been changing and was about to put on a dress. If this was the case, she didn't want to spare the time at a moment of some apparent importance, and when she appeared at the front door, she was wearing the pale-pink robe with the fluffy collar that I had seen once before. I was surprised that the door had been locked.

"I want you to see something, Gid," she whispered. Her foul mood had changed into one of alertness and crisp balance.

She tiptoed through the hallway and the other rooms to the kitchen, where she stood signaling me to keep silence. She and Barry had found somewhere an old meetinghouse bench, which they kept against a wall beside the kitchen door as a repository for hats, coats and incoming or outgoing packages. This bench had been pulled away from its usual mooring, and Herman Driscoll, the Young Intellectual, was lying on it, unconscious. Asleep? Certainly. Drunk? I thought this more than likely.

"Where . . . ?" I think I managed this one word.

"I just found him here," Gretchen whispered. "He must have wandered in and gone right to sleep."

I doubted the plausibility of so simple an explanation.

Herman badly needed a shave, of course, and almost certainly a bath; the evidence of his night on the shore and the moors and both on and in the Crying Swamp was everywhere upon him. Anyone in Dinton would have taken one look and called this representative of capital a plain bum.

"My God!" I said.

"Sh-h-h-h!"

"I don't think he's going to wake up right away," I said in a low voice, but not whispering. "What are you planning to do with him?"

"I don't know. That's what I was going to ask you. I don't think Ruth Ellen should see him."

"Put it the other way around. Maybe he shouldn't see Ruth Ellen—at least not right away."

"I guess so. Anyway, there he is. He can't have suffered any broken bones."

"He's so much ahead with his training for the United States marines."

"Is he going into the marines?"

"Not that I know of."

"Then what are you talking about?"

"Katie says things like that, and when I'm not thinking, I drop into the habit. Anyway, the lost is found. This character isn't a subject for worry as the situation now stands."

"If I can only get him out of the house!"

"Don't you think he'll walk out eventually?"

"This is not funny. I wouldn't want to have somebody find him here. Would you like a cup of coffee, Gid?"

I said yes, I would like a cup of coffee. There was none freshly made, and Gretchen used the instant kind. We ignored the Young Intellectual, conversing in ordinary tones; yet we were not ignoring him entirely, since he occupied his share of the kitchen and had begun snoring gently.

It wasn't just somebody who found all three of us—Herman Driscoll on his bench, Gretchen and I finishing our coffee at one end of the refectory table—it was Ruth Ellen. She paused in the doorway.

"So the Herman is still laid out," she said.

Gretchen asked sharply what she meant, and Ruth Ellen divulged carelessly that she had discovered the Young Intellectual at the end of his wanderings and had guided him to this place of refuge. The explanation remained inadequate, but Ruth Ellen cut off further questioning.

"Oh, drop it, please. There's something a lot more urgent—Rufe Handmore is about to arrive at the front door with an imperfect stranger."

"What do you mean?"

Instead of answering her mother, Ruth Ellen said, "Listen!"

It couldn't have been much more than sixty seconds before a knocking sounded at the front door of the house.

"Nice timing," said Ruth Ellen. "I got here just in time to give you warning."

I suppose the warning, scant as it was, did serve a purpose. We managed to get the kitchen door closed upon the sleeping Young

Intellectual, and I arranged myself in the living room while Gretchen admitted the visitors. Rufe Handmore's companion was the stranger with whom he had been standing in front of the paper store, the one I had taken for a salesman.

"This is Mr. Carter," Rufe said, beginning a formal, important introduction. "He's from the F.B.I. Meet Gid Lester, Mr. Carter."

Mr. Carter produced an identification card with one swift movement and held it so that we could compare its small photograph with his full reality. The two matched. He returned the card to his pocket.

"You didn't flash your badge," said Ruth Ellen. She had come in silently from the kitchen. Mr. Carter gave her a cold look.

"Which route did you drive down on?" she asked.

"I don't remember."

"I thought maybe you could tell me whether they've finished the underpass near the Pickwick Grill."

"No," said Mr. Carter.

"You're not needed here, Ruth Ellen," said Gretchen.

"I wouldn't miss it for anything."

"We'll see about that," said Mr. Carter.

Rufe Handmore broke in with his best Statehouse voice. "Everything's going to be friendly. Mr. Carter here is collecting the answers to a few questions."

Ruth Ellen accepted her dismissal, and Gretchen sat down, twisting her fingers. Although I had thought Henry Spinney's story preposterous, it had at least given me some forewarning of the F.B.I. intervention, which had now so strangely materialized. For Gretchen the warning had been of the slightest and shortest. Of course, she would be amazed and alarmed—increasingly alarmed as her amazement yielded to the compulsion of reality.

"I won't take much of your time, Mrs. Johnson," said Mr. Carter. "This is just the kind of inquiry that comes along now and then, and I feel sure you'll want to co-operate with this investigation. Representative Handmore is giving me a sort of neighborly escort—making it clear that there's no hostility of interest here. I'd like to ask a few questions of you and your husband."

Mr. Carter belonged to the F.B.I., but he had muffed Rufe Handmore's introduction. He hadn't caught my name.

"He isn't my husband," Gretchen said. "This is our neighbor, Mr. Lester."

Mr. Carter surveyed the informality of Gretchen's robe and its possible inadequacies. His face held no expression whatever.

"If you don't mind waiting outside or somewhere for just a few minutes, I have some questions for you, Mr. Lester."

"I don't mind waiting," I said, "and then again I do. What disturbs me, waiting or not, is the time, money and nonsense spent by Mr. J. Edgar Hoover's organization over the location of a few surveyor's stakes in the township of Dinton."

"If you don't mind," said Mr. Carter.

"Come on outside, Gid," said Rufe.

I went, the heat and pressure of my anger rising by the moment. Rufe and I sat on the front steps.

"Gid," said he, "who said anything about Mr. Carter being here in relation to the matter of surveyor's stakes?"

"What the hell else, then? As a matter of fact, Henry Spinney told me."

"Nobody should pay any heed to what Henry Spinney says. I'm not supposed to say anything in advance of Mr. Carter's asking questions, but I don't mind telling you, Gid, that this is no kind of fooling around. It has to do with marked bills."

Rufe wasn't supposed to tell me that, but no force in heaven or on earth, moral or otherwise, would have kept him from the importance of being the one to convey the information.

"Marked bills," he repeated, clasping his hands about one knee and leaning back. "Here in Dinton. Right here in Dinton."

"You've left out something, Rufe. There's always the plain Manila envelope that goes with the marked bills."

He looked at me, apparently decided my remark was frivolous and not an indication of inside knowledge.

"It could get into all the papers," he said.

"You haven't made much sense so far, Rufe. You'll have to do better."

"I can do better, Gid. Bribery—you know what it means in Washington if somebody important, somebody high up, is smeared with it. Bribery, I mean. If somebody close to the administration is smeared, the administration is bound to go to considerable lengths to, well, clear the man's name. Even if it means having J. Edgar Hoover send an agent to Dinton."

"I'm beginning to understand you, Rufe. The man's name in this case would be Professor Jon Hamilton."

"I didn't tell you that, Gid. I didn't bring Professor Hamilton into this conversation in any way, shape or fashion."

"No, Rufe, you didn't." He was pleased at my tribute to his discretion. "The inference I drew was from the fact that Professor Hamilton showed up here so suddenly."

"I heard he was here."

"Rufe, you knew damn well."

"All right, Gid, but I'm not doing any loose talking. I know how to keep my mouth shut. Anyway, nobody's got anything on the professor. Not now."

"What do you mean, not now?"

"You know as well as I do, Gid, that this whole stink has been raised over the road project, which I could have put through in the first place without any to-do. Now don't fly off the handle, Gid. I know you took a position and you're sticking to it, or else you got stuck with it. All the same, deep down, Gid, you don't want to fight the cow that gives off good milk. You don't want to fight all the rest of us, Gid. This road is going to bring prosperity to Dinton.

"Now, like I say, the professor has come out for the road, which he absolutely meant to do right along, which will be plain to anybody who looks at the record, such as it is. Governor Ferrick will say the professor favored the road—he told me so himself only yesterday."

"If he told you that, he told you a damned lie, and you know it, Rufe."

"This has been a complicated negotiation with a certain amount of fine points. You have to look at it that way, which is the only sensible way. What I'm getting at is in a nutshell. Inasmuch as the professor favors the road, he wouldn't possibly have been taking marked bills against it. And a man don't give bribes contrary to his side of the case, any way you look at it, least of all a man in Professor Hamilton's position."

I sat in silence, trying to digest this indigestible concoction of deceit, fallacy, politics and gall. Rufe had at least filled the gap that Katie had pointed out in her conversation with me: the professor's accountability, as she put it. His motive. He was going along with the road project in order to clear himself or, perhaps, beyond the point Rufe had tried to make, he was carrying out political orders that happened to be personally convenient. Yet all this remained vague. It still didn't make old-fashioned country sense, though perhaps it meant suburban sense.

"Nobody has to have all the answers in this kind of mix-up," said Rufe. "At the same time, it looks kind of funny that Ellie Kempton has took off for a visit to his cousin in Duluth."

"I didn't know Ellie had gone."

"He went sudden. He had some words with Sparrow—and Sparrow's lucky if he don't get indicted—and right after that Ellie took off."

This part was understandable. Ellie knew more about the marked bills than anyone in Dinton, barring Katie, Henry Spinney and myself, and Ellie wouldn't favor being questioned by the F.B.I.

This front-step conversation had occupied only a few minutes, and it seemed to be complete. There was nothing more to be said between us. But I had plenty to say in the wrathful colloquy of my own mind, and it was upon this colloquy that Mr. Carter of the F.B.I. intruded when he opened the door and said, "Mr. Lester, will you come in, please?"

Gretchen obviously had gone upstairs. Ruth Ellen was not in sight, but I would have bet that she was not far out of listening distance. Mr. Carter invited me to be seated in the dining room so that he could use the surface of the table for making notes.

"This is a funny affair, Mr. Lester. Nothing to it, really. As you may possibly have heard, Professor Hamilton has been made the object of certain allegations. This fact has become known in Dinton, and there's no harm in my mentioning it to you, though in strictest confidence. The less mystery between us, the better."

"All right, what do you want to know?"

He didn't like my manner, but he didn't choose to alter his own. "There's a matter of certain marked bills." He waited.

"Do you want to know where they came from? Do you want to know who marked them?" I asked.

"Naturally I do."

"Do you want to know who passed them and who got them?"

"Yes, I sure do! Let's get on with it."

I knew there was a certain amount of suspense; why wouldn't I know? I was building it up myself purposely, without thought of assistance from any outside source such as a noise that now came from the kitchen. Mr. Carter got up, crossed the room, and opened the kitchen door. Ruth Ellen had pushed the meeting-house bench back against the wall and covered Herman Driscoll with a heavy rug, the bulges of which did not appear overly suspicious. That is, they might have interested a Boy Scout but not Mr. Carter of the F.B.I., and I couldn't blame him. Dinton is not an environment that encourages suspicion—or wasn't until highways took so high a place in national culture.

We returned to our seats. I had an idea that Ruth Ellen was somewhere about, but I hadn't seen her.

"You were going to say, Mr. Lester . . ."

"I was going to say, Mr. Carter, that I stand on my constitutional rights. I decline to answer any of your damned impertinent questions on the ground that to do so might tend to incriminate and degrade me. As the newspaper headlines usually put it, I choose to take the Fifth Amendment."

So here I was, foursquare with Henry Spinney, over the shadow line of the moon-struck fringe. This wasn't what I wanted, and I experienced an ominous qualm as I departed from the norm of my life so far, the behavior of a dignified member of the community, its heritage and tradition, and an executive of an important, ancient business firm in Boston, who ate an apple at his desk before starting work in the morning. All this was, I say, a tug. But I had no intention of being led by Mr. Carter's questions through a narrative that would include a description of the professor jumping from a second-story window without his pants, an account of the Manila envelope, Katie's improvisation, her marking of the bills, and heaven knows what else. The crazy business ran on and on, not helped any by the flavor that Henry Spinney could impart to it.

So Mr. Carter and I sat facing each other with detestation on both sides. I can't remember what he said, but I assume he must have said something intended to modify my attitude. My own brief comment was derived from a long-ago boyhood.

"Mum!" I said.

I suppose we might have gone on sitting there indefinitely if it had not been for another noise, unmistakable this time, in the kitchen. Mr. Carter and I reached the door in a dead heat.

The outside door had been flung wide open, the rug was on the floor, the bench deserted. Ruth Ellen stood in the middle of the floor as calm and softly persuasive as Indian summer.

"Hello," she said.

"Where's Herman?" I asked.

"He just went. He was in a hurry. I think he never wants to come back. Do you mind?"

"No, I don't mind, especially the last part."

"Who's Herman?" Mr. Carter asked, looking at me.

"I decline to answer on the ground . . ."

"Never mind!"

"He's a boy," said Ruth Ellen.

"A boy?"

"A young man. Old enough to get into trouble. You'd assume that, with your training. Otherwise he wouldn't have scrammed out of here like a bat out of hell."

"What do you know about my training?"

"You're from the F.B.I., aren't you?" Mr. Carter couldn't deny that he was. He stood mute. "That's why Herman left in such a hurry. He didn't want to be questioned about the assault."

"What assault?"

"Oh, it wasn't anything, really. I pushed him off a cliff, which I suppose was technically an assault, and after that he got mixed up in his directions and spent a whole night wandering around. It wasn't my fault that he started drinking to keep off the chill. The chill was nothing much, if anything at all, and he shouldn't have had liquor on him. The liquor proves he had an improper motive when he started out in the moonlight with a girl."

"What girl?"

"Me. At this point Herman is a badly confused young man. When he found out the F.B.I. was after him, he lit out. He lit out fast."

"Listen, young lady, if I hear it right, he didn't assault you— you assaulted him."

"Kind of."

"Then what was he afraid of?"

"Don't you see? If he had assaulted me, it would have been the normal thing, assuming he isn't a pansy, which I don't think he is. But the fact that I assaulted him gave him a consciousness of guilt. His image was suffering, and I imagine he was suffering some himself."

"I still don't see why he wanted to get out of here so fast."

"Oh, I told him the F.B.I wanted to interrogate him. Didn't I have it right? You would have questioned him if you had found him sleeping it off in the kitchen, wouldn't you?"

Mr. Carter seemed to meditate. I judged that, looking at Ruth Ellen's serenity and having listened to a sample of the dialectic with which she was amply stored—you could see it was straining to come out—he decided there was no useful comment to make. But he did ask one further question.

"What do you know about those marked bills?"

"Not a goddamned thing," said Ruth Ellen with an utterly convincing sweetness and innocence.

When I arrived at my own house, Katie regarded me with more than usual thoughtfulness until finally she said, "Gid, you've been up to something. Don't you dare deny it."

"I've no intention of denying it. You know I've been up to something."

"I'll sit down first. Now tell me. What?"

"I've just taken the Fifth Amendment."

"Don't you stand there and tell me any such nonsense."

"It's nonsense, but I did it. We're all mad here."

"You and Henry Spinney."

"That's right."

Then I told her the story in all its unreality.

"I guess you did right, Gid, though I hate to say so. When you start out with the professor and his pants—I mean without his pants—you're bound to end up in some peculiar consequence."

I don't know why the silence now should have been awkward, but it was. Ruth Ellen's arrival therefore seemed timely, even though her first act was to walk across the room and turn on a small table radio, which usually supplied Katie and me with Boston news.

An excited voice from the airways said, "This is your overhead traffic monitor, talking to you from a helicopter just over the southerly rim of the metropolitan area. Traffic is badly choked on the Southeast Expressway—there's a truck overturned near the Neponset traffic circle with cars backed up for a mile and a half. Some kind of trouble has developed near the Dorchester gas tank —I'll let you folks know as soon as we get a better view.

"Now for the central artery—things are clearing up nicely after the two-hour delay we told you about on the three o'clock broadcast. Northbound traffic on Route 28 is heavy. . . ."

I got up, prepared to turn off the intruding voice, but Ruth Ellen was ahead of me.

"Oh, Jeez," she said. "It's all so normal."

"Why for goodness sake," said Katie, "what do you care about traffic up Boston way?"

"I don't know."

"You don't know?"

"Maybe it's just my generation. We have to be with it. Maybe it's like comic books, only different. You get kind of indoctrinated." She sat down, and for a little while we talked about the most recent happenings in Dinton.

"What do you think I'd better do next?" We had no idea what she meant. "I'll bring you up to date. Things don't just happen, you know. It's people that make things happen, like with this road deal. Are we going to let the powers of evil put it through?"

"I hope not," Katie said.

"Well, so what? Moral force is so much garbage, politics all the more so. You need action. Mr. Spinney has the right idea, but he takes too much out in talk. He doesn't know it, but he and I have been working together—he put those stakes out, and I had a hell of a job moving them. Nice timing, as it turned out."

"I was off the track," said Katie. "I didn't guess it was you."

"Then I got rid of Herman. We had to get him the hell out of here."

"What's to keep him from coming back?" asked Katie.

"There's an absence of wild horses to drag him back," said Ruth Ellen. She added, "If you will pardon the classical allusion."

I wasn't so sure—but I wasn't sure of anything at the moment.

"I asked you what I had better do next," she said.

"Maybe we'd better not know what you're going to do next," said Katie. Then, as Ruth Ellen went out, Katie said to me, "What are *we* going to do next?"

"I don't know. What can we do?"

"For that matter, what have we done so far?"

"All the usual things. In a democracy . . ."

"You shut up," said Katie. "What you're saying is that we haven't done one damn thing. Not one damn thing that could help."

"Maybe you're right. The thing was rigged against us from the start."

"We've been mostly sitting around."

"Well, what could we do?"

"Something. Anything."

"I haven't the slightest idea what you mean."

"Henry Spinney did something. Ruth Ellen did something."

"All right, did they help or did they hinder?"

"I say they helped," said Katie. "They not only helped but they kept us entertained."

That last I could admit, but I thought it best to offer no comment.

"The usual things," said Katie. "The usual things—a meeting, a petition or two, resolutions, smooth talk back and forth with the Governor. What the hell, Gid. I say, what the hell."

"I don't know what you're getting at."

"What I'm getting at is that we should do some unusual things for a change. We should get smart."

"That's easy to say."

"Easy to do. I began to see daylight ahead when we found out how Ruth Ellen handled that young man, Driscoll. She got rid of him."

"Who do you think we ought to get rid of?"

"You're not being funny, Gid. What I mean is we should carry the fight to the opposition."

"All right. You've got something in mind. What is it?"

"Only a glimmer, but let's get started. Who do you think the weak spot is in the army of the opposition?"

"Who?"

"I'd say Jared Bartlett."

"Why? He stands to make a lot of money out of the road."

"That's what he thinks. You might get him to think different."

I knew better than to argue or even to comment. I sat quietly, listening to Katie. She was bringing us to the brink of action. I hoped she wouldn't land us in jail or get us involved in a suit for slander with high damages.

～◦

For the sake of greater importance, I telephoned Jared Bartlett and asked him to meet me in the lane. He came willingly enough. We spoke about the weather, of course, and after that I didn't say much for perhaps five minutes. Hands in our pockets, we walked along the route of the proposed road, my moodiness obviously affecting him somewhat.

"I don't know about that land scheme at the Point," I said when I got around to it.

"What do you mean, Gid?"

"They tell me it's blown up. I hear the young fellow has left town. I hear it on good authority that he won't be back. It looks as if the whole scheme was just talk."

The day was a drab one. The prospect toward the Crying Swamp had taken on a dismal character.

"Maybe," said Jared. "All the same, there's money to be made in land at the Point."

"More money in land somewhere else, from what I hear. The water's bold at the Point. A pier wouldn't stand through winter gales, and there's no shelter for small craft in summer."

"Are you saying that's what the young fellow found out?"

"I think it's likely."

"There's still the road."

"Well, yes."

"What are you getting at, Gid?"

"I'm not sure, but I think Henry Spinney knows something. He's kept pretty quiet lately."

"Henry Spinney!"

"I know what you're thinking."

"He's always nosing around. He could have found out something, at that."

"Say what you like about Henry. He's got a head on his shoulders."

"You don't know who you can trust, what with Ellie running off, and what with all this F.B.I. fooling around. What do you make of it, Gid?"

"I don't like to say, Jared. Ellie went in a hurry, and he must have had a reason. I hear that Gretchen Johnson thinks we should have another meeting at the courthouse, on the same principle as the first one."

"No, no, Gid. Meetings are no good."

"You may be right, Jared."

"But you don't think so?"

"The way things are, a man don't know what to think." He recognized his own idiom and looked at me sharply. I said, "Of course, you know Barry Johnson has come around to favoring the road."

"I heard. Some say he wants a four-lane highway through here."

"I don't know how many lanes."

"Four lanes would be kind of foolish."

"It's taxpayers' money, Jared. The more foolish, the more likely."

"We could have the road with just two lanes. It would be a good paying road for the town."

"What do you think Rufe Handmore is up to?"

"What do you mean?"

"What do you think I mean?"

"Is he planning to feather his own nest out of this?"

"It would be human. You know Rufe as well as I do."

"They're all alike," said Jared.

That was the end of our conversation, and I wasn't satisfied. I could see Jared was hanging on to the idea of the road. But I went right away to see Henry Spinney, and after that Henry and Jared had a talk.

❧

Henry told me about it in a conversation that went on to include elaborations of his own.

"You worried him," Henry said. "No doubt about it. I told him I heard the new road was to be two lanes now, with land-taking for four lanes later. I told him the contract was going to be let to O'Donnell and Yellenti, Inc. I forgot the name you gave me, so I took this out of the Boston papers. O'Donnell and Yellenti build a lot of roads and bridges and are always being investigated. Jared began to look worse than glum. He could see his chance of hiring out his trucks had gone dead."

"So I guess the next thing is to have another meeting at the courthouse."

"It's better than something else. Goddamnit, Gid, we've got to go on taking chances."

❧

Of course, I knew Gretchen would want another meeting, and she did, as soon as I suggested it to her. She saw no reason for optimism, and I'm not sure that Katie and I saw too much, but meetings are a civic-minded housewife's particular thing. She began to show renewed animation, and two or three times when Katie felt moved to pry into the situation, Gretchen was busy on the telephone.

"Telephonitis," Katie said to me. "But she didn't introduce it here. Lots of our own Dinton people have had it bad."

The new meeting was set for a Thursday evening, and on the previous afternoon I took the first chance to intercept Jared Bartlett.

"Have you seen Barry Johnson?" I asked him.

"Yup. He had heard I was weakening, and he wanted to talk road."

"I'm not surprised."

"He played it pretty cute, didn't he? Pretending to be on our side."

"Whose side do you mean?"

"Dinton people. We got a right to run our own affairs."

"But Jared, you were in favor of the road right from the beginning."

"Everybody's in favor of roads, in a manner of speaking, but we don't have to be dictated to. There's plenty of places for roads, and I don't mind admitting I might have been a little hasty about this particular location. Leads nowhere, never will lead anywhere."

"You think the land scheme was just bait?"

"Looks so, Gid. Did you hear the contract was going to those big Boston crooks, O'Donnell and Yellenti?"

"I did hear something to that effect."

"Once they get in here they'll hog everything. We're liable never to get them out."

"But if all this activity brings a lot of money into town . . ."

"Gid, you know one thing? Just one thing always holds true in Dinton. We ain't for sale. Now take this Professor Hamilton—he ain't our kind. Here he comes, all the way from Washington, telling us we've got to have a road. Changed his mind, he says. What sort of kindergarten foolishness is that? Everybody knows he was passing out bills."

"Well," I said, "I hope you're going to be at the meeting, Jared."

He guessed he would, and we parted. He had gone only a short distance, though, when he called to me, "Gid." I waited while he retraced his steps. "Another thing. How about this oddball girl of the Johnsons'? How does she stand?"

"Don't fret about that girl."

"Well, I hope I don't need to. What I notice is she's always talking about route numbers. You can't go from here to Wilton Corners without her asking what route you took."

"It's her generation, Jared."

"Routes," said Jared. "It's a goddamned crazy world. When we first began talking road, it never occurred to me that before we could draw breath we'd be numbered off. I'm for roads, but I'm against numbering off except when nobody can help it."

"You don't drive outside the county much, Jared."

"Not a mile if I can help it, not any more. Last time I was in Boston I got stalled in some artery or other that nobody ever told me what it was. I don't know to this day where it is. When I finally managed to cut off, expecting to drive around a block, I was all of a sudden on an overpass and I damn near had to go clear to Worcester."

He started off again. I didn't move right away, though. I looked after him with amazement. I had made the discovery that Jared Bartlett, the real Jared Bartlett, was an antihighway man, just as Barry Johnson was a prohighway man. Something of that sort couldn't possibly be in their chromosomes, but it must be almost as fundamental, and no matter on what side they talked at one time or another, they were, without volition, what they had to be.

Any reassurance derived from this conversation didn't last long, though. Henry Spinney told me later with chagrin that Jared Bartlett wasn't planning to speak at the meeting. He might not even go. He didn't want to get upset in his stomach.

❧

The subject continued to hang over the town that night and the next day. You couldn't conclude that the climate had changed, or public opinion, either, because Rufe Handmore had never grinned more in his life. He was seen on the street with Professor Hamilton, thus reminding his constituents that those who move in high places are likely to be seen together on an intimate footing.

Gretchen called us on the telephone a couple of times, but we didn't see her. We asked her how things looked, and she asked us how things looked. How much had we gained, if anything?

I wished we knew, and Katie wished so also, but the people you met on the day of the meeting weren't talking. They had clammed up, and maybe the continued presence of the F.B.I., rumored but not confirmed, had something to do with this attitude. Professor Hamilton, at least, had stayed over for the meeting and was engaging voters in conversation.

So here we were again, in the slickly varnished grand-jury room at the courthouse, but instead of April the month was August, and elegiac rose-of-Sharon bushes bloomed in lavender and pale mauve on the courthouse lawn. The room filled early, and there were standees at the rear.

"You can smell them," said Katie. "I wish they'd thin out."

But we knew they wouldn't. More would come and peer over their shoulders and stamp and cough so that the ones in front couldn't hear. But that would be later. The hour of eight had arrived, and Gretchen, neat and crisp in pale blue, her face beautiful, and a bit cruel, too, if you knew her—for vengeance was now compounded with her deep resolve on the road question—stood to rap for order.

"Makes it worse for her, Barry sleeping away from home," said Katie.

"This meeting is called because of very urgent requests," Gretchen said. "There seems to be a feeling that some vital factors remain to be discussed in relation to the road that either will or will not be built between the lane—you all know the lane—and the Point. Discussion is now in order."

Katie had been craning around. She whispered, "Jared Bartlett isn't here."

But his wife, Charlotte, was. Her voice was asking, "Where's Ellie Kempton? He ought to be here. We ought to hear from Ellie."

"I understand he's visiting a cousin in Duluth," Gretchen said.

"I heard San Francisco," said Charlotte Bartlett. "I never knew anybody to have cousins so convenient in so many places."

Her remark was followed by general laughter.

Rufe Handmore rose, a little to the left of Katie and me, and one row of seats to the rear. Jon Hamilton was seated on one side of him and Barry Johnson on the other.

"Madam Chairman," Rufe began, "Ellie's absence at this particular time has no particular significance. It never was up to Ellie to make any decisions on this matter on the policy level. It was only up to Ellie to do what was voted and what there was money for. Now, to get down to the gist of things, I am asking the courtesy of the floor for a distinguished visitor, Professor Jon Hamilton, who has something to say that is of the most material importance to the township and county of Dinton, which is why he has the desire to address this meeting."

"I hear no objection, and Professor Hamilton may speak," said Gretchen.

The distinguished professor rose and began punctiliously. "Madam Chairman, ladies and gentlemen, I come before you in a peculiar light, as I well realize, because when I first visited your lovely, enterprising little town I was opposed to this road. But I was not in possession of all the facts. In addition to investigating with the greatest care, I have reviewed with a number of high officials in Washington—and with a number of city planners—the proper avenues of development for the town of Dinton.

"I have also talked at length with Representative Handmore, and I must say to you here tonight that we see eye to eye. The issue is more than the building of a road; it is a decision whether or not Dinton chooses to relate to the larger community of which it must of necessity be a part. . . ."

He went on at considerable length, smoother than I had imagined he could be, secure in his authority, secure also in his reliance on the town's instinct of self-interest. I noticed that Katie was glancing around the room with close attention.

"I believe they're swallowing it hook, line and sinker," she said.

This was a disquieting judgment, for Katie usually saw clearly. Finally Jon sat down. Rufe Handmore reached across and shook his hand.

"Madam Chairman," said Henry Spinney, rising up with his shipshape manner and bulk. Since this form of address had been started, it was pretty sure to run through the whole evening until someone got too excited to remember.

"Madam Chairman," said Henry Spinney again. Gretchen had been too disturbed to recognize him at once, and a further pause was unexpectedly filled.

"Henry Spinney," said Ella Clifford, "you shut up!" She sat, then bobbed out of her seat again and said, "You shut up and sit down."

Henry looked around, astonished, but such a stamping of feet and clapping of hands, combined with catcalls, persuaded him to follow Ella's injunction. Probably, too, he realized already that his function of muddying the waters had been fulfilled; the meeting now wanted to face the issue head on.

"Madam Chairman," Ella said, on her feet for a third time, "what I've said before I say now. Anyone would lay out so much as fifty cents on that road ought to be put away for good. We taxpayers have enough to contend with."

Mrs. Alder expressed the same view, and then Charlotte Bartlett, too jumpy to wait to be recognized, her voice shaking but determined, half rose and said, "I believe Ella's right, and I should have known enough to say so before. Somebody ought to stand up in this room and speak out for the rights of the people who live here in Dinton and pay taxes. I never understood we needed any instruction from professors or anybody who looks like them, least of all professors who bring Mr. J. Edgar Hoover into our midst, and I say nothing like that has ever happened before in this town's history."

"Madam Chairman." The voice was Barry's, and he stood up with complete poise and confidence. "I may say that I have paid taxes in Dinton for a number of years. I have the interest of the town close at heart, and I seem to recall that the position I hold today in regard to this road is precisely the same as that held by

Mrs. Bartlett, the previous speaker. What has happened to bring about this change of front I can't begin to imagine. . . ."

"Shady work, that's what," said Charlotte Bartlett loudly, not hesitating to interrupt him. "And interference with the rights of Dinton. I don't care about any newcomers and outsiders who may settle here and pay the taxes they can well afford to pay, and if they can't, let them go somewhere else. My people have lived in Dinton for close on to two hundred years, and I know what I'm talking about. If this new road goes through, we'll have big Boston Eyetalians in cahoots with Statehouse politicians, and where will our rights be? I say there's real important things to consider, such as having our dealings clean and aboveboard and no F.B.I. snooping around corners and for all I know peeping through our windows."

"No, no, Charlotte, that's too extreme," said Rufe Handmore, forgetting parliamentary procedure.

"Ain't extreme enough," said someone. I think it was Mrs. Abbot Parker, because she added, without a breath in between, "You couldn't get past the Crying Swamp, anyway, not without spending a heap of money. I'd like to know where this money is coming from and whose pockets it's going into. Looks to me like crooked work somewhere."

"Madam Chairman," said Rufe, his neck reddening, "I rise to a point of order."

There were cries of "Sit down!" from standees in the rear.

Gretchen rapped. "Representative Handmore has the floor. He is entitled to the courtesy of being heard."

"I don't have much to say," Rufe began. "You all know me and how I've represented this town on Beacon Hill to the best of my ability and the best of my conscience. . . ." He went on in this style for several rotund minutes, then suddenly changed his tone. "I don't have to stand here and be stabbed in the back because I've put the town of Dinton in a way to more prosperity than there's been around here at any time in the twentieth century—or any other century."

He sat down amid loud stamping and whistling. Gretchen rapped for order.

"Madam Chairman," said Amos Godfrey, one of our retired citizens who was an authority on Dinton gossip, especially scandal, because he lounged in the post office or the bank or the paper store, having nothing else to do—nor should he have had, I think, at his thin, rheumy-eyed age of eighty-one. "It appears to me there's a case here that ought by rights to be submitted to the Attorney General. I been listening to all sides of this thing, and I'm telling you my conclusion. Roads is nothing to me personally. I ain't going anywhere. I guess I'm the only one in this whole United States that ain't involved up to the teeth in roads— I got through using them a good while back, and I ain't regretting it. Now I forget the rest of what I was going to say, but more than likely I've said enough."

We didn't expect to hear from any of the three selectmen of the town, but the chairman of the board, Alpheus Nickerson, stood up. I was surprised at his political temerity in coming to the meeting at all.

"Maybe an investigation might be a good thing," he said. "We ain't accustomed to having the F.B.I. down on us in Dinton. That's something we might like to consider. Meantime, there's no use worrying about the road. There can't be anything done without the town voting its share, and I didn't need to hear what I've heard tonight to know that Dinton ain't going to vote a cent— not to go ahead with any such project dictated from the outside. I don't mean any particular disrespect to Professor Hamilton—if he is a professor. That could be looked into. As for Rufe Handmore, we all know Rufe's all right. We don't need to hold it against him that he got caught in this queer business. Any man is likely to get caught. Rufe's all right."

"Let's go," said Katie to me. "There'll never be a meeting in Dinton with a nicer ending than that."

I needed an instant longer to recognize that phenomenon of democracy, the switch, the turnabout, the about-face. The imagination of Henry Spinney and Ruth Ellen had kept things roiled, had gained time, until at last in the confusion our planning—Katie's and mine—freed from old habit, had touched a secret spring, perhaps deeper than Jared Bartlett's concern about hiring out his trucks. Just when the moment of overturn had come might take some time to analyze; it was almost as if the town had been all one way for all these months, then—as if it were the most natural thing in the world—had reversed itself.

Katie and I got up and started an exodus that choked off any formal adjournment. Alpheus Nickerson had sensed the reversal sooner than anyone else; he had been a selectman long enough to know about these things. And I judged that by this time everybody thought just as Katie and I did, except for Professor Hamilton and Barry Johnson. I couldn't be sure of Rufe Handmore's ideas, but he had plenty of reason to let things close on the theme expressed by Alpheus.

Katie and I walked home, tranquil with relief and satisfied retrospect.

"So that's over," she said, "unless there's some legal hocuspocus."

"There won't be. The F.B.I. isn't that imbecilic, and even with this Fifth Amendment business the crazy nothingness must be apparent. Whatever pressures have been put upon the professor, he'll hardly have to worry any more. He played his part out, and the thing was removed from his hands."

"Everybody in the world today is in favor of roads except you and me and Amos Godfrey."

"Henry Spinney, too."

"Yes, him too. I never knew it was possible to shut him up."

But Henry, emerging from the courthouse, had winked at me and walked away grinning. Henry had got what he wanted.

"We mustn't forget Gretchen," I said. "She's sacrificed her marriage. . . ."

"Sacrificed, rats!" Katie said. "She'll always have a bed to get into, and you can bet Barry won't be off the reservation long.

About Jared Bartlett, it was smart of him to stay home. Charlotte's the talker in that family, and they both know it."

It was after we had reached our house that I indulged in a mild boast.

"When I cut loose in the style of Henry Spinney and Ruth Ellen, things began to happen."

"You didn't do any such thing. You just dropped naturally into the old Dinton custom of sharp practice, same as the others. You as good as lied to Jared Bartlett, and you know it. You finally up and met 'em on their own ground."

"Maybe. I still don't believe the end justifies the means."

"In this case, Gid, there isn't any end. They'll be building four-lane and six-lane roads round and round the world until nothing is left except streaks of blacktop."

"Anyway, we've saved Dinton."

"For the time being," Katie said. "Come on, Gid, it's time for us to go to bed."